OTHER WORKS BY NIKOO KAFI MCGOLDRICK AND JAMES MCGOLDRICK

Writing as

MAY MCGOLDRICK

JAN COFFEY AND NIK JAMES

MAY MCGOLDRICK NOVELS

A Midsummer Wedding

The Thistle and the Rose

Angel of Skye (Macpherson Trilogy Book 1)

Heart of Gold (Book 2)

Beauty of the Mist (Book 3)

Macpherson Trilogy (Box Set)

The Intended

Flame

Tess and the Highlander

The Dreamer (Highland Treasure Trilogy Book 1)

The Enchantress (Book 2)

The Firebrand (Book 3)

Highland Treasure Trilogy Box Set

Much Ado About Highlanders (Scottish Relic Trilogy Book 1)

Taming the Highlander (Book 2)

Tempest in the Highlands (Book 3)

Scottish Relic Trilogy Box Set

Love and Mayhem

The Promise (Pennington Family)

The Rebel

Secret Vows Box Set

Borrowed Dreams (Scottish Dream Trilogy Book 1)

Captured Dreams (Book 2)

Dreams of Destiny (Book 3)

Scottish Dream Trilogy Box Set

Romancing the Scot

Sweet Home Highland Christmas

It Happened in the Highlands

Sleepless in Scotland

Dearest Millie

How to Ditch a Duke

A Prince in the Pantry

Jane Austen Cannot Marry!

Highland Crown (Royal Highlander Series Book 1)

Highland Jewel (Book 2)

Highland Sword (Book 3)

Ghost of the Thames

Thanksgiving in Connecticut

Made in Heaven

Marriage of Minds: Collaborative Writing *(Nonfiction)*

Step Write Up: Writing Exercises for 21st Century *(Nonfiction)*

Aquarian

Omid's Shadow

SLEEPLESS IN SCOTLAND

MAY MCGOLDRICK

Book Duo Creative

Thank you for choosing *Sleepless in Scotland*. In the event that you enjoy this book, please consider sharing the good word(s) by leaving a review, or connect with the authors.

Dedicated with Love to the

Longtime Readers of May McGoldrick Novels.

You give us tremendous support

and encouragement.

❦ I ❦

Edinburgh, Scotland
June 1818

AS TWO FIGURES hurried past the dark, dripping walls of St. Giles, the bells in the tower tolled eleven. They were late.

High Street, which formed the spine of Edinburgh's Old Town and ran from Castle Hill down to the palace, still pulsed with life despite the foul weather and the hour. A handful of revelers spilled out of a tavern door across the cobbled street, led by a pair shouting at one another and ready to brawl. Beneath the flickering oil lamps, others gathered to witness the imminent battle. And under the meager cover provided by overhangs and shop doorways, homeless people huddled together against the damp and turned frightened eyes on the impending violence.

Phoebe Pennington glanced up at the crown steeple of the cathedral, lost in the darkness and mist. Pulling up the collar of her coat against the persistent drizzle, she tried to match the strides of Duncan Turner, the surly Highlander she employed for nights like this. Dressed in men's clothing as she was tonight, she expected no one to give them a second glance, but she was no fool. Occasionally, the places she needed to go required a strong arm, quick reflexes, and a thorough knowledge of the streets. As a former Edinburgh constable, dismissed after being injured on duty, Duncan possessed all of that.

This was one of those occasions.

Phoebe had never before been to the Vaults beneath South Bridge. Originally designed to form the arched supports for the bridge that spanned the urban valley known since the Dark Ages as Cowgate, the Vaults were now infamous as the seediest portion of the cellars, tunnels, and caverns that formed Edinburgh's underground city.

Not fifty paces on, Phoebe found the dark wynd she'd been directed to take and looked at Duncan. He nodded wordlessly. As they turned into the alleyway, a meek voice called out from a murky niche.

"Spare a ha'penny, sir?"

A small, ragged girl appeared, keeping her distance from them. Phoebe stopped. In the darkness behind her, a bundle of rags stirred and the sound of a woman's wheezing cough reached Phoebe's ears.

"What are you doing here so late?"

Weariness clouded the girl's eyes. "Me mum's sick."

Phoebe didn't have to ask. This had to be another case of the sick being put out of a poorhouse.

Looking at this ragged figure before her, Phoebe felt a flush of anger wash through her. With a commission due to arrive from London to inspect the poorhouses, administrators all over the city had been covertly emptying their facilities for the past month of the sick and of those too old to work. The streets of Edinburgh, from the Grassmarket to Leith, were now crawling with women and children like these two.

And this was precisely the reason why she was meeting her informant tonight.

Secretly writing for the *Edinburgh Review* and using an assumed name to hide her identity even from the editors, Phoebe had been producing articles about corruption and providing a voice for those who could not make themselves heard.

What was happening now to the city's poor was a disgrace, and she intended to expose it. The man she was meeting tonight had records of the evictions and minutes of meetings. Proof she could use in her articles.

She felt Duncan's impatient presence behind her.

"Can your mother walk?" she asked. Getting a nod from the girl, she continued. "Rouse her and go down High Street to the close just past the Bull's Head Tavern. It's not far. At the end of the close, you'll find a house with a green lantern in the window. They'll take you in. Understand me?"

"Aye. Thank ye, sir."

The government was failing these two, but shelters like the ones her sister Jo funded were scattered across the city.

"Good girl." Phoebe put a coin into her hand and watched her retreat into the darkness.

Starting down the twisting wynd, she could feel the man at her shoulder biting his tongue as they walked.

"Say what you have to say, Duncan," she ordered in low voice.

"You can't save them all, m'lady," he growled, his Highland burr echoing down the wet alleyway.

"I know that, but I can help the ones I find," she replied in a whisper. "And don't call me '*m'lady*.'"

"Aye, but that lassie could've been a badger worker for some thug lying in wait for us."

"That's why I have you," she replied.

Duncan huffed and gestured down the passageway. "Why the Vaults?"

"I didn't choose the place. He did. He wouldn't meet me anywhere but there. Show a wee bit of that Highland courage I keep hearing about." Phoebe slipped on the wet cobbles but caught herself. Twisting down the hill between crumbling stone tenements looming four or five stories above them, the wynd was treacherously slick.

"Courage? You know me. Everyone in Edinburgh knows me. I'm the man what took a bullet from Mad Jack Knox and still dragged him in," Duncan said, bristling. "I know the ways of these back alleys better than any man in Auld Reekie, and I'm telling you, it ain't a good thing, you going down there. And when my wife finds out I agreed to come down here with you, she'll nail my hide to the door of St. Giles back there."

Phoebe smiled in the dark, thinking it was a good thing there *was* someone Duncan was afraid of. After she heard the former constable had lost his job, she'd helped him set himself up as a mercantile agent. He was now serving as a supplier in the city's efforts to begin installing gas lights on the streets.

As they continued on, she eyed the deep shadows of doorways and stone steps leading to the basements. It was a dark and treacherous maze, but they had to be close.

A moment later, Duncan put his shoulder to a low

door in a wall, and Phoebe heard the scrape of a heavy rock moving back across the floor. He went in first, then turned and waved her in.

The dim light from the alleyway did little to illuminate the cellar, and the musty, tomblike smell of damp earth and vermin immediately assaulted her senses. On one wall, a stone stairway led to an upper floor, but he gestured past it.

"We'll follow this through to the Vaults," he said in a low voice. "Stay behind me and look sharp for thugs and other scoundrels. Many a robber has been known to hide out in rooms like these."

She nodded and followed him through the darkness into another chamber, marveling at his ability to pick his way along in the near pitch blackness. Passing through another door, Phoebe saw they'd reached the Vaults.

Like dungeons she'd seen in old Norman keeps in the south of England, arched passageways led off into the darkness. Far-off sounds of men's voices and the shrill laugh of a woman echoed along the stone walls.

In the distance, a lamp flickered outside a larger archway with a dingy, red cloth hanging across the opening for a door.

"So where's your man?" the Highlander growled.

"He said he'd meet us there," she told him, leading him toward the makeshift red door. "I'm paying too much for him to leave us in the cold."

At the doorway, she paused. A smoky, sickly sweet odor hung in the air. Phoebe's correspondence with the clerk asked her to be here. He'd be waiting, and there'd be a quick exchange. For a dozen heartbeats, her feet remained rooted in place. She listened to the sounds from inside and breathed in the distinctive smell.

"This is a drug den." Duncan scowled. "The man's an opium eater?"

"So it seems." She pulled open the curtain.

The barrel-vaulted chamber beyond was wide and deep, lit by candles perched in arched, catacomb-like shelves along the outside walls. Through the low-hanging smoke, Phoebe could see straw pallets, occupied by both men and women, lining the floor. Jacketless attendants scurried about, carrying trays with pipes and hot coals.

She peered in, but Duncan grabbed her elbow. "You can't go in there. They'll sort you for a blueblood in a wink. And if you're a toff who's not indulging, then you're a mark for every thug in Old Town."

Phoebe was no fool. She knew she couldn't go in. "If he is in there, I want to see him."

"You wait here and don't move." Duncan stepped past her.

As her bodyguard stalked between the rows of pallets, an attendant met him and, after a brief exchange, led the Highlander deeper into the vault. He already knew the clerk's name and a brief description. She hoped that was enough.

Phoebe thought of the kind of people who visited a den like this. The confidence she had about her source and the credibility of the documents he was willing to produce were quickly losing ground. Though published under a false name, her articles were respected as honest commentary on the politics of the city. She was not about to have her reputation destroyed by inaccuracies or lies.

Without warning, a body that seemed to be no more than skin and bones barreled into her at a high speed, jarring her and knocking the curtain from her hand. She reached out to steady the falling creature. A young lad, almost a man in height, looked frantically over her shoulder.

"What's wrong?"

The boy twisted free of her grasp and lurched off, stumbling and banging into a stone wall as he ran.

As she watched his retreating back in astonishment, Phoebe moved away from the door and directly into the path of a man, dressed in black, who nearly upended her as he rushed past.

She barely caught a glimpse of him as she tried to regain her balance. But the chill she felt was unmistakable. He was the dark movement one sees at the edge of the woods. The wind that howls and scratches at the windows on a winter night. He was the shadow of evil. The image of Death—with hooded robe and scythe— flashed before her eyes. He was Satan here to collect a soul.

A cry came back down the passageway.

"Let me live!" the voice echoed. "Don't!"

The lad hadn't escaped. The sounds of a scuffle reached her. Phoebe's heart drummed in fear, and her stomach rose into her throat. Murder.

"Duncan," she called. The red curtain lay thick and heavy across the door.

She couldn't wait for him. Phoebe didn't know how she gathered the courage to take a step, then two. But she was going after them.

Holding her walking stick like a club, she took off down the passageway. Not forty paces along, she came upon the two, struggling in an archway where a stout door stood ajar.

The attacker, cloaked all in black, was flesh and blood.

He was half pushing, half dragging the boy, who was fighting as if he knew his life depended on it.

Phoebe didn't hesitate but attacked, swinging her cane as she rushed at them. The first blow struck the man's back, drawing a bark of pain. Swinging the stick again, she landed one on his shoulder, but the assailant latched onto it, yanked it from her grip, and sent it clattering against a wall.

The boy, freed, scuttled past her and was gone.

Unarmed, facing a monster she wasn't strong enough to fight or fast enough to run away from, she backed away, looking for a route to escape. The assailant came at her, and she kicked at him, landing a booted foot hard in his crotch.

He was staggered for an instant, but she only managed to move two steps away when he came at her like an enraged bull. Phoebe saw, almost too late, the blade gleaming in his hand as he slashed at her face. She ducked back and felt the point of the knife slice her throat above her coat collar.

He came at her again, and she kicked at his hand. The knife flew from his grip.

She turned to run and saw stone steps leading downward. Escape. But as she reached the top step, he caught hold of her ulster, jerking her backward as his fist caught her below the eye.

The sharp blow numbed her face, and Phoebe felt her knees give as she tipped backward into the shadowy void.

Ian Kerr Bell ducked his head beneath the top of an archway and tried to ignore the nauseating odor of decay and death that permeated the air and the very stones down here.

The Vaults. Level after level of vile, stinking corruption. A rat's nest of depravity and crime.

Here, beneath the bustling shops and taverns of South Bridge, this catacomb of rooms and passageways, originally used as storage space and workshops for the businesses above, had long ago been left to decay, closed off by the crumbling walls of tenement buildings crowding up against them.

Ian knew that when the businesses above sealed off access to the lower levels, new occupants found their way in. The hellish labyrinth of cramped, dark chambers soon housed the poorest of the city's poor. Illegal pubs found a place to operate. Gambling hells. Brothels. And worse.

No sunlight, no fresh air, no clean water. No law either, other than the law of the streets. Robbery and murder were everyday events in the Vaults.

But with every problem—even murder, he thought grimly—intrepid entrepreneurs saw opportunity. The dead had value. A market for cadavers had sprung up in Edinburgh. Bodies were in demand by anatomists. The city's medical schools bought every corpse they could get their hands on.

Corpses like those of his sister.

Three years. Three years since Sarah had gone missing. The last time anyone saw her alive, she'd been browsing in a dress shop on South Bridge with a friend. And then she was gone. Vanished into thin air amidst crowds of people who frequented the busy stretch of markets every day.

As Deputy Lieutenant of Fife and a justice of the peace, Ian was a man of consequence. He had power and connections. But with all of this influence, it had still taken him months to solve the riddle of his sister's disappearance.

She'd been murdered and left in the Vaults. Her precious body had been stripped of all finery, and her corpse sold to the surgeons at the university. It was only by gaining access to the meticulous records kept by clerks and anatomy students that Ian had been able to identify his sister. Four broken bones that Sarah had suffered in her right arm falling from a horse at the age of eleven had matched the injuries described in detail during the dissection of the "unknown female subject."

Struggling to breathe despite the familiar knot in his throat, Ian ducked through another archway. Even after learning what had become of his sister, he continued to come down here. He had to.

Finding her remains and moving them to the church crypt at Bellhorne did little to ease the pain. Her murderer had never been discovered. The mystery of how she'd become separated from her friend and found her way down here continued to plague him. Although Sarah was only twenty at the time, Ian knew she was smart and alert and wise beyond her years. She wasn't reckless. She wouldn't put herself in danger. There was no possibility of her coming down here willingly. Three years ago, the place was no less infamous for the dangers lurking here. The reputation of the Vaults was enough to keep any rational person away.

As he moved along the passageway, an echo of a scuffle and a soft cry drew Ian's attention to the darkness at the top of a flight of stairs ahead of him. He'd often used his stout walking stick as a weapon down here, and he prepared to use it again.

Many times over the past three years he'd come upon some poor soul being attacked. More times than he could remember he'd intervened and managed to save a life, even if it were only for that night. And there were many times when he'd come upon victims left to die. Some had been beaten or stabbed. Many were drunk to the point of oblivion. Some were burning with fever.

As he reached the stairwell, a body came tumbling from the top, landing in a heap at his feet.

Peering up the stairs, he saw no one in the darkness of the upper level but heard the faint echoes of distant voices. Whoever this fellow had been fighting, the opponent didn't want to pursue the encounter.

Ian crouched beside the body. The man was facedown, his legs akimbo on the lower steps and his ulster thrown up over his head. His hat lay nearby.

"Hard fall," he commented.

No response. As Ian pushed the coat down to turn him over, he was stunned when his fingers brushed against soft hair braided and pinned in a coil.

"Bloody hell," he muttered. "You're a woman."

He gently rolled her. The passageway was too dark for him to make out her features. She was unconscious, but she was breathing. He guessed she must have struck her head at least once as she fell.

"I don't know what reckless game you were playing in coming down here, but I won't leave you to it."

Juggling the walking stick, Ian picked her up and started back in the direction he'd come. Tall for a woman but light enough to be carried easily, she lay completely limp in his arms.

Random possibilities of who she was and what she was doing down here ran through his mind. The men's clothing piqued his curiosity. And the quality of the wool greatcoat told him she wasn't one of the legions of poor who took shelter down here. Of course, she could easily have stolen the clothes.

Retracing his steps, he made his way up several flights of stairs and eventually emerged in an alley that led to the street level of the bridge.

His valet, Lucas Crawford, was waiting by the carriage, and Ian saw him exchange a look with the driver. Neither was surprised at the sight of their master surfacing from the Vaults with a body. The driver opened the door as Lucas approached to help.

"Netted yourself a trout tonight, Captain?"

Ian shook his head. "No net required. This one dropped in my lap."

"Och, it's a woman!" Lucas exclaimed, peering at her face as Ian carried her past a streetlamp. She stirred and moaned, but then was silent again.

"Well, she's alive, at least," the valet said, sounding relieved.

Reaching the carriage, Ian deposited her on a seat and inspected her for bleeding. She had a small lump on her head and a welt forming just below her eye, but he saw no stab wounds.

Lucas looked over his shoulder. "And she's a bonnie lass as well."

Ian glanced into her face. He sat back suddenly. He knew her.

Bloody hell.

Ian's brain threatened to explode. It was almost too much to fathom. Alone. In men's clothes. In the middle of the night. In the most dangerous place in Scotland.

And he knew the vile corruption that lay at the top of

those steps where he found her. The wretchedness that consumed the Vaults.

Of all the places for a young woman to be traipsing through, why the *devil* was she in there?

Dressed like a man. Fighting . . . *fighting!* And with God-knows-who. Running for her life, from the looks of it.

He'd like to think she was a fool, but he knew she wasn't. He'd known her for years. His temper grew even hotter at the thought that this woman at one time had a connection with his sister. Sarah had socialized with the family, considered her a friend, and looked up to her with respect. She'd often visited their home at Baronsford when they were in residence. And invited her to come and stay with them at Bellhorne.

Why such foolhardy behavior? He seethed. He couldn't get past that question. She could have died down there tonight, murdered just as his sister had been.

"Do you know her, Captain?" his valet asked.

"Blast me," he cursed, staring. "She's Lady Phoebe Pennington, the Lord Justice's younger sister."

⚜ 2 ⚜

A VAGUE SENSE of awareness returned.

The boy. He got away. She saw him run. One thing to be thankful for.

The thought gave her mind some relief, but it did little to soothe her body's aches. Phoebe felt like a cleaver had split her skull in two, and where she'd been punched, her face was throbbing dreadfully. She didn't know how long she'd lain unconscious in the Vaults, but the pain beneath her eye told her she was alive, at least. Her limbs seemed to be intact, and she was still wearing the men's clothing she'd donned before setting out with Duncan tonight.

Duncan. He'd be beside himself when he came out and found her missing.

The pounding in her head wouldn't let up, but she forced herself to focus past the pain and pay attention to her surroundings. She was propped up in the angle of a bench seat, her head lying against a cushioned side wall. From the smell of leather and the whinny of an impatient horse outside, she knew she was in a carriage, and it wasn't moving.

Phoebe opened her eyes a slit and peeked through her lashes, but quickly shut them tight. Two others occupied the carriage with her, and one of them was hovering over her, too close for comfort. Still, she sensed no threat.

She let her head roll slightly, and the cravat she'd worn rubbed against her throat. Stinging pain brought back her memory of what happened in the Vaults. Hearing the lad's cry, she had to go after him. Never in her life had Phoebe been in a situation where a murder was being committed. She couldn't stand by and let it happen.

Cold sweat spread across her brow even now at the recollection of the knife in the man's hand. He'd intended to kill. *To kill.* And once she'd interfered, his fury turned to her.

Her throat. She was cut. But it had to be only a scratch, for she'd survived. Every muscle in her body tensed as she relived the fight in her mind. Hitting him with the cane wasn't enough. She'd kicked him. Her arms weren't long enough nor strong enough to keep him away. She'd kicked him again. Finally, Phoebe had found some use for her long legs. She wanted to laugh, but she couldn't. Everything in her mind was a jumble. One moment she was chasing after an evil spirit, the next her boots were connecting with a man's flesh. And now she was here.

The pain in her skull was not helping her reassert order to her thoughts.

Her hat was missing. Her rescuers must already know she was a woman. She tried to build the courage to open her eyes again.

"Do you know her, Captain?"

Captain. Phoebe forced herself to focus. She was rescued by a captain. The memories of the fight tried to claw to the front, but she pushed them back. Captain.

Since the war with the French, many men still used their rank. The names and faces and voices of her brothers' friends came to mind. She avoided most social events, but twice a year Baronsford put on the most eagerly attended balls in Scotland, and her parents made it mandatory for her to attend.

She wished he would say more. Perhaps she knew him. But she didn't want to know him. Tonight, coming here to the Vaults . . . she cringed at the thought of how horribly her family would react to find where she'd been.

"Blast me." The voice was deep and angry. "She's Lady Phoebe Pennington, the Lord Justice's younger sister."

The tone of each syllable emphasized the displeasure of the speaker.

She knew the voice. Her curiosity bested her, and she opened her eyes to be sure.

Damnation. Captain Ian Bell of Bellhorne, Fife.

Her throat tightened. Sarah. Her dear friend. The memory of her fight in the Vaults disappeared. The headache was forgotten. Her thoughts shifted and focused on an innocent life lost.

Sarah's shocking disappearance and the news that came much later of the recovery of her remains had been horrifying. She was her friend. Aside from her sister Millie, her closest friend. To this day, Phoebe had nightmares about the shocking business. Sarah's young life had been lost, her body defiled in a public dissection, and her family cast into a permanent state of tumult. Mrs. Bell, shut away in the family's estate in Fife, had become estranged from society. She accepted no invitations and saw no guests. And Phoebe had heard that Sarah's brother, Ian, scoured Edinburgh's underworld at night, continually searching for the person or people responsible for his sister's death.

"Captain Bell," she managed to croak.

The devil as well should take her. Why did she have to be rescued by him? The one man who had every reason to escort her this very moment to her family's home and demand an audience with her father or either of her brothers. She had no doubt he'd happily watch as they skinned her alive.

"Out, Lucas. Leave us."

The sharpness of the order was expected.

The valet climbed out and shut the door of the carriage as Phoebe willed her foot to stop tapping nervously. Even in the dim light, she felt the weight of the man's glare.

Lectures. Threats. She expected it. But silence hung as ominously as a noose between them. One fist perched solidly on a muscular thigh. Her gaze moved upward over the broad chest to his stern face. He remained perfectly still, except for the sinews in his jaw that clenched and unclenched repeatedly. Much of his face lay in shadow, but she had no trouble seeing that his eyes were watching her with the intensity of a great cat studying his prey.

At a much younger age, long before tragedy struck the Bell family, Phoebe had entertained many fanciful dreams about Captain Bell. But she was six years younger than the war hero, and he was only gradually recovering from recent battle wounds. He barely acknowledged her existence. He ignored her subtle overtures. He never knew of her hidden affection.

"Now," he snapped. "Explain yourself."

No formality at all in his manner of address. His tone was sharp and barely civil. Phoebe felt herself squirm slightly, but she fought the urge to look away.

No one. No one but Millie and Duncan knew of the career she'd already established herself in as a journalist. Women—particularly women of her class—simply did not pursue such indecently "public" endeavors. An earl's daughter, Phoebe had been born to wealth and privilege. Philanthropy was allowed, and a passionate hobby might be acceptable. But a career—particularly one that occasionally endangered her life—was entirely beyond the pale.

Nevertheless, Phoebe was doing it, and she was good at what she did. Her writing, albeit published anonymously, continued to strike at the heart of corruption and injustice, and she already felt a sense of pride in her efforts. Still, she couldn't explain any of that to this man. Not now, to be sure. How could she? She'd never yet felt she could tell her own family.

Phoebe loved her family too much. Knowing what she was doing would simply distress them unnecessarily.

"I wasn't down in the Vaults alone," she began, trying to play down the danger she'd faced. "I had a bodyguard with me, and the man was perfectly capable of protecting me. But we were separated for a moment and—"

"Clearly, you were not protected," he cut in even more sharply. "The truth now. Why were you down there?"

He wanted details that she wasn't about to reveal. She considered sharing what she'd witnessed about the lad and the man chasing after him. But although she'd justified it to herself, her actions would be construed as foolish. She could have been murdered. And that still didn't explain why she'd gone there in the first place.

"Charity work. I was down there looking for poor families that have been driven out of the poorhouses in recent weeks. The old and infirm. Any who are unable to work. Women and children have been inundating my sister Jo's charity houses, but many more don't know there are such options. I went into the Vaults to help direct—"

"I'm quite certain Lady Josephine," he snapped, interrupting again, "only a fortnight before her wedding, knows nothing of your reckless behavior. And I would be willing to wager neither does your father. Nor your brothers. They're all at Baronsford, are they not?"

Phoebe struggled not to match the edge in his tone. She *was* speaking the truth . . . in part. Edinburgh's dispossessed were the cause for her being here. Her article could expose the political maneuvering and benefit those poor souls put out on the streets.

He wasn't waiting for her to respond. "Take us to Baronsford," he ordered, directing his man standing outside to ride with the driver.

"No!" she cried out. "You can take me to my family's townhouse on Heriot Row. My sister Millie is in town. She's expecting me back tonight, and she'll be beside herself with worry if I don't return. Please. She and I are to travel to the Borders together."

The carriage began to move along the stone pavement. No orders were issued to alter the route.

"Does your sister know about this?" He gestured to her attire.

"Of course not," she lied. Actually, Millie had helped her dress in men's clothing before she left the house. "No one in my family knows."

A dark brow arched, and he continued to stare at her. "A moment ago, you said Lady Josephine—"

"I never said Jo knew anything about where I was going tonight." She threw up her hands in frustration. "Can you please stop the carriage and allow me to explain properly?"

Her words seemed to fall on deaf ears. The brooding Scot made no move to halt the carriage.

"Please, Captain."

The thought of arriving at Baronsford just after dawn with Captain Bell, only to have him rouse the earl to report where he found his daughter was unthinkable. But there was no escaping him. She had to convince him, but the stubbornness in his look was daunting.

"I'll tell you everything. The truth, as damning as it is." Her fingers clutched the edge of the leather seats. "Captain, you know me. I was a friend to your sister. Many times, I was a guest at Bellhorne. Please give me a chance."

The carriage wheels hit a rut, jerking the passengers, and Phoebe put a hand to her throbbing head.

"Very well." He called to the driver to stop. "Out with it."

Damnation. She let out a frustrated breath. Sarah's tragedy had hardened this man to any honest plea she might make. And he was not one to be reasoned with. She needed a believable fabrication that would satisfy his curiosity.

A report of her whereabouts—and the situation in which he found her—couldn't reach her family. At least not until she'd had a chance to explain to them the entire situation. Including her writing.

Hopefully, that would be never.

Her brothers went to war and pursued creditable careers afterward. Jo was an angel of mercy, touching the lives of so many. Millie was already the family peacemaker, and her heart of gold defined the meaning of understanding and encouragement and selflessness. Phoebe was the only black sheep. Already well on her way to spinsterhood, she lived with her head in the clouds and her pen to paper, off in some dreamland. At least, that's how her family saw her.

It had taken her many years to realize who she was, what she could do, and how to go about doing it. She'd been blessed with a gift, and she'd be damned if she wouldn't use it for the good of others. She wasn't willing to give that up.

The captain stirred impatiently. "I see that we stopped prematurely."

"A man," she said as he started to call out to the driver.

Ian Bell's gaze snapped back to her face. He was large and imposing, but Phoebe had spent her whole life dealing with her father and brothers.

"I went there in search of a certain man of my acquaintance."

Well, that was true, she thought.

"A beau . . . of sorts. A young man my family knows nothing about, and I'm certain they would disapprove of him if they learned of our liaison. Up until an hour ago, I imagined I was in love with him. After what I witnessed in those Vaults, however, that is no longer the case."

With this single lie, Phoebe knew she was ruining any positive impression he might have had. With just a few words, her character—in his eyes—was damaged, if not destroyed. But what did she care, if she could avoid exposing her true calling to the world and her family? She was twenty-seven years old, and she had no interest in matrimony. And she very much doubted Captain Bell was a gossip.

She could only hope he would see her as unworthy of his time and effort in exposing her.

He leaned back in his seat, much of his face disappearing in the shadows, but the grim line on his lips clearly demonstrated his disapproval.

"As bad as this all seems," she continued, gesturing toward her attire and feeling encouraged. "Tonight was a blessing. Tonight I woke up. I now know what a vile scoundrel he is. And I shall never see him again. I can promise you I shall not waste even one moment regretting the loss of our relationship."

"What is the name of this man you were meeting?"

"We weren't meeting. I was looking for him. But his name is of no consequence. He and I are done. Finished," she said in the most somber tone she could muster. "I pray you won't ask another word about him. That foolish chapter in my life is over."

His scowl became almost fierce. "Were you fighting with him at the top of the stairs?"

The lad's frightened face, as he stared over her shoulder, came back to her. His cry for help. Phoebe shivered and resettled herself in the seat. She hoped he had a shelter far from the dangers of the Vaults.

"Were you fighting with your lover?"

The sound of the word "lover" made it more damning, for Ian Bell was the only man she'd ever dreamed of in such terms.

"No. I found him in . . . in an opium den not far from there." She shook her head. "There, now do you understand why I'm finished with him?"

"You, Lady Phoebe Pennington, went into a drug den?"

"No. Of course not."

"You said he was in the opium den."

"But *I* didn't go in. My bodyguard went in. That's how we were separated."

"Then who knocked you down the steps?"

"I don't know! I didn't see his face."

She wanted to tell him about the black-garbed man, but right now whatever she said only led to another question. He was trying to break down her story. He gave her no time to think. And the irritating pain in her skull was no help. She needed time to sort through the fact and the fiction she was weaving.

Phoebe recalled Sarah's complaints about the brother. Even as a young man, he'd been extremely protective of his sister and his mother. And he was by nature impatient and always too quick to issue a verdict.

"Please allow me to explain, Captain, from the beginning."

"I'm waiting."

His gaze was direct and piercing. Phoebe took a deep breath. She needed to end this inquisition, and that would never happen while the carriage was pointed toward Baronsford.

"While I explain everything that happened tonight, could we at least head to my family's townhouse? I've said before that my sister Millie must be sick with worry. I was expected back long before now." She gave him the exact address in the New Town section of Edinburgh.

Every request had to be analyzed and stewed over before he responded. As she waited, she tried to fight down the anger beginning to burn within her. She also began to wonder how she could ever have been foolish enough to be attracted to him in her youth. Obviously, she knew nothing of his mule-headedness in those innocent, untroubled times. From his dubious expression, she sensed that the phrase "give her an inch and she'll take an ell" might be passing through his thick head right now. She had to do something.

"Duncan Turner, the former Edinburgh constable, was my escort when I went down into the Vaults," she offered. "Perhaps you know him. The man is tall, strong, and knowledgeable. He and his wife are both acquaintances of mine."

Phoebe thought the mention of her bodyguard's name might put Captain Bell's mind at ease, and she was certain that Duncan would not reveal her secret if her inquisitor decided to track him down.

The captain gave no indication of either knowing or not knowing the man, but he called up to the driver and gave him the address.

Phoebe waited until the carriage rolled down the street again.

"I went to the Vaults tonight because I'd heard rumors about the gentleman that I was seeing."

"So he's a gentleman?"

"Not in my eyes. Not after tonight," she said, continuing to speak quickly to take away his chance of asking questions. She knew it was easy to be caught in your own web of lies once you began spinning it.

"The worm is an opium addict. He intended to use me and my fortune. I heard some rumors, and I came tonight with Duncan to confirm them. And it's the truth. I saw him in that horrid place. Not that I walked in there myself, but I saw him from the curtained entrance. Then

I sent Duncan in to inform him that any correspondence between us was finished. I wanted him to know that I'll not be receiving him in the future. I shall not be accepting any letters from him, and I'm not interested in any excuses or tales of woe. There will be no communication of any sort. Done. Finished. And I'm relieved. So relieved."

She brought a fist to her lips, pretending to calm her unsteady breath. Phoebe wished she were a better actress. Still, perhaps he'd be empathetic enough to allow her some grace by changing the subject.

"What happened on top of the stairs?" he demanded in the same hard tone. The man was positively a Torquemada.

At least now she could tell the truth, and Phoebe was thankful for that.

"I was waiting in the passageway for Duncan to come out of that place and escort me back to where I belong. Suddenly . . ." Phoebe paused, realizing the consequences of speaking the truth. A woman chasing after an assailant, armed only with a walking stick.

He would think her imprudent, at the very least, and possibly insane. And Phoebe would have to agree with him. Also, she had no doubt he'd insist on immediately taking her back to Baronsford. And again, she wouldn't blame him. What she'd done *was* foolhardy. But she had no regrets. She would do it again.

"Suddenly?" he asked. "If your purpose is to keep me in suspense, it's working."

Phoebe sat up and straightened her coat, deciding what she could say. "Suddenly a man grabbed me from behind and dragged me like a sheep into the shadows. He held a knife to my throat."

She touched her neck where the knife wound still stung. She held her fingers to the light coming through the window and stared at the smear of blood.

"The deuce! The blackguard cut you." His hand closed around her wrist as he moved directly across from her. "Let me see."

He didn't give her a chance to object but lifted her chin and quickly untied the cravat.

Amusing. Awkward. Mildly embarrassing. She couldn't summon quite the right words to clarify the feeling rushing through her at the sensation of her legs tucked between his, her head tipped back while Captain Ian Bell leaned close, inspecting and touching the sensitive skin of her throat.

"I'm fine. I believe he only nicked me," she managed to say, fighting a delicious shiver as his thumb brushed one last path down to the top of her collarbone.

"Who was he? The man who grabbed you?"

Her skin felt cold when he released her and sat back. He remained seated across from her.

"I never had a good look into his face." She'd fought him with all her strength, but there was nothing about him that she could describe, except his evil spirit. "It was dark, and the attack happened so quickly. But he was about my height. Perhaps a bit taller. He was quite strong."

"What else?"

She frowned as the confrontation played out again in her mind. He was dragging the lad somewhere when she'd reached them.

"I think he had a destination in mind. Someplace nearby. And the way he wielded the knife, I can't help but think he's used it before."

His stony gaze turned to the window and the dark houses they were passing, and Phoebe scolded herself for saying too much. She had without a doubt reminded him of his sister's murder. The muscles along his jawbone twitched.

From the moment she'd opened her eyes and recognized him, she'd been trying to make up stories that would satisfy his questions and curiosity. Now, with Captain Bell's attention directed somewhere else, she studied him.

The touch of grey in his sideburns showed how much he'd aged since the last time she'd seen him. It was the day of Sarah's funeral. His mother had been absent. He'd looked as if he was carrying the weight of the world on his shoulders, and she'd wanted to reach out to him. There was so much she'd wanted to say about Sarah, about the lost friend who'd been like a sister to her. But she couldn't. Phoebe had realized whatever words she said, they would be about her own loss. And though her emotions were raw, she couldn't allow herself to fall apart while he was nobly struggling to retain his own composure.

On that miserable winter day, while the skies shed tears of grief over the young woman's life, Captain Bell barely acknowledged the scores of people attending. He was distant, unapproachable. He was very much the same now.

Phoebe recognized Heriot Row as the carriage rounded a corner. They were only a block away from the townhouse.

She reached out and touched his hand, drawing his attention back to her.

"Thank you," she said softly. "Thank you for saving my life."

The carriage rolled to a stop in front of the residence.

"Please believe that I learned a lesson tonight. And I will never, ever do such a foolish thing again." She had no desire to return to the Vaults. That was the truth. But as far as going after an assailant in a similar situation, Phoebe had little control over what she would do.

A footman emerged from the house and ran down the steps to the carriage. Phoebe sent her rescuer one last look. "I don't know when we shall see each other again. But please know that I am forever indebted to you."

As the footman opened the door, Ian climbed out and offered her his hand.

"I shall see you in less than a fortnight, Lady Phoebe," he told her. "At Baronsford."

Her foot slipped on the step, and she would have gone down on her face if Ian hadn't held her up.

"A fortnight?" she asked, realizing she sounded like a fool.

"At the ball your family hosts," he said gravely. "I'm suddenly inclined to accept their gracious invitation. I believe that will provide the perfect opportunity to pay my respects and speak with your family."

The impenetrable mist, suspended like a wet shroud, pressed into the doorways and sills of grey stone buildings, barely visible along the wide street. For any soul unfortunate enough to be abroad on a night like this, there was no escaping the wet, oppressive chill. It settled thick and damp on the skin, leaving its bitter scent of primeval ash and decay. It soaked through clothing, seeped into flesh, and settled into bone, a cold reminder of the dark and endless fate that claims all.

In the light of day, one might think that moments like this gave birth to tales of Grendel and his kind, of monsters that rose out of swamps and lakes and oceans to destroy and to devour. The stuff of poets and false heroes, safe beneath a shining sun.

But tonight, no sun shone to chase away fears. No moon hung in the sky. No stars dotted the firmament. Tonight, death was more than a story, more than a dispirited feeling, more than a cold, unsettled sensation. Tonight, in the shadows of South Bridge in the city of Edinburgh, death was a living presence, a cold and heartless predator. A serpent, coiled and motionless. Watching. Waiting.

He stared from the darkness as the captain carried his prize to the carriage. The interloper who'd muddled the purity of his kill. Lucas Crawford, standing outside the carriage, looked in his direction. He melted farther into the shadow. He'd had the boy in his grasp. Another lamb to slaughter. He felt his knife ready to enter the flesh. But the boy escaped. Because of him.

Him? Not him. Her.

A surprise, for a moment. But the clothing was only a disguise. He saw her face.

Cold rage coursed through him. Like a she-devil, the woman fought him, attacked him, forcing him to release his kill.

The boy ran. As if he could escape him. No one escaped him. He had a destiny that he must fulfill. All those lost souls called to him. *Vengeance*, they cried. *Kill*.

His gaze focused on the carriage. The street, so empty

and silent. They were not moving. Perhaps she broke her neck falling down those steps. It was dark, but he saw her face. Did she see his?

He held up the knife, the blood still on his blade. The smell of it filled his lungs. A few more steps and it would have been over. He could have killed them both.

Meddler. Anger pulsed through him.

"And you, Captain Bell. Hunting in the shadows for some faceless creature. What do you imagine I am? What do you envision when you dream of these Vaults? You don't even know how close you've been. How close. Turn her out. Leave her in the street."

Today was the day. He needed to kill and he would. For all of them.

The captain spoke to his valet, who relayed the command as he climbed up top. What was the word he said?

Baronsford.

The driver called to his team to walk on, and the carriage began to move south along the bridge.

"You've slipped from my reach. From my blade of destiny. From immortality. For now." The mist swirled and the carriage disappeared. "Baronsford. Very well. I'll find out who you are. I'll find you, meddler."

In the distance, a mad hound barked at the night and then grew silent. The Vaults behind him beckoned.

Another lamb awaited.

※　3　※

Baronsford
The Borders

TWICE A YEAR the grand ballroom at Baronsford opened
its magnificent doors to the public. With its vaulted
ceiling rising a full two stories above the dance floor, its
classically framed doors and windows, its ornate gold-leaf
decorations, and its carved figures of Roman deities
peering out from their arched niches, the huge Palladian-
style room welcomed the family's guests from all over
England and Scotland.

Most of those attending would never have guessed
that for the rest of the year, this same great room had
been used by generations of Pennington children as they
played makeshift games of bowl and nine-pins, blind
man's bluff, and shuttlecock. And the narrow, marble-
railed gallery high above, supported by Ionic columns set
into the walls, had provided a wonderful place to run
races on rainy summer days.

Today, however, an orchestra was seated there, above the open doors, and the melodious sounds of Handel filled the room. The waltzes would come later.

Phoebe's attention was not on the orchestra, nor the great vases overflowing with flowers, nor the tables filled with refreshments. She barely spared a glance at the assembled partygoers in their finest gowns and evening clothes, moving across the wide floor with its mosaic design of the gold, white, and grey marble tile. Phoebe's eyes were fixed on the entrance door between Jupiter and Venus, and the anxiety clutching at her stomach wouldn't ease its grip.

She and her sister Millie were standing by the open doors leading to a veranda. Behind them, the setting sun spread golden rays across the rolling fields beyond the gardens. But she wasn't interested in that either. She was watching only the late arrivals trickling in.

Then, at the precise moment the musicians paused between movements, a crystal cup crashed to the floor nearby, causing her to jump.

The two women turned to see their brother Gregory gliding quickly toward Ella, his newly acquired six-year-old daughter, who was pointing an accusing finger at the shattered pieces of glass and the red punch that had spattered her white party dress and slippers.

With a word of thanks to a footman who had leapt into action to clear the mess, Gregory scooped Ella up and, after a brief whisper to the little girl, they both turned to the gathering, smiled, and bowed. From across the room, the sound of the earl's gruff laugh broke the silence, and the music began again.

"This is why I love our family," Millie said proudly. "We are never boring."

As Gregory came by them with Ella still in his arms, the younger sister asked if he needed help. The little girl shook her head.

"Shona laid out two dresses for me," Ella told them in a confidential tone that could be heard on the far side of the ballroom. She nodded toward Gregory. "Gag told her to."

"I can't *imagine* what made me think to do that," he said with a wink at his sisters.

As he started for the door, Phoebe turned her attention again to the entrance. Maybe he wasn't coming, she thought hopefully.

The majority of the guests had already arrived, but a stir by the door drew everyone's attention. As the butler announced the arrival, Phoebe couldn't help but smile with pride as her older sister Jo, married just the day before, swept into Baronsford's ballroom with an air of quiet confidence that was so new to her. Coming through escorted by her handsome husband, Captain Wynne Melfort, and her new stepson, Cuffe, Jo smiled and greeted well-wishers as they moved directly toward the receiving line.

"She looks beautiful," Millie said, sighing happily. "Imagine. A second chance at love after so many years."

"Heartwarming," Phoebe replied.

"Captain Wentworth is a good man, but I'd say he's lucky to have her."

She agreed. "And no shots needed to be fired this time around."

A broken engagement, a duel at dawn between their brother Hugh and Wentworth, and sixteen years later the couple had found each other again. More than once over the past few days, it had occurred to Phoebe that she might be better off if she gave up writing for the newspaper and instead penned a romantic novel about her sister Jo and Wynne. Their story certainly had all the elements.

Phoebe's eyes once again swept over the heads of the assembled crowd toward the entry door. It was too early to feel any real sense of relief, but Captain Bell had not yet made an appearance.

Perhaps he changed his mind, she prayed. Or was delayed on some governmental business in Fife. Or was set upon by a gang of highwaymen.

I should have hired a gang of highwaymen. A weak smile tugged at her lips.

Not far from the ballroom door, their mother and father greeted guests with Grace and their brother Hugh beside them.

Lyon Pennington, Earl of Aytoun, and Hugh, Viscount Greysteil, were doing their best to appear cordial, but Phoebe knew neither one really enjoyed the formalities of the ball. The annual Summer Ball and Christmas Assembly were an institution at Baronsford, and the family would continue the tradition. Despite the dreadful injuries that nearly killed their father as a young man, she was certain he'd be leading his beloved wife onto the dance floor soon enough.

"You can now breathe," Millie teased when the last guests were announced, and the receiving line broke up. "You are safely back again in your family's arms. Perhaps Captain Bell decided no intrusion was necessary."

Phoebe nodded hopefully. Though she trusted her sister implicitly, she hadn't wanted to worry her with all the details of the attack and her intervention in the Vaults. She only told her she'd gotten separated from her bodyguard and fallen down a flight of stone steps in the darkness. Captain Bell had found her. He was so upset by Phoebe being there that he'd threatened to expose her adventure to the earl. But that was all Millie knew.

That same night, Duncan had turned up at the family's townhouse, looking terribly distraught. He was sick at the thought that she was lost or injured, or worse. It did little to relieve him when she informed him of everything that occurred.

In fact, Phoebe didn't think she'd ever seen the Highlander as enraged. He was quite clear that he didn't see her actions as compassionate and brave. She'd acted recklessly and stupidly. He threatened *never* to accept a job with her again.

By then, her headache had improved somewhat, and she gave him her word that she would be far more cautious in the future. When Duncan's temper had cooled, Phoebe told him she'd had to reveal his name to Captain Bell. And she trusted him not to say anything about her profession if he were approached by the man.

An elderly couple who were friends of the family paused to comment on the success of the ball, chatting with them a moment before moving on.

"I hope you're giving up on that horrid Leech person as a source," Millie said in a low voice when they were gone. Her sister knew all about him. She served as Phoebe's first reader for every article before she sent her work on to her editor at the *Edinburgh Review*.

"I can't," Phoebe whispered back. "He has solid proof I need for the column. When Duncan confronted him, he reiterated that he has irrefutable documentation. And I believe him."

"But you won't go back to that terrible place, will you?" Millie asked.

"No more going to the Vaults."

"Where will you meet him?"

"Someplace much safer," Phoebe assured her. "He needs the money I've offered. Now I know why. Still, once I get back to Edinburgh, I'll have Duncan make the arrangements."

The two sisters watched Hugh and Grace dancing for a moment, and Phoebe was relieved to see her parents deep in conversation with their oldest friends, the Earl of Stanmore and his wife.

"You know, perhaps it's time you told Father what you're doing. If *you* do it, then you have nothing to fear from . . ." She stopped, and Phoebe realized her sister was staring at the door.

She turned to look, and her heart sank. Captain Bell was standing in the ballroom, and their gazes locked over the crowd. Heads turned to him, and a wave of murmurs swept through the room.

Even for those who knew nothing of the tragic circumstances surrounding his family, Ian Bell cut a dashing figure and drew the eyes of those around him. Except for his impeccably white cravat, he was dressed all in ebony from top to toe. His black brocade waistcoat of satin was buttoned high with a collar that framed the angular lines of a stern, handsome face.

The men of her family were all tall, but he towered over those around him. But for the hints of grey at the temples, the color of his hair nearly matched his clothing, and he wore it longer than was currently fashionable. Even the shadow of whiskers on his face gave him the careless look of a man who gave no thought at all to what others might think of him.

His dark eyes remained fixed on her face, and Phoebe felt unexpected heat pool in her treacherous stomach. Memories of those impetuous, golden days of her youth returned. The rogue could still set her insides on fire.

Then, with an almost imperceptible nod, he turned and looked across to where Hugh and Grace had ended their dance.

Without any hesitation, he started toward them.

"Damnation," Phoebe muttered. "I've got to stop him."

Ian had timed his late arrival intentionally. He was here to see and speak to one person and only one. Phoebe Pennington. Based on what he'd learned from their discussion in the carriage, however, and from everything he'd been able to ascertain about her story since, he was certain any conversation tonight would be more productive if it were initiated by her. Otherwise, he'd never get a straight answer out of her.

He asked the butler not to introduce him when he entered. Having been pretty much absent from social gatherings such as this for nearly a decade—because of the war and his recovery and his sister's death—he didn't want to draw the attention of acquaintances asking about him or about his mother. He had no interest in mingling. And he definitely didn't want to give anyone the erroneous impression that he would be accepting other invitations.

Scanning the crowd, he immediately found Phoebe standing by the open doors to the veranda. She was taller than most women, including her younger sister who stood beside her. For a moment, all he could do was stare.

She was wearing a regal red robe over a white short-sleeved dress. The border of gold embroidery captured the rays of the setting sun behind her. The ribbon intended to keep the mass of dark curls arranged atop her head was inadequate for the task, and ringlets hung loosely around her face.

His gaze moved over the perfect symmetry of her expressive face. He knew her eyes were a dark shade of blue, and they shone with intelligence and intensity during a discussion. Sitting across from her in his carriage, he'd been teased by those lips, with their fullness and color.

His mind focused. A scarf of red silk encircled her throat, covering her wound.

He was here for a reason, and it was essential that he speak to her.

His plan. Ian found the earl and the countess speaking with some guests in the far corner of the ballroom. A number of people around him had already recognized him. He heard his name rippling outward through the assembled guests. Her brother, Viscount Greysteil, was just finishing a dance with his wife. Perfect, he thought.

He looked in Phoebe's direction again. As he'd hoped, she discovered his arrival. Their gazes connected across the ballroom. He fought back a smile when her eyes narrowed with displeasure. Ian nodded in greeting and started toward her brother.

Before he'd gone half the distance across the dance floor, she slid into his path, effectively blocking him.

"Captain Bell."

This close, he saw little evidence of any bruise under

her eye. However handsome he'd thought her in his carriage, the impression didn't come close in comparison with how striking she was in the well-lit ballroom.

"Lady Phoebe." He bowed and she curtsied.

"How delightful of you to accept the invitation. My mother and sister-in-law were under the impression that once again you'd deprive us of your company."

He arced one brow, well aware of the eavesdropping audience hemming them in. "As I mentioned to you in Edinburgh when we met last, I wouldn't miss it this year."

The bonniest of blushes colored her cheeks.

"Now, if you'll forgive me, I need to give my regards to—"

"And if I recall, when we parted, you asked for the first dance. Did you not, Captain?"

Ian looked into those shining blue eyes, sparkling with challenge. The moment hung in the air between them, and he heard more whispers of his and her name. If he wished to see her squirm a little, he knew he would be waiting a long while. Phoebe Pennington was far too independent and sure of herself.

He bowed and stretched a hand out to her. "You honor me."

She slid her gloved fingers on top of his, and they moved toward the dance floor. Anyone watching would have believed their little lie as she granted him a rare smile.

"I believe this is the first time I've ever been asked to dance by a young lady," he told her. "Did you knock anyone over running across the ballroom?"

"You should accept more invitations, Captain. I'm certain there are quite a few ladies here tonight who would happily ambush you."

"But I suspect if our last meeting had been different, you wouldn't be one of them."

She opened her pretty mouth to say something but thought better of it and pressed her lips together.

A waltz was announced, and as the two of them moved to join the large circle of dancers, he caught Greysteil's gaze over Phoebe's head. Both men nodded in greeting.

His partner's head turned to follow his gaze, and she saw her brother.

"I hope you're not thinking of abandoning me, Captain."

He shook his head. "The night is young, and I'm certain both the earl and the viscount will be happy to meet with me in private for a few minutes after we finish this dance."

He hid his amusement as she took his hand and forcefully positioned it on her waist.

The music started, the two of them turning together and dancing into the space vacated by the next couple as the whole circle moved in a slow, whirling motion.

He felt the tension in the rigidity of her steps and in the way she avoided looking into his face. They were close, but miles apart. Her forehead was creased and her cheeks were flushed. He imagined her having an argument with him now while he was deprived of hearing a single word.

"And you were saying?"

Blue eyes narrowed, meeting his.

"I did as I promised and came to Baronsford the next morning. I thanked you already for what you did for me. Why can't you let it end at that, Captain? Why keep threatening to expose me to my family?"

"Because you lied."

Ian was charmed to see how dark the blue irises turned as his words sank in.

"Everything I said was nearly the truth."

"You lied," he repeated, spinning them faster as the music picked up in tempo.

Sounds of giddy laughter surrounded them, but the hilarity had no effect on the unblinking gaze or the clipped sharpness of the words.

"How can I defend myself when I have no idea what your accusation pertains to?"

He waited to answer until the music once again slowed. "I spoke with your man Turner."

Phoebe went flat-footed for a moment, but he slipped his hand around to the middle of her back and guided both of them into the turn.

"What did Duncan tell you?"

Deuced little, he thought. The former Edinburgh constable was devoted to her. He was not going to be pressured into revealing anything about why Lady Phoebe had hired him to escort her to the Vaults. But when it came to corroborating falsehoods . . . well, the man wouldn't cross that line.

"There was no beau. No lover," he told her. "You followed no manipulating cad to that drug den." The man actually said Lady Phoebe's secrets were hers to keep or reveal, but that Mrs. Turner would "ne'er cook another morsel if he did one solitary thing that might injure her ladyship's reputation."

The music tempo increased again, and she held on to him tightly as he turned them in the heightening frenzy of the dance.

"Why did you go there?" The respectable distance

between them had diminished nearly to an embrace. The constant turning had her clutching onto his arm. "I'm giving you one last opportunity."

"After the dance," she whispered breathlessly, her face flushed. "Please meet me in the gardens outside my brother's study. I'll explain everything to you then. I promise."

Too soon, in his opinion, the dance came to an end. Laughter and applause filled the room, but the two stood still, facing each other, the tension palpable in the narrow space between them.

He bowed, and as she curtsied, he saw her cast a glance over his shoulder. An instant later, she backed toward the crowd. When he turned around, Viscount Greysteil was waiting.

"I'm delighted you're here, Captain. We hadn't been expecting you."

❧ 4 ☙

PHOEBE LOOKED BACK along the path toward the veranda. The sun was gone, leaving behind a thick blanket of red and gold beneath the deepening blue of the twilight sky. Distant sounds of the party emanated from the open ball-room doors. Music mingled with occasional laughter and voices, intermittently sharpened and muffled by the soft breeze that carried it to the walled garden outside of Hugh's study. Still, there was no sign of him.

Captain Bell had visited Baronsford before, she told herself. He'd have no trouble finding his way. That is, if he was coming.

"He'll come. He *will*," she muttered, starting to pace to calm her agitation. At the end of a garden path, beyond the orchards, where the meadows fell away to the lake, darkness was already claiming the rolling hills of the deer park. Around her, a mist was beginning to rise from the fields.

I'm delighted you're here, Captain. We hadn't been expecting you.

She'd heard her brother's greeting as she walked away from the dance floor. Hugh might be delighted that Ian Bell was here, but Phoebe certainly wasn't.

"Why can't you let it go?" she asked under her breath.

She knew why. She wasn't blind. Ian had been mourning his sister for three years. And it was his nature to worry about others and try to prevent a similar tragedy from occurring. Especially to a person he knew.

Of course, she was more than simply a person he knew. Sarah had been closer in age to Millie, but the bond of friendship had been stronger with Phoebe. And she knew the reasons. They each had an independent nature and a sense of adventure. They shared a love of books and poetry and stories. They were both tall, almost the same height. Their stature was hardly a requirement to establish them as friends, but it served as one more link between them. And there were a hundred more things that bonded the two young women.

For a moment the music and the dance were back in her thoughts. To be held so close, to feel Captain Bell's strong hands on her waist, on the small of her back. Her body relived the movement, each step in perfect harmony even as his words wreaked havoc in her mind. She'd never seen eyes like his, nearly black with a rim of silver encircling the irises. They'd held her captive throughout the dance.

Feelings she'd had for him from before kept pushing into her mind like the strains of a song that would not be forgotten. The song was distracting and somewhat embarrassing. And try as she might, she couldn't ignore it.

But Phoebe had other, more important things to consider. The present situation was too stressful. She liked her life. She loved what she did. She wanted to get back to it. She hated the possibility of being exposed by someone else, and the certainty of disaster that would follow if she were. She now knew what the "sword of Damocles" meant.

"Damnation," she muttered, turning on her heel and walking back along the same path.

She couldn't blame Duncan either. She'd put herself under that dangling blade. The Highlander was an honorable man. He would say nothing that would demean or endanger her—especially to a gentleman who might be considered a suitable matrimonial possibility. His wife had delivered many a kindly lecture to Phoebe extolling the benefits of marriage and family. It was a favorite topic of hers. And Duncan shared her sentiments.

No, Phoebe alone had caused the current difficulty she was facing. Except for that weasel, Leech. He too was responsible. But she never should have agreed to meet him in the Vaults. They could have met in a thousand other places.

"You didn't think it through," she scolded herself.

The hoot of an owl quite close by was immediately answered by another down by the loch. Servants were beginning to light torches in the gardens at the far end of the west wing and along the paths. Light poured from a number of windows on the upper floors and from Hugh's study. In the distance, the music of a waltz ended.

"Will you make me wait all night?" she said aloud, growing restless as she looked back down the path.

Millie was right. She should have spoken to her family before tonight. It was childish not to make a clean breast of it, and she was hardly a child.

But she could not approach her father. He was too stubborn to understand. Everyone in the family was of the opinion that she had inherited the Earl of Aytoun's temperament. "Like two bulls" was the way her brother Gregory once put it. Perhaps it was true. The two of them never seemed able to listen to the other.

Not her mother either. The husband and wife had no secrets, and the two had always operated as a united front. Growing up, Phoebe and her siblings knew there was no divide and conquer when it came to getting one's way.

No point in talking to Gregory about it. He had too much to worry about with Freya expecting, and with a precocious six-year-old to raise. And Jo was out of the question. For the first time in her life, their older sister was immersed in happiness. Phoebe would never dream of casting a shadow of worry over that.

"Hugh?" she mused, immediately frowning at the thought. She had a feeling the Lord Justice would drag her into his courtroom and prosecute her for trespassing in the Vaults, just to teach her a lesson.

No, she had to speak to Grace. She was the bravest woman Phoebe had ever met. She'd grown up on battle-fields. She knew what women were capable of doing, and she was not one to accept any ridiculous confines based on a person's gender. She would understand. Grace had also lived in some of the greatest royal courts of the conti-nent, and she knew how politicians worked. Her sister-in-law could convey this information to her husband without upsetting him. Look what she'd done for Jo and Wynne Melfort. She had known exactly how to soften a blow and mediate when there was danger of a disaster.

"Why didn't I think of it sooner?"

She looked in the direction of the ballroom. The scoundrel was not coming.

"Do you always talk to yourself?"

She jumped, pressing her hand to her heart as she whirled to face him. Ian was leaning against an archway, his arms folded across his broad chest. He was silhouetted by the light from the study window. Phoebe fought the urge to shower him with a string of curses. Of course, he wouldn't walk through the gardens to find her; he came through the house.

"Did I frighten you?" he asked.

"Yes, as a matter of fact, you did."

"I'm glad. You should be frightened more often."

"By whom? You?"

"Not me." He unfolded his arms and drew himself up to his full height. "But you *should* be frightened of going places where you don't belong. Of exposing yourself to danger unnecessarily. Of trusting people you shouldn't. Of dressing like a man. Of lying to your family . . . and to those who save your life. And about that—"

She put up a hand to stop him. "I appreciate your concern, Captain. I accept all that you say."

He scoffed. "I don't believe it."

"Is it that you don't believe I appreciate your concern or that I'm capable of conceding I was in error? Or both? Or perhaps you've been practicing this admonishment for the past fortnight and you want to make sure you get in every word."

"You'll say anything to evade the issue at hand, won't you?"

"Perhaps you've brought your schoolmaster's switch and will require I kiss the rod when you're done?"

"Now that's a thought."

Phoebe saw a smile tugging at his lips.

She tended to intimidate men with her quick tongue and her willingness to argue. She knew she could be somewhat persistent—perhaps obstinate at times—in refusing to concede even minor points. Millie claimed she did it to push men away. But Ian Bell didn't seem at all put off by her nature. She took a deep breath, forcing a change in her manner.

"I apologize, Captain," she said. "I know you've come out here to give me another chance to explain." *And you've not mentioned the Edinburgh misadventure to my brother*, she finished silently.

He remained where he was, and she didn't know if he was dubious or amused.

"Let me put your doubts to rest," she said softly. "Please ask your questions."

It was understandable that he did not entirely trust her.

"I've had plenty of time to think of that incident," Phoebe continued when he said nothing. She touched the scarf at her throat. Every night since her return to Baronsford, she'd awakened in a cold sweat. The frightened lad appeared in her dreams again and again. Some nights she couldn't get to him fast enough. Other nights, she was the one being chased by a fiendish assailant. She faced this in her sleep. But what of reality? The horror of what could have happened to her down there was a constant companion. She could have been killed when she fought him at the top of the steps. And if Captain Bell weren't at the bottom, she would be dead now for sure, as she guessed the murderer would have come after her.

"I *am* grateful to you for saving my life. And as far as the fabrications . . ."

She paused, smoothing the front of her dress. The moment of reckoning was here.

"I'm a writer." The words tumbled out and she hesitated, half expecting a great chasm to open beneath her feet. "And I was in the Vaults with Duncan that night to research a project I'm working on right now."

The truth was out. She should have felt lighter in saying it. But the frown that now creased the man's brow told her she might only have succeeded in opening Pandora's box. And she didn't wish to tell him more.

A person's political inclinations determined how he viewed the newspaper she wrote for and her columns. She was a heroic social crusader to some but a troublemaking demon to others. She didn't know for certain, but she could only imagine Captain Bell was firmly in the Tory camp. His father, having made his fortune in Baltimore, had returned from America on the eve of the revolution there. And the son had proven his value on the battlefield and now served as a high-level administrator in Fife. It would only make sense that they would be on opposite ends of the political spectrum with regard to support for the government.

"Your uncle's wife, Gwyneth Douglas Pennington, isn't she a novelist?" he asked.

His statement surprised and relieved her. Captain Bell knew of her aunt's writing, and she heard no hint of scorn or condemnation in his voice. Gwyneth's work was published pseudonymously, but the subject of her writing was far less problematic than Phoebe's.

"Yes, for many years she's been quite successful with her adventure novels. How did you know about it?"

"Sarah was a great fan of her work," he told her. "So is my mother."

"Of course. I knew that." Phoebe had given her friend some of those novels and arranged for Sarah to meet Gwyneth at Baronsford when her aunt and uncle were visiting. But it surprised her to know that Captain Bell was familiar with his sister and mother's choice of authors and books.

"Is that what you do? Write romantic adventures?"

Phoebe decided evasion was in order. If that's what he thought, it was close enough to the truth. In any event, it would have to do. "My aunt has always been my idol, but I'm only at the start of my calling. I'm still feeling my way, as it were."

He nodded but didn't seem convinced. "But you haven't mentioned any of this to your family?"

"I have. Well, I mean they know of my aspirations. They've encouraged me to pursue it on some level. There is a collection of fables in Baronsford's library right now that I put together from the stories Ohenewaa told us."

"Ohenewaa?"

"She was a freed African woman who was a grandmother to all of us as we grew up." Phoebe never forgot how happy her mother had been when she presented the printed collection to her. "What my family doesn't know is that I foolishly put myself in such grave danger in Edinburgh that night. I went there to gain firsthand knowledge of the Vaults. It was a mistake."

She saw no reason to draw Millie into any of this. Phoebe slid her hands along the embroidered belt that ran beneath her breasts and looked along the path. She couldn't remain in one place. Pacing suited her restless nature, especially when she didn't care to tell the absolute truth.

"Would you care to walk, Lady Phoebe?"

"That would be very nice. I love the scent of flowers in the evening, don't you? You have lovely gardens at Bellhorne. The roses should be blooming at this time of the year, I believe."

"They are," he said, falling in beside her. "But you wouldn't be thinking of changing the topic, I hope."

"No, of course not."

They walked in silence for a moment. The music in the ballroom had stopped, and in the distance, the faint yipping of a brood of young foxes could be heard.

"Going into the Vaults was more reckless than anything I've ever done." Her words were heartfelt, and she hoped he recognized that. "And you found me. You must know how terrified I was. I know how close I came to catastrophe. I'll never do that again. I assure you."

They reached a wall at the bottom of the garden. In the orchard beyond, apple trees stood in neat rows like burly night sentinels.

"You don't *know* how close you came," the captain said brusquely. "A man was killed there that same night."

"A man?" Her nightmares abruptly became reality. Had she saved the lad only to have him be caught again? "Was he old? Young?"

"I don't know his age." He pressed a fist into his other hand. "The murder was discovered by a constable the next day as two men were carrying the body through Cowgate toward the medical college."

Her chin dropped, and she stared at the dark paving stones between his boots and her skirts. Duncan had warned her, but she'd heard before about the villainy and dangers lurking in every shadow. Life lost its value when you ventured into those catacombs and the twisting alleyways surrounding it. But the warnings hadn't dissuaded her from going.

Her thoughts cleared. She'd battled only one man.

"Two men?" she asked.

"Workmen. Not the murderers."

"Horrible. I . . ." Words seemed insignificant in the face of something so awful. She wanted to know if the boy she fought for had been the victim, but there was no way for her to find out. And what difference would it make? A human being had died.

"The men said they found the body in an alcove not far from the place where your attacker approached you."

Unexpected tears threatened to break free, but she fought them back and looked away.

"The throat was slashed. That was enough to cause the victim's death. But then the murderer made another cut, from the chin to the navel."

Her hand flew to her neck. Her wounds were healing, but the memory of those moments in the dark passageway—the hot panic, the fight for the boy's life and then her own—wasn't fading. And now, to learn what happened afterward stung her badly. She'd fought a battle only to find out later she'd lost.

The captain injected no added drama into his voice. The facts were harsh enough.

"Over the past three years, I've learned of or seen with my own eyes over a dozen corpses with the same wounds. All of them were found in the Vaults or in the wynds of Cowgate and Canongate. All in the same vicinity. And these are just the bodies that were recovered before they could be sold and dissected by anatomists. I have no way of knowing exactly how many have died by the same hand."

Her stomach churned. She recalled the impression of malevolence when the man passed, before she knew him for what he was. She *felt* the evil he exuded.

"Someone is killing in a *consistent* manner?" she asked, unable to ignore a chill that had taken root in her very bones. Whatever horrors had infected her dreams, they were nothing compared to this grim assertion. "One person is doing all of those killings?"

"Yes. A cold-blooded hunter who is manic enough to leave a distinct mark. A signature, so to speak."

Phoebe turned away from him, trying to force air into her lungs. After the incident in the Vaults and the exchange of only a few words with Ian, the vague idea of a criminal underbelly existing in the world became an ugly and horrifying reality. She had grappled with a murderer.

She was relieved when she felt him press his hand into the small of her back, steering her back toward the house.

"I've said too much, Lady Phoebe. I apologize for telling you all of this."

His candid description only now struck her as surprising. How many men, she wondered, would have been so blunt? So graphic? Women were to be sheltered from the sordid and the horrific.

"Do not apologize. I was there, Captain. The man I fought with could surely have been the killer. He could have been responsible for the other man's death. For all those other deaths."

His hand remained on her back, a gentle caress giving her support and comfort through the layers of her dress.

She wondered if any person had seen another attack,

someone who'd been as close as she was. Someone who could identify him. For a moment, it had been only the two of them, predator and prey. She'd felt this killer's knife slashing toward her throat. But the Vaults were too dark, the moment too frenzied. She'd been too blinded by fear and the need to fight to look at his face. But he saw her.

She glanced out into the night. He could be out there in the darkness now. Waiting to strike. To finish what he'd begun.

The thought flashed through her mind that perhaps Sarah had been the victim of this same man. But she was hesitant to ask, unwilling to dig at wounds Ian was still nursing.

They paused by the door leading into the house, and Phoebe felt an odd sense of loss when he removed his hand from her back.

"This tragedy is only one incident amid a morass of corruption and murder that is rampant in the rookeries of Edinburgh." His face was in shadow. "I don't know what your novel pertains to. But please, don't ever, *ever*, place yourself in such danger again."

Captain Bell had kept her secret. He hadn't exposed Phoebe to her family. He believed the partial truth she'd told him. She was grateful for that. But it was his concern that touched her more deeply than she would ever have imagined. She felt the emotion—the pain— that laced his words. He was thinking also of his sister, Sarah.

"I am sorry," she said softly, touching his arm. "I've said a great deal, but nothing excuses what happened."

She stared at his chest, not trusting herself to look into his eyes. Sadness, like some hot poker, wedged itself into her breast and pried loose a long-buried regret; she'd not had the courage to speak the words in her heart at Sarah's funeral.

"The most upsetting part of all of this right now is knowing what I've done to you. Of dragging up bitter memories. For that, I can offer no excuse. Sarah was my friend. I loved her dearly. But then the tragedy struck. She was in our lives one day, and the next, she was gone." She heard her voice quaking. His face wavered in her vision as tears burned her eyes. "Whatever feelings of loss I had, I know they were nothing compared to what you suffered. The prolonged search for her. And then . . . the day of the funeral . . . seeing how you suffered . . ."

A single tear broke free and found a path down her cheek. Another followed, and she dashed them away.

He pulled her roughly into his arms, and she went willingly. Her hands found their way around his middle. Her face pressed against his heart.

The workings of her disposition—how she felt and even acted—were always so extreme. Right now, her heart ached because of what he'd suffered, because of what she'd made him suffer.

"Forgive me. I didn't intend to dredge up the tragedy of Sarah's death."

"There's nothing to forgive. You cared for her," he said in low voice. "Do you think she's ever far from my thoughts?"

"No," Phoebe murmured. "How could she be?"

Ian caressed her back and then, taking hold of her arms, pushed her just far enough away to look into her face.

"Promise me you'll never again put yourself in that kind of danger."

"I promise."

They stood still, his hands on her arms, their bodies so close.

And suddenly, the rest of the world ceased to exist. There was Ian. His face, with its hard edges and rugged lines. She saw tenderness and vulnerability in his eyes. She'd longed for this moment for much of her life.

Before she could even think to stop herself, Phoebe raised her hand to his cheek. She felt the rough shadow of whiskers, and then the tips of her fingers moved to his lips. They were surprisingly soft. Their gazes locked, and she saw hunger in his eyes.

She withdrew her hand, knowing she'd gone too far. "I shouldn't have—"

He crushed her lips beneath his, silencing her. Phoebe's palms pressed against his chest, but her body wouldn't muster the strength to push him away. It had been so long since she'd felt a spark from any man's kiss, but never had she felt the scorching heat that Ian ignited in her now.

He deepened the kiss and her knees grew weak. She leaned back against the stone walls of the building. He followed, pressing against her. Excitement blazed a delicious path through her veins. She wanted him even closer. Her hands moved up and slipped around his neck, and she molded her soft curves against his hard, powerful body.

The dreams of youth were back. Far too many times she'd imagined this, pictured herself wrapped in Ian's embrace, protected by the shadows of the night, lost in the passion of their kiss.

Phoebe knew the moment a sense of urgency seized him. His arms tightened around her. The pressure of his lips increased, and she melted into the kiss. His tongue was soft and insistent, and she opened to him as he started sampling, tasting, learning the texture of her mouth.

Never before had her body burned like this, seared by the mere touch of lips and tongue. Never before had she wanted more of this. But she wanted it now. Her tongue responded to his, becoming bolder by the moment as his taste, his scent, the pressure of his body dazed her. The heat, the raw desire growing within her was unlike anything she'd ever imagined.

Phoebe didn't even hear the sound until Ian broke off the kiss abruptly and stepped back. Two people were approaching along the path from the ballroom. They were talking and laughing. Ian stood staring silently into her eyes, and she burned with excitement, nearly over-whelmed by what had just happened.

The intruders stopped at the entrance to the garden when the music began again. The two were here to stay.

"I have to go to Bellhorne for a few days," Ian told her, his voice sounding strained.

"I'll be returning to Edinburgh at the end of this week." She didn't know what made her speak so candidly about her plans. Yes, she did. She was offering him a chance to call on her if he chose to.

"Edinburgh, it is, then." A smile tugged at his lip. "Will you promise not to cause any trouble or put yourself in any danger until I get back?"

He was asking too much of her. She still had an inflammatory article to write. And she still needed Mr. Leech's information.

"Until you get back," she promised.

The wind, foul with the dead salt smells of the harbor and fish, whipped across the darkened town, yanking at shutters and roofs of thatch and scattering the sleep of those huddled within. Windows rattled fiercely, as if marauders from the marshes were beating at the panes, threatening entry. Children clung to each other in their beds and cried out that the death crone had come. Ragged clouds scudded across the face of the dying moon, and out in the raging sea, battered sailing men clung to crude miniatures of loved ones while their ships rose and fell, shuddered and groaned. If this was summer, what evil would descend with the bitter northern blasts of winter?

But monsters did not roam abroad. They dwelled within.

He pushed the papers on the table away and rose to secure the window latch. It had been a night not much different from this one when he began his journey. When he first heard them.

You've been chosen. Avenge us.

He'd not yet reached his fifteenth birthday when he stumbled out into the dark street to answer the summons.

The man came into his path by accident, stumbling from the tavern. The sounds of carousing followed him out the door, but the drunkard came alone.

His knife burned in his hand. It was the same tool he used to sharpen his pens, trim the wick. But when the voices called, the blade took on new life. It was Excalibur, the claymore of the Wallace, the sword of Drogheda.

Avenge us.

As he drew the cutting edge across the drunkard's throat, he felt the Fire of the Ages ignite within him. Power surged through his veins. The sweet, copper smell of blood flooded his senses, overwhelming the foul odor of the bog.

Finish. Mark him. As they did to us. Mark him.

He left the mark. And it was done.

Until they spoke to him, the Chosen, again. And again. And again . . .

$\maltese$ *5* $\maltese$

Bellhorne Castle
Fife, Scotland

AT THE TOP of the rise, Ian reined in his mount and looked south toward the distant Firth of Forth, glistening under the noonday sun. Taking off his hat, he breathed in the smell of the first haying as he waited for his estate manager, Mr. Raeburn, to catch up.

He'd grown up on this land. He knew every field and lane, every sparkling brook, and every green glen. He knew every tenant and every fisherman in the village. Bellhorne was his home.

He'd left it for the first time during the wars. Purchasing a commission in the cavalry, Ian had served "with distinction" in Germany and Denmark and then on the Peninsula. Badly wounded and taken by the French at Talavera, he'd only learned of his father's passing after he was released. So he'd come home to Bellhorne to recover and take over the duties that went along with running a vast estate. And that included the care of his mother and sister.

The horrors of war, however, had left deep and invisible wounds that continued to pain him long after his body had healed. Riding through these hills and fields provided his only escape.

Day and night, through every season and every kind of weather, he'd push his horse at breakneck speeds in an effort to exhaust himself. What he'd witnessed and done in the wars, what he'd suffered in the French prison at Lille, continued to haunt his sleep. But the pain that plagued him then was nothing compared to what Sarah's loss brought later.

After her murder, this land that had once been imbued with memories of youthful innocence became a sharp and constant reminder of his sister and how he'd failed to protect her.

And now he had only his mother left.

Ian forced his attention to the north end of the valley that led down to the fishing village. The four connected towers of Bellhorne Castle were just visible above the trees of the surrounding deer park. He was sure that Fiona Bell would already be on the terrace overlooking the beloved garden, arranging roses she'd just cut to grace their dinner table.

As sweet as the roses she cherished, his mother was even more fragile in body and mind.

Ian wasn't looking forward to dinner, but he saw it as his duty. Everything at Bellhorne was now arranged to maintain the delusional world in which his mother lived. And that included keeping her away from all but a limited number of neighbors and friends who were party to the elaborate charade.

Ian's gaze wandered down to the meadow bordering the loch, and the painful knot in his chest grew in size. It was there that he taught Sarah to ride when she was not yet five. On so many cold, wet mornings, they'd fished that loch together, cut off from the rest of the world by Fife's heavy mists. He expelled a long breath.

It was so difficult being home. There was no getting around it.

Raeburn spurred his sturdy mare up the hill and stopped beside him. Since Sarah's death, the man had been carrying more than his share of responsibility for the running of Bellhorne.

Immediately, his estate manager's attention was drawn to one of the tenant's cottages below. A cow was standing half in the door of the place.

"Blasted old codger," he said, shaking his head in disgust. "If I've told the rascal once, I've told him a dozen times. I'll not have him keeping that bloody cow in his cottage."

Ian donned his hat again. "Never mind, Raeburn. The work is getting done. The farms are doing well enough. Everywhere I look, I see evidence of your hard work."

The manager began to mutter, but he seemed satisfied with the acknowledgment he received from Ian.

"Let's go down to the house. Dinner will be served shortly, and I don't want to keep my mother waiting."

As they rode down the hill, Raeburn filled him in on the progress of a new dairy barn under construction.

"Perhaps tomorrow we can ride out there, and I'll show you what still needs to be done."

As the farm manager finished talking about tenants and grain yield and the fine summer weather, Ian thought of what an idyllic place Bellhorne would be for a poet or a writer.

Phoebe. He guessed she'd be in Edinburgh before he returned.

The recollection of their kiss came back to him, causing a tightening in his loins. The fullness of her lips, the curve of her long body against his, the soft yearning sound in the back of her throat. Thinking about it now, he was well aware that something was happening between them. Something that caused the secure ties he kept on his control to snap.

He hadn't followed her into the garden to kiss her. He wanted answers, and he felt she should know about the murder. She needed to understand the potential fate she had narrowly escaped. He wanted her to be frightened. He wasn't entirely certain he'd accomplished that goal.

Phoebe Pennington enjoyed wealth and position as the fourth child of the Earl and Countess Aytoun, and Ian knew her family allowed her great latitude to do as she pleased. She was, however, upset to think they would learn about her traipsing through the Vaults. But what family wouldn't fear for a daughter's safety in such circumstances?

Her face took shape in his memory again, and he was astonished by the force of his attraction to her. Phoebe, whom he'd seen many times while Sarah was still alive, had barely drawn his notice. He'd never appreciated her vibrant beauty, never enjoyed her quick tongue and passionate nature. He knew nothing of her adventurous nature.

He was fascinated by her.

Then, there were the words she'd spoken to him in the

garden about the day of Sarah's funeral. *Seeing how you suffered.*

"I hope you won't be offended, Captain," Raeburn said, breaking into his thoughts. "But my wife and I have been entertaining a cousin of hers for the past few days, so we'll need to excuse ourselves from dinner today. But the old bore is leaving for Edinburgh in the morning, praise the Lord, and I told your mother that we'd be honored to join the family tomorrow instead."

Ian nodded. He was tremendously grateful for the people who visited Fiona, even when he was away. Raeburn's wife was an especially kind and stalwart supporter.

"Would you happen to know Mrs. Raeburn's opinion on how my mother is faring?"

"Aye, sir. We were speaking of it just the other day," the manager told him. "She says, more so than before, Mrs. Bell's humor reflects the manner of those around her. When the housekeeper grumbles at a servant, your mother gets the grumbles, as well. And Dr. Thornton, with his blunt words and gruff ways, can agitate her. But the minister, Mr. Garioch, can always put a smile on her lips. And of course, there's your cousin, Mrs. Young. An angel she is, that woman. She couldn't be kinder if she were Mrs. Bell's own flesh and blood, and she cheers your mother to no end. The woman is a godsend."

One of the best things Ian had done after Sarah's disappearance was to invite his widowed cousin Alice back from Baltimore to live at Bellhorne and serve as his mother's companion. As for the doctor, the minister, and the rest of them, he could not imagine a more trustworthy group to help him protect his mother from the horror of Sarah's death.

Leaving his horse at the stables, Ian was greeted at the house by the butler.

"Has Dr. Thornton arrived?" he asked.

"Just so, Captain. All the guests are in the garden with Mrs. Bell and Mrs. Young. Eight will be dining, sir."

"Very good. If my mother asks, tell her I'll be down shortly."

Lucas had his dinner attire ready for him upstairs. As Ian cleaned up and dressed, he reminded himself that he needed to find a private moment with the doctor. Last month, Thornton spoke of a physician he planned to visit in Edinburgh. The man was an expert in pathologies affecting the heart. He hoped to find out if there was a correlation between the occasional bouts of dizziness afflicting Ian's mother and her weakened heart.

Ian paused a moment in the stone archway leading into the garden before making his presence known. A couple from the village and their daughter comprised the additional members of the party. Right now the guests looked like a small flock of sheep following the bell-wether. They were making their way out of a lane of late-flowering azaleas.

His mother took great pride in these grounds. Before he was born, she'd overseen the planting of the endless rows of flowers, herbaceous plants, and even vegetables. On the wide grassy lanes that separated the beds, Ian and the other estate children had run footraces past sweetly scented summer flowers—a blur of red and yellow, blue and white. Even now, he could recall his mother on her knees amongst the flora, laughing and waving as they sailed past.

But of all the plants in that magical garden, what she prized most dearly were her roses.

"One planted for every year of my daughter's life," Fiona would tell her visitors. Even now, he could see her leaning on her ivory-headed cane, gesturing to individual roses, white and pink and red, as the group meandered along a garden wall. Talking incessantly, she was pointing out the colors and no doubt sharing a wealth of information about each bush.

Ian noted the shawl around her shoulders. It was thicker and warmer than the ones she usually wore this time of the year. Alice walked just behind, occasionally putting out a hand to assist her.

Sorrow formed a clenched fist in his chest. Fiona Bell was only in her fifties, but grey hair and a stooped back and uncertain steps suggested someone much older. It was as if each of the three years since Sarah's death had aged her a decade. And whenever Ian returned to Bellhorne, which was at least once or twice a month, it seemed to him that his mother failed even more.

The group was near enough for him to hear now.

"Did I ever mention that I lost two children between my son and Sarah?" she asked of her audience. She didn't wait for an answer but continued. "Twin boys."

It was an oft-told story, one that those in attendance had surely heard numerous times. Ian was obliged to the guests for their attention and show of sympathy as they allowed the older woman to repeat her tale.

His brothers. Ian had been only three years old, and his vague memories were more from the retelling of the difficult six months from the boys' birth to their deaths. They'd battled one ailment after the other until a fever had taken them. And then seven years had passed before Sarah was born.

"My first daughter. My only daughter," Fiona said

happily, touching the delicate pink flowers on a rose bush. "My husband brought me a single rose right after he first laid eyes on our beautiful child. And that started our ritual. One a year we've planted ever since, on Sarah's birthday."

The wife of the couple from the village praised the garden and asked about the work that went into caring for it. Ian's mother was more than happy to elaborate. They continued down the row of roses, and a moment later they were out of earshot.

The visits, these dinners, the moments when Fiona retold stories of her life and showed the guests her precious rose garden all meant a great deal to her. These were now the only times she showed a hint of the lively woman she once was.

Ian moved into the garden, and Mr. Garioch was the first to see him. The minister was standing with Dr. Thornton, who was gesturing with his customary animation as he spoke. Garioch pointed out Ian's arrival, and the two men crossed the grassy lanes to join him.

"Quite happy you've returned in time for some socializing before dinner, Captain," the minister said, turning his back to the small group following Ian's mother.

"Mr. Garioch arrived a wee bit early this afternoon," Dr. Thornton clarified. "And the man has already had his fill of the attentions of the ladies. Particularly the lass there. She persists in asking his opinion on every insignificant matter she can think of."

Ian saw the young woman cast a forlorn look in their direction, and her mother nudged her to pay attention to Mrs. Bell. For as long as Ian's family had known the minister, he'd always had that effect on women. Extremely handsome to the point of being occasionally referred to as "beautiful" by the ladies, Peter Garioch commanded the interest of the female members of the parish with his bright blue eyes, golden hair, and soft, pleasant manner. Dr. Thornton, on the other hand, stood in sharp contrast with his craggy, battle-scarred face and curt, gruff ways. The man suffered no fools and was known to give vent to his volatile temper when he thought a patient was wasting his time.

The girl was even now attempting to break free and come in their direction, but the firm hand of the mother kept her where she was.

"But if you don't wish their adulation," the doctor advised brusquely, "then don't treat them as you do. You only encourage it. So gentle and understanding, even when the silly chit was complaining about trifles."

"It is my duty, Thornton, to treat all the Lord's creatures in the same kindly manner, regardless of their gender. And that includes you."

"And you think I give a tinker's da— . . . a moment's pause to how you speak to me!" the doctor grouched indignantly.

Ian knew the two bachelors were capable of arguing about this topic, and any other, for hours, but right now he had no interest in knowing what Garioch's sermon pertained to last Sunday. Nor was he particularly interested in the fact that every female patient the doctor attended to this week insisted on telling him all about the minister's scriptural observations. He glanced toward his mother and her companions. They'd be completing their tour of the gardens shortly, and Ian wanted to speak to the doctor before dinner.

"Your visit to Edinburgh," he broke in, addressing Thornton. "Did you have the opportunity of speaking with your colleague at the medical college about my mother?"

"I didn't. An urgent matter came up while I was there, and I didn't have time to see him." Thornton did not provide any further details but turned his gaze toward his patient. "But I did write to him two days ago and invited him to come to Fife for a visit. It would be better if your mother were seen by him personally."

Fiona Bell had been diagnosed with angina a decade ago, and Ian had been encouraging her to let him arrange for a trip to Edinburgh or London. He wanted her to be regularly examined by an expert, as she had been in the years preceding Sarah's disappearance. But since then, she refused to leave Bellhorne and scoffed at the idea of seeing any other doctor besides Thornton. And although Ian trusted the man's medical capabilities, he also agreed with the doctor that a second opinion by an expert was a necessity.

"As you know," Ian said, "she may be resistant."

"I'll help the doctor to persuade her, Captain," the minister put in.

"I should hear back from Edinburgh soon enough," Thornton assured him as Fiona's voice reached them. The group appeared to have completed their turn in the garden. "I'll make the arrangements."

"Ah, Ian. You're back," his mother cried out upon seeing him. He couldn't ignore the note of relief in her tone as well as the shadow that had crept over the older woman's demeanor. He hadn't noticed it when he watched her from the garden arch.

Ian went to his mother and kissed her on the cheek. As he welcomed the guests from the village, Fiona said nothing but held his arm tightly against her. He sent his cousin a questioning look, but she simply shook her head and gestured toward the gardens.

The guests lined up to proceed into the dining room, and Alice accepted the arms of both the minister and the doctor while the young lady from the village looked on peevishly at the arrangement.

As Ian escorted his mother toward the house, she sighed heavily and looked over her shoulder at the gardens.

"What's wrong, Mother?"

She was twisting the carved handle of her cane with thin, pale hands. "Sarah's roses."

"What about them?"

She sighed again unhappily.

"The twentieth. The rose we planted for Sarah's twentieth birthday. Do you remember it?" she asked, her voice quavering. "She wanted to plant it herself. She got right down on her hands and knees. My sweet girl was covered in dirt; she ruined a dress that day. But she didn't care. Do you . . . do you . . . ?"

"I remember clearly," he said. "She wanted to plant a Scots Rose, a double-bloom white rose, different from the others."

"'My rose will have a halo of perfume and produce everlasting points of beauty,' she'd said," Fiona whispered. "And she was right. Year after year, that one plant has continued to put the rest of the garden to shame."

She brought a fist to her mouth.

"Did someone cut flowers without your permission?"

She shook her head, her aging eyes brimming with tears.

"Please, tell me what's gone wrong?" he asked, ready to go back into the garden to correct whatever was amiss.

He hated seeing her upset. It was contrary to everything he was trying to do.

When he'd gone to war, Fiona had wept bitterly at the thought of losing him. Sarah told him later how grievously their mother had suffered. With every passing week and month and year, she'd grown physically frailer. Worse, something in her spirit had weakened, as if a thin blade had punctured her soul, allowing her very essence to bleed out slowly, steadily.

All the stories about the terrible months when they thought he'd died on the battlefield still tore at him. His father had been morose, inconsolable, and the tiny rend in Fiona's soul had become a gaping fissure. Having no news of how he'd died or where he was buried only compounded their suffering. Finally, the strain had been too much, and his father fell, struck down with apoplexy as he wandered alone through the fields one evening.

Only a fortnight later, word arrived at Bellhorne that Ian was alive in a French prison. But it was too late.

Upon Ian's return, his mother recovered. Her attachment to her children helped Fiona to get through the loss of her husband, though her health would never be the same.

Ian knew losing a daughter would be the final blow, however. She would never survive.

As much as it nearly killed him to live in a world of lies and fabrications, he would do anything to spare her even a moment's sorrow. He'd failed in his duty of protecting his sister. He'd be damned if he let his mother suffer anymore.

"Her white rose is dying," Fiona said in a pained voice. "The flowers budded but have struggled to open, and now the leaves are turning brown. It's the only one that is dying, and nothing I do is helping."

The twentieth. Three more roses had been added since, each on her birthday, each of them planted under the pretense that his sister was alive and living in America. But the one that had to die, of course, was the rose Sarah had planted with her very own hands.

His sweet, lost sister. The one constant breath of happiness and life in this family.

Ian brought his mother's hand to his lips. "This autumn, on her birthday, we can plant two shrubs. One new and one to replace the twentieth."

A tear rolled down the pale, lined face. "It won't be the same."

He didn't know what to say, what to offer to make her forget about the roses. For three years, reading letters of his own invention, filled with tales of Sarah's adventures in America had been enough. But no more.

"I want her to come back," she said, waving her walking stick at him. "And before you object and tell me all the things my daughter is involved in with your father's estate in Baltimore, tell her I'm only asking for a visit. A *visit*. That's not much to ask, is it?"

Ian looked into the teary eyes of the woman who meant the world to him and was lost for words.

"She listens to you, Ian. You two have a bond stronger than most brothers and sisters. If you ask, she'll not deny you. So please, ask her for me. Make it happen."

It was agony for him to lie, and Ian had done plenty of it until now. *Make it happen.*

"Please, bring my Sarah back for one visit before I die."

The final words were a dagger driven into his chest.

He didn't want to think about her dying. She was his mother. He was connected to her, flesh and blood and heart and soul. He could never see her suffer.

"I'll try to make it happen. I'll ask her in my next letter," he said. He was lying yet again, but for her, he would take eternal damnation and never flinch.

Fiona looked up at him in surprise. Then there was a smile, followed by her rippling laugh that had been absent from Bellhorne since Sarah's disappearance.

"She's coming home. Back from America," she cheered, turning to their guests.

Ian looked over her head at the startled faces of his cousin, Garioch, and Thornton.

Another lie. Another brick in the wall of falsehoods he'd constructed.

But where would it end? How long would he allow his mother to cling to hopes he himself had been building in her? How long could he protect her from the truth?

The time was coming nearer when he would need to tell her that no letters, no pleas, and no miracles would ever bring Sarah back home again.

$\maltese$ *6* $\maltese$

MIDAFTERNOON on the last day of June, and the city pulsed with life. And Phoebe loved it.

She loved the crowded bustle of Edinburgh's streets. As her carriage descended from the narrow confines of West Bow into the more open space of the Grassmarket, her driver inched his way through the crowds of workers and carters and vendors and ever-present gangs of ragged, barefoot street urchins. High in the tenements lining the muddy streets, women hung out laundry on makeshift drying poles. The doors of shops and tradesmen stood open to the summer warmth, and all along the way, people hurried by, intent on their busy lives.

Leaving the house in New Town, they'd made their way around the marshy North Loch and picked up Duncan at the lower end of Warrender's Close, already deep in the shadows cast by the fortress high above.

Safety. Caution. Discretion. Phoebe was diligently attending to everything she'd promised her sister-in-law during their long talk at Baronsford. Grace now knew what she did, the newspaper she wrote for, and the assumed name she wrote under. Phoebe wasn't surprised to find out that Grace was familiar with her work. The woman was an avid reader with an astonishing memory, and they talked in detail about the four columns she'd written so far.

Phoebe had no desire to add to the worries of those she loved, however, so the trip to the Vaults was not part of the discussion. Neither was the attack and her fight with a faceless killer. Still, Grace made her sit through a somewhat lengthy lecture about the need for safety, caution, and discretion.

So much like Grace, she thought now, looking out the carriage window. Not a word to discourage her from pursuing her passion. Just the careful collection and organization of information about Phoebe's vocation to be used in constructing the argument she would use later when she put her husband Hugh's mind at ease.

Her vocation. She smiled, already feeling vindicated.

Grace would tell Hugh, and his reaction would no doubt influence how their parents received the news.

Phoebe knew they'd still be somewhat anxious. As far as society was concerned, someone of her class traveling such a path, particularly a woman, would be perceived as scandalous. But the Penningtons as a family had a history of scandal. They also occupied a position in society that the ton and those in power could not afford to ignore. She was only living up to the family's legacy. As Millie said, they would never be boring.

Still, 'relieved' was the best way to describe how she felt. As was Millie, knowing she wasn't betraying their family by keeping Phoebe's secret.

As her driver approached Candlemaker Row, a small

flock of sheep being driven to market crossed in front of them, and the two young shepherds eyed the carriage with curiosity.

"We're here, m'lady," Duncan said, glaring out at the city he knew so well.

"I can see," she replied, anticipation bubbling inside. She had the article penned in her mind already. The tone, the argument, the conclusion. The call to action that she hoped readers would seize once they read it. The documented information Leech was to provide about the old and the infirm being thrown out into the cold would serve as the beating heart of the column.

The carriage stopped by an arched opening in the high stone wall. Beyond an iron gate, a dozen steps led up into Greyfriars Kirkyard. The gate was open, but no one appeared to be going in or out of the burial ground. It was well known that Bloody Mackenzie's ghost haunted the cemetery at all hours. Few people wanted to encounter the angry spirit of the old Covenanter, even in broad daylight.

It was the perfect place to meet with Leech and get the papers Phoebe needed for her column.

"The blasted scoundrel had better be here," Duncan huffed as he opened the carriage door. One thing she particularly liked about the Highlander was he never minced words with her. "Because I'm getting a wee bit tired of this scab's bloody antics."

Duncan had told Phoebe that when he found the nearly insensible Leech in the opium den in the Vaults, the man didn't have the papers on him. He'd gone through his things thoroughly. And though he'd admittedly been ready to shake the "sorry rum gagger" awake and force him to produce the documents, Duncan thought it better to report the situation to Phoebe. By that time she had already disappeared.

"You stay right here in the carriage, m'lady."

"In the carriage. I know."

"And no getting out to get a breath of air."

"I understand, Duncan."

"Nor to stretch your legs."

"Out, Highlander." She pointed at the door.

"Mind now," he warned. "The likes of you has no business sallying about in a neighborhood such as this."

Phoebe was about to argue his "likes of you" comment and make him understand she was tougher than he was giving her credit for, but she decided against it. She wanted Leech's information. "Don't worry. I know what to do."

His snort made it clear he didn't believe her. Nonetheless, he climbed out into the narrow street.

Watching through the open window, Phoebe saw him make a warning gesture to her driver before going through the archway and up the steps into the kirkyard.

She smiled to herself. Her conversation with Grace was already paying off. Aside from discussing Phoebe's writing, they'd also spoken about survival and pursuing one's interests as a woman in today's society. Her sister-in-law was an expert at succeeding in that. During the years before arriving in Scotland, she'd accompanied her father —an Irish colonel in Napoleon's army—from one battle-field to the next. She'd had the freedom to go where she wished. But she'd remained by his side and become an essential aide to him, safeguarding highly valued state secrets.

Grace had suggested that Phoebe practice the art of compromise in dealing with her father. Instead of constant conflict, she could give in a little, on occasion. Then, when she needed to communicate with him about something important, he'd be more open to understanding and respecting her wishes.

Compromise. It was a term almost entirely foreign to Phoebe's language and temperament. But she was willing to give it a try. And not only in dealing with her father, but with Duncan and Captain Bell, as well.

Suddenly, a trickle of sweat ran down her spine. She was being watched. Phoebe looked out the window away from the kirkyard. A man in a dark cloak stood in the open door of a shop, staring. His hat was pulled low, but fierce eyes bore into hers. Before she could act on her discomfort, an oxcart piled high with barrels briefly blocked her view of the shop, and when the wagon had rumbled past, the man was gone. She looked up and down the road, but there was no sign of him. For a moment she didn't know if she'd imagined it.

As Phoebe's pulse slowed, she decided all the words of warning she'd been getting recently were affecting her. From Duncan. From Grace.

From Captain Bell. His warning was the one she took most seriously, and she hadn't stopped thinking about him.

Mooning over a man was not an activity she was very familiar with, and daydreaming was hardly her style, but this week she'd found herself spending far too many hours mulling over every word she and the captain had exchanged in the garden. The kiss they shared had been deeply unsettling. Since that night, anticipation regarding when she was going to see him again had continually preyed upon her state of mind. Would he call on her? Perhaps her feelings weren't reciprocated by him. The uncertainty was maddening. There were moments these past few days when she'd felt as if she were fifteen again.

The change he wrought in her was too sudden, too sweetly disturbing, and she struggled to make some sense of it.

He was definitely disrupting not just her thoughts but her life. "I can't allow you to do that."

"Allow me to do what?"

Jolted by the suddenness and the nearness of Ian's voice, Phoebe sat back hard against the seat. It took her a moment to recover.

"How could you do this?" she said finally.

"What did I do?" Ian asked innocently, standing by the open window of the carriage. He took off his hat and raked his fingers through his black hair.

The dark blue color of his cutaway coat and the blue brocade of his waistcoat created a sharp contrast from the buff breeches. He put one mud-spattered boot on the carriage step, but it was his face that made her heart beat faster. He looked even more handsome than when they stood together in the garden.

"Showing up so unexpectedly. Appearing out of thin air." She glared at him as fiercely as she could. "What happened to civil greetings?"

He brushed a spot of mud from the hat he held and then bowed. "Good afternoon, Lady Phoebe."

"Now you're mocking me." She pointed a finger at him accusingly. "You gave me a shock, Captain."

"I hope not an unpleasant one."

"I never . . . well, I hardly expected to see you here."

"May I?" he asked, motioning to join her in the carriage.

Before answering, Phoebe pretended to arrange her skirts as she glanced at the kirkyard gate. Duncan could be back at any moment. She didn't think the exchange with Leech would take much time. That is, if the clerk honored their appointment this time.

Captain Bell was waiting for an answer. She couldn't refuse him.

"Yes, of course."

The gentleman climbed in, sparking all the feelings she'd been trying to curb since the last time they met.

He sat across from her, and his long legs adjusted to fit into the limited space. He laid a package wrapped in paper and string on the seat beside his hat.

As he settled back, he observed her face, studying every detail as if he were seeing her for the first time. His gaze lingered on her lips. Her cheeks had caught fire the moment she saw him, and beneath his stare, the heat intensified. Phoebe wondered if he too had been thinking of their last meeting.

She forced herself to look at the packet.

"Did you return from Bellhorne today, Captain?" she asked.

"I did. I left this morning."

"Your mother? I hope she's well."

"As well as can be expected."

A furrow immediately creased his forehead, and that told her more about Mrs. Bell's condition than his words were conveying. Phoebe's heart went out to her friend's mother, and she wished she had the time to hear more, but this wasn't the moment. She didn't know what to do about Duncan.

She nodded at the wrapped parcel.

"Do you have business in this neighborhood?"

"My business is with you." He gestured toward the street outside. "But I didn't expect to be conducting it here."

"What do you mean?"

"Just that I was surprised to catch up to you in a neighborhood like this, and only a short distance from South Bridge and the Vaults."

Like him or not, flustered by his presence or not, she objected to his implication that she was not living up to her promise.

"I'm sitting in a carriage, Captain," she retorted, "with a driver and a groom riding above."

"I saw them."

"It's broad daylight." She nodded toward the open window. "And those are hardworking Scots, going about their business."

"Indeed. One of those hardworking Scots is back there tending to my horse right now."

"They pose no threat," she continued, trying not to be swayed by his attempt at humor. "And you have no reason to be critical of me."

"Was I being critical of you, Lady Phoebe?"

"I believe you were." She glared at him. "The accusation was clear enough in your tone."

"Are you feeling a wee bit guilty?"

If he were being hostile, dictatorial, or even patronizing, she'd know exactly how to deal with it. But he wasn't. He was simply teasing her, and the hint of a smile told her he was enjoying it.

"I'm not feeling guilty at all about being here. I have no reason to. But you and I have a history, as you well know."

His gaze moved to her lips again. "Yes, we do."

"I'm talking about the Vaults," she said, trying to stay on topic. "It's true that I stretched the truth at the time. You found me out. But I promised to exercise caution in the future. And I am."

"And that's why you sent Duncan Turner into the kirkyard a few moments ago instead of going in there yourself."

She stared at him a moment. "So you *have* been following me, Captain Bell."

"Not intentionally."

"Now *that* sounds like an evasion, I'd say." She quirked an eyebrow at him. "Either you have been following me or you haven't."

"I didn't intend to chase you down here, but I wanted to deliver a gift."

"A gift?" *A gift.* Damnation. The man knew how to spoil an argument.

She glanced at the parcel on the seat beside him. The shape of it made her think it was a book. He picked it up.

"A gift." He laid it carelessly on his muscular thigh. "When I went to deliver it at your family's townhouse, you were just stepping into your carriage to leave."

"You could easily have approached me when we stopped at Warrender's Close."

"That's true. But by then my curiosity was aroused."

"That's somewhat forward of you, wouldn't you say, Captain?" she said, teasing him now.

"Also true. But I wanted to be sure my gift was not

being given in vain." He paused, drumming his fingers on the parcel. "You owe me no explanation, of course, but would you be kind enough to tell me why you're here?"

She didn't have to answer him, but there was no harm in him knowing. He'd not betrayed her confidence, and she wanted to show him she deserved his trust.

"I told you before. I like to do research for my work," she explained affably. "I'm sitting here while Mr. Turner gathers information for me in the kirkyard."

Phoebe hoped he wouldn't ask anything more specific about what she was waiting for. He didn't disappoint her.

"Then I'd say this is an appropriate time to give you this." He held the package out to her.

She smiled, undoing the wrapping. Inside, there was a printed but unbound manuscript. Few things made Phoebe happier than receiving the gift of a book, but this was particularly special. She read the title aloud. "*A History of South Bridge and Its Environs.*"

"This is an advance copy of a soon-to-be-published monograph, written by a friend of mine," he explained. "In it, he covers the past four decades from the original conception of the bridge to the construction to the problems that have evolved since, including a detailed discussion of the Vaults."

She leafed excitedly through the first few pages.

"There is nothing you could wish to know about the Vaults that is not documented there. Drawings, a map, surprisingly candid descriptions of the businesses that have occupied the space, both above and below. He even includes a section about the ghosts that now allegedly haunt it." He paused as his voice grew somber. "Although, as we both know, the monsters down there are quite real."

Phoebe was astonished and heartened that he should find such a precious source of information for her. Even though she'd been untruthful with him about why she'd gone into the Vaults, he'd believed her and had gone as far as bringing her this gem. She struggled for the right words to thank him.

"Now you never need to go down there again."

"I never shall. I gave you my word." She pressed both palms on the pages as if swearing on something holy. "Thank you. I'll treasure this always."

Highly impractical and inconvenient feelings pulsed through her. He surprised her. Charmed her. As if she weren't attracted to him enough.

"You said this will soon be published. I'll make certain we purchase a copy for Baronsford's library. Also, I'll order copies for the town houses here and in London. And for Melbury Hall."

"I didn't give you this early copy so you would single-handedly buy out the entire printing." He laughed. "Archibald Constable is a dominant force in Edinburgh publishing. I like the man, but he doesn't need that kind of support. I hear he's making a great deal of money from several novels by a neighbor of yours in Melrose, Walter Scott. Nonetheless, I'm certain the scoundrel would be delighted to have you buy dozens of copies."

Phoebe wished she could tell him everything. The *Edinburgh Review*—the newspaper she wrote for—was funded by Archibald Constable. But if Ian approved of the publisher for his friend's work, she wondered whether he'd be as approving of her secret.

A man, writing a historical account of a bridge.

A woman, penning articles that exposed fraud in corrupt establishments.

Duncan came through the kirkyard gate, putting an end to her internal debate. The Highlander was carrying a parcel under his arm, but he paused in the street, realizing someone else was in the carriage.

"Captain, would you care to accompany me and my sister Millie on a walk up to Arthur's Seat sometime this week?"

He looked at her warily. "Propositioning me again?"

"That's what happens when you bring me gifts. I can't help myself."

He smiled. "So your invitation has nothing to do with Mr. Turner waiting to rejoin you. You're saying your sudden desire to be rid of me is completely unrelated to the constable's return?"

Captain Bell was far too astute.

"As a matter of fact, I *do* wish to be rid of you at this moment." She smoothed the dress across her lap. "But I'd be delighted to see you again. Are you interested?"

"Would the day after tomorrow suit you and Lady Millie?" he responded. "Or do you have other business scheduled for that day?"

She didn't care what might be on her schedule. Her only regret was that it was two days off. "Very good. Wednesday it is, then."

He bowed his head and took his leave. As he began to climb from the carriage, however, she touched his hand.

"Thank you," she said again. "Thank you for this book. I shall treasure it and care for it."

He took her fingers in his.

"The book is quite unimportant in the grand scheme. What I want you to treasure and care for is your own safety and well-being."

She watched him walk away from the carriage. He and

Duncan exchanged a greeting as the two men passed each other. Phoebe's attention turned to the manuscript on her lap, and she wondered if Captain Bell would be searching for a map or a manuscript relating to Greyfriars Kirkyard next.

It was her own fault. She'd given him plenty of reason to worry about her. She wondered if the time would ever come that he'd be calling on a social visit instead.

"I hope this is worth all you paid," Duncan said, climbing to the carriage and handing her a thin packet.

Phoebe's eagerness regarding what was inside was gone. Her thoughts still dwelt on the man who'd just left. She looked out the window in time to see Captain Bell wheel his horse about and ride off toward the Grassmarket.

Chaos broke out in an instant. The end of what appeared to be a weapon poked through the carriage window. Phoebe jerked back out of the way as Duncan leaped across her lap and caught the wrist of the hand holding it. A boy's yelp rang out on the street as the constable yanked the arm in, twisting it fiercely.

"Fock me," the voice cried out in pain. "Fock, yer hurting me. Nay, don't! I meant no harm."

Phoebe grabbed the object that had been pushed through the window. Recognition brought enormous relief. Her walking stick. The one she'd used on the killer and lost.

"Don't hurt him." She leaned closer and put her hand on Duncan's arm.

The same thin, hairless face, the same cracking voice caught between boyhood and manhood. She had but one clear look at him that night, the moment he'd glanced over her shoulder in fear at his pursuer, but she had no doubt.

"I know him."

Duncan eased the pressure on the arm but didn't release him.

"You're alive. Good Lord, I'm so happy to see you're alive."

She'd thought the worst. The loss of any life was tragic, but to think of someone this young murdered by a ruthless killer had eaten away at her faith in humanity.

"Aye, alive 'cept for I'm about to have my arm broke off." He yelped again as Duncan sat back, pulling him securely against the outside of the carriage. "I found your stick. I was just giving it back."

"What's your name?" Phoebe asked.

He tried to pull free instead of answering her.

"Answer the lady," Duncan threatened, encouraging him with a slight twist of the wrist.

"Jock." He grimaced. "Jock Rokeby."

"Where do you live, Jock?"

The boy had no interest in answering. He tugged and pulled instead.

"There's a gang of them, m'lady," Duncan answered under his breath. "They live down there. Some of them born in the Vaults. Others forced to dwell there. None of them doing any good in the world."

"So this what I get for doing good?" Jock griped. "Lemme go."

"I can help you," Phoebe said urgently, her mind racing to figure out which of Jo's houses could handle a boy his age. Unfortunately, none immediately came to mind; they were prepared to accept women and children. Still, she'd figure out something.

"Aye. Fine. I thank ye, m'lady." Jock's tone was considerably less hysterical. "Folks is looking. If yer bruiser here'll let me go, I'll sit nice with you and we can talk."

Phoebe nodded, waving off Duncan as he began to protest. The constable let go of the arm and pushed the door open. The boy was off and running like a long-legged rabbit.

Phoebe immediately jumped out, ready to go after him, but Duncan's hold on her arm stopped her. A moment later the lad had disappeared down Cowgate.

"You'll never catch him, m'lady. Him and his gang know every nook and cranny from the Grassmarket to Leith Wynd." He released her arm and backed away a step. "Nights, they go down to the Vaults."

Phoebe recalled the boy's screams the night of the attack. The same thing could happen again. A killer haunted those Vaults. "He's in danger there, Duncan."

He nodded. "No argument, but that's his lot. And those urchins know who comes and goes. That's how he found you. Let him be."

They might know the secrets of those underground byways. They might know how to survive among the addicts and the gamblers and the others who frequented the Vaults, but Jock couldn't protect himself against the kind of demonic force they both faced down there. No one could.

"But I can help him."

"We've had this talk before, m'lady. You can't save all of them by giving them money or shelter. That's all 'here today and gone tomorrow.'" The former constable held the carriage door open for her to get back in. "But maybe you could do something by putting to use what's in that packet from Leech. What do you say?"

.   .   .

"A gaping chasm has opened in the earth and swallowed me up, Millie," Phoebe said. "There's no bottom to it. I just keep falling farther and farther into an endless gloom."

"You're being extremely dramatic."

Phoebe didn't think she was being either extreme or dramatic.

"What I've written is no good to me. I can't use any of it." She tossed the packet of papers she'd gotten from Leech onto the table and started pacing the room again.

After the incident in which she found young Jock Rokeby was alive, only to have him run away, Phoebe was more motivated than ever before to write this article. Perhaps there was something she could do with her pen. True, it might be of no help with Jock's immediate future, but it could help so many others.

After she dropped Duncan off, she'd begun to peruse the documents the clerk had given the former constable. That was when the abyss yawned beneath her.

By the time she arrived at their Heriot Row townhouse, Phoebe was distraught, and Millie had quickly ushered her into the library.

"Even what I know to be true is useless. These documents have ruined me."

"Why? What's wrong?" Millie asked, picking up the papers and sitting on a chair to go through them. "What happened?"

For her entire life, for as long as she could remember, the injustices and cruelty inflicted on the poor had given her family a cause to fight. Her father, the Earl of Aytoun, had been a champion for the victims of the

Highland clearances, battling his peers over the mass evictions and the cruel treatment of tenants. Their mother, having found Jo as an infant in a vagrant camp near Baronsford, had immediately adopted her and raised her as their own. Jo's own efforts in creating a home for women and children at the Tower House in the Borders, as well as supporting similar homes in Edinburgh, were exemplary.

Phoebe remembered clearly the day she'd decided to get into the fight. One summer day less than a year ago, while hunting through the library at Baronsford for something to read, she'd come across a pile of yellowed decades-old copies of a weekly publication named *The Bee,* which reported statistical accounts of Scotland and parish information on the poor.

In one edition, a writer named James Anderson compared the treatment of the poor in England and Scotland, concluding that the system in the south was "groaning under the influence of laws" aimed at punishing the poverty-stricken, whereas he considered the destitute in Scotland were "abundantly supplied with all that their wants require."

Knowing how the poor were treated in Scotland, Phoebe had become incensed. If one person could use his pen to create a rosy portrait of a terrible situation, she'd decided, then she could use hers to report the truth.

And then, several months ago, news had come that a Select Committee from London was to visit soon. Immediately, she'd heard the report that the charity houses in the city and in Glasgow had begun to turn out the old and the sick. To look like a model of benign efficiency, only the healthy, hardworking, and satisfied poor would be seen during the visit. No inadequacies would be displayed.

It was a travesty that Phoebe had intended to expose. Until now.

"These minutes of a meeting held in Bailie Fife's Close are quite damning," Millie said as Phoebe paced back toward her. "The members of the Edinburgh City Parish are in attendance, and they give the directive."

"Exactly! Bailie Fife's Close!" Phoebe wailed. "*Why* does this need to be from the Orphan Hospital? Why couldn't he give me the minutes for a meeting at the Charity Poorhouse in Port Bristo or Canongate Poorhouse? I'm certain Leech took the minutes for all of those meetings."

Millie paged through a few more sheets. "I think what you have here will serve you well. One can safely assume the suggestions coming from the parish were the same for every institution scheduled to be visited by the London Committee."

"No. What's in there is no good to me."

"I understand the people of Edinburgh have a fondness for this institution since it's the oldest charity in the city," Millie said reasonably, continuing to leaf through the pages. "But what you're writing is a commentary on governance in the city. You're not discrediting the good these places do."

Phoebe took the document out of her sister's hand and showed her the page that had created such havoc in her mind. "Here. Read these names."

"The list of the board of directors." Millie scanned the names and then she looked up in surprise. "Captain Ian Bell."

"A benefactor *and* a director of the Orphan Hospital," Phoebe said, wringing her hands.

"Do you think he could have known about the eviction of the sick? According to the minutes, he wasn't in attendance at this meeting."

"Of course, he couldn't know," she snapped, suddenly angry her sister could think for a moment he was capable of such cruelty. "He volunteers his time. He donates his money. And he does all of it quietly with no need for accolades. But can you imagine the consequences if I wrote an article that exposed all of this? His name would be dragged into it."

Phoebe threw her hands in the air and resumed her pacing again. She didn't know which upset her more right now. Not being able to complete her column or the probability that writing it would besmirch Ian's name.

"What are you going to do?" Millie asked.

"I can't cause him more agony after what he's suffered. Not after everything he's gone through, losing his sister like that." And not after saving her life, she continued silently. And, Lord help her, not after how she'd begun to feel for him. "I have no choice. I can't write the column."

Millie sat in silence, looking intently at her. They were only two years apart in age, and Phoebe knew her sister's expressions too well.

"Come out and say it."

"All right." Millie organized the papers on her lap. "If it had been any other person, you'd have written the article. But Captain Bell is different. Finally, there exists on this planet a man who has some influence with you."

"He has no influence," she protested. "My decisions are mine. My own conscience dictates right and wrong. I simply cannot justify doing an injustice to a man of good character while attempting to expose this problem."

She wasn't going soft.

"So you think Captain Bell is a good man?"

"Of course he is. And you know it too."

"And you think he's handsome?"

"You know I do. And you do too. And so does every woman in Edinburgh with two eyes in her head."

"But you're the woman who encountered him in the Vaults. And you're the only one who danced with him at the ball. And I don't recall anyone else spending time with him in the garden that night."

Phoebe had said nothing to her sister about their kiss, only telling her that Captain Bell assumed she was a novelist like their aunt Gwyneth and that he'd been very understanding.

"Oh, that's not all," Millie continued, not allowing her to interrupt. "You told me he followed you across the city to the Grassmarket, just to bring you a gift today. And you're going walking together to Arthur's Seat."

"But you're coming with us."

The young sister sighed. "Admit it, Phoebe. Captain Bell has an influence with you because you like him. You always have. But there is no 'happily ever after' in sight the way things stand now. You haven't entrusted him with the truth."

She wanted to argue that Ian's assumptions weren't far from the truth. But with Millie, she couldn't pretend it was so, so Phoebe stayed silent.

"He is showing extraordinary interest, but are you suited for each other? You're headstrong and stubborn, and I suspect he is too. You have an independent spirit, but his life has taught him to take command." She laid the stack of papers to the side. "But the most damning part is that you have a talent for pushing men away. You intimidate them."

Hearing the truth hurt. Millie stood and embraced her

before drawing back and looking intently into Phoebe's face.

"I am happy for you. I truly am. But your relationship with the captain has the potential of being either a very romantic love story or a heart-wrenching tragedy, depending on what you do next."

"What I do next?"

"Yes. To have him, to keep him, you need to consider making a compromise . . . in your life and in your writing and in what you want for your future. You have to change."

Compromise. Phoebe wondered if Millie and Grace had already been talking. Everyone wanted her to change.

Trust, the foundation of society. Trust binds one person to the other. Trust lifts people up and makes them whole. Trust creates faith in a leader and belief in heaven.

Trust is what leads the lamb to slaughter.

He hadn't set out to kill Sarah Bell. His blade was still hot from the kill, and the voices had grown silent. But when he emerged from the wynd and turned onto the South Bridge, she saw him. They stood face-to-face. There was no mistaking. No passing by. They exchanged greetings. She expressed her surprise at seeing him. She looked curiously at the clothes he only wore in the city. She was visiting with a friend who was in the shop, she said. Why was he there?

She was trusting. Luring her down to the Vaults was simple. He mentioned a name she knew. She was hurt, and he was going for help. If she would accompany him and stay with her for a moment. Down this wynd. Through here. Be careful on these dark steps.

She felt little pain. He'd known her since she was a child. But she had to die.

And now this one. Phoebe Pennington. She saw his face, and that made her a threat. To him. To everything he needed to do.

He would be patient, find his moment, and then strike.

❧ 7 ❧

LADY MILLIE PENNINGTON received Ian in a manner that could only be described as open and friendly. After telling him that her sister would be down shortly, however, she offered her apologies for not being able to join them for the outing. She had another engagement, but she'd be pleased to accompany them next time if they desired it.

Ian was frankly pleased with the arrangement, but the irritation darkening Phoebe's expression as she sailed down the stairs and into his carriage suggested her feelings were somewhat different.

As they started across town toward Arthur's Seat, he waited for the cloud to pass, but her continued silence indicated there was no foreseeable end to her mood. When he attempted to engage her in light conversation about the neighborhood and the day and their destination, she was largely unresponsive for much of that too.

"We can go back," he told her finally. They'd reached the foot of Calton Hill. Beyond the Bridewell Prison,

Arthur's Seat and the Salisbury Crags rose majestically in the distance. "You and I alone. With no chaperone. If you're at all concerned—"

"Do you really think I give a straw about what others might think of us walking out together?" she asked, interrupting him.

He raised a brow, watching the storm brewing behind her deep blue eyes and expecting more thunder to follow. "Well?"

"My sister, if you must know. I'm upset because we were arguing before you arrived."

"I couldn't tell from Lady Millie's welcome and hospitality that there was any problem."

"That's because she is just like my mother," Phoebe groused. "She has no difficulty speaking her mind, ordering me about. And she has no right. She's younger than I. She disagrees with me, causes me to lose my temper, and then I rage at her like a fishwife. And through it all, her poise never falters. She never shows that she's upset at all. It's infuriating."

Ian sat back in the seat, admiring Phoebe's flushed cheeks. Over the cream-colored muslin dress, the blue spencer jacket she wore matched the color of her eyes. She was punishing the reticule she held in her lap. She turned her gaze out the carriage window. Her lips were moving, though the murmurs were usually inaudible, and the ribbons of her straw bonnet danced beneath her chin in agreement.

"There should be some advantage to being fourth out of five children, one would think."

He waited, sensing the answer was not his to supply. He was correct. She continued her dialogue as if he were not there.

"*Should be* is clearly not the same as *is*." She cut down a dozen pedestrians with her fierce frown. Luckily, they were unaware of the injuries they suffered. "Shouldn't I have authority over *someone* in my family?"

"Pardon me for breaking in." Ian tapped his boot against her foot. "But are you upset because of the lecture Lady Millie gave you or because you think you might have hurt your sister's feelings in the course of that discussion?"

She started to reply but stopped. Her lips immediately thinned, and her chin dropped.

Ian thought of his own family. No father to take advice from. No brothers to argue with. No sister to care for and spoil. Only a mother whom he continuously lied to with the hope that sparing her the pain of the real world would somehow keep her alive and reasonably content. He had none of the familial connections that defined Phoebe Pennington's life.

"You're very perceptive. Millie's advice is always thoughtful and well-intended." She tossed her reticule onto the seat beside her. "She was only trying to help me with a problem that I brought to her, and I was entirely too harsh."

Phoebe was privileged, but she was not shallow or spoiled. She was volatile, but she was also deeply affectionate.

She touched his knee and immediately drew her hand back. "I must sound like an ungrateful harpy. I should be thankful I have a sister like Millie. I should never have given vent to such silly complaining as this." She paused. "Especially in front of you. I am sorry."

Her compassion regarding his loss touched him once again.

Ian was attracted to her beauty, her fire, and her wit. As he looked across at her now, he knew his heart was opening to her in a way that he'd never allowed with any other woman.

But there was so much more about her that he wanted to know. There were questions that he'd never asked. To start with, he was curious about the story she was writing now. She never talked about it. Ian had friends who were writers, and you couldn't stop them from explaining in elaborate detail the work they were penning, all the while moaning about their lack of progress.

Two days ago near the Grassmarket, she'd been anxiously awaiting whatever it was that Duncan Turner was collecting for her in the kirkyard. But she'd kept her own counsel about it and hadn't even offered him a clue. The Vaults. The kirkyard. Where would she go next? He'd promised himself he wouldn't ask her. He'd wait for her to offer information voluntarily. But that didn't stop him from worrying.

"I'm quite happy that you share your tales of family with me. I feel privileged, in fact," he said. "I am also curious to know what two sisters might argue about with such passion."

He could tell by the way she picked up her reticule and began toying with it that she wasn't too keen on sharing any details. But he waited.

"To be honest, the argument was fairly one-sided." She looked out the window again. "But it was about nothing of importance."

Phoebe was not a very good actress, however. The blush rising in her fair complexion immediately gave her away. Ian had a strong feeling he'd been the topic of their discussion. Perhaps the wisdom of today's outing was questioned by the younger sister.

He had no strong impression of Millie. He knew her but didn't think of her in any certain manner. He had no idea what she thought of him either. Like Phoebe, the youngest Pennington was still unattached, though she was of marriageable age. Still, from what he was hearing, he could imagine her providing the voice of reason to her older sister's passionate nature.

"Have you ever before made the walk up to Arthur's Seat?" he asked, trying to draw her back.

She shook her head. "It's surprising that we haven't, I suppose. Millie and I talked about it dozens of times."

They'd passed the gates of the palace and were drawing near the walking path leading up to the Crags and then to Arthur's Seat itself.

"What is that smell?" she exclaimed.

"That's coming from the bogs." He looked out and pointed. "You can see the top of the dykes. The rain washes the waste of the Old Town right into the low area and it collects here. You won't smell it once we've been climbing a while."

Troubled blue eyes met his. "Like everything else in life, unpleasantness is hardly noticed once we separate ourselves from it."

"I have a feeling we're no longer speaking of the bogs."

Their hours together had been few, but Ian was already beginning to feel he knew her well. Phoebe's face was a window into her mind. Right now, he could see an argument simmering inside of her, but she was fighting the urge to voice it.

"You're far better company when you say what you're thinking."

She sent him an incredulous look. "You *want* me to speak my mind."

"I insist on it."

"And how will you react, I wonder, if you don't like what you hear?"

"Why should that worry you?" He shrugged. "I've always enjoyed a lively discussion."

"But I just told you I sometimes get carried away in an argument. I say things that can be hurtful."

"My skin is fairly thick. Besides, how can we understand another person's views on any topic unless we listen to them? Isn't that how we learn?"

She gnawed at her bottom lip as she considered his words. "You're honestly interested in learning my views?"

He nodded. "I am, indeed. And I hope you might be interested in learning mine in return."

"What happens if our perspectives put us at odds with each other?"

"I've never known two people to agree on everything," he replied. "And if we do disagree, then perhaps one of us will convince the other. Even if we don't, we both walk away from the discussion with a clearer perspective, having heard the other's reasoning."

She was squeezing the life out of that reticule. "Do you mean what you say or are you trying to be accommodating because this is our first outing together?"

"I've known you . . . let me see . . . for how many years?"

"Seven years this autumn. But the years of my friendship with Sarah have nothing to do with this conversation."

Ian stopped himself from laughing. "Fine, then I consider the first night when I carried you out of the

Vaults to be our first outing. Then there was our walk in the gardens at Baronsford. My brief visit with you in your carriage in the Grassmarket could be counted as our third time together. So this is clearly our fourth outing. However, I would be happy to cede the point, if that is our first argument."

She didn't smile, her face as solemn as a gravedigger's.

"But yes," he continued, "I meant what I said. I should very much like to know your opinions about things."

She hesitated only long enough to draw breath.

"These bogs accumulate waste water from the town. But we choose not to notice the foulness of the situation. We hold our noses and pass by as quickly as we can." She paused and looked out at the folk walking on the road before turning her attention back to him. "It seems to me this is the same as when those who can help the sick or the destitute ignore them. Or worse, to decide that only the strongest of the unfortunates deserve our assistance."

"We have no disagreement on that account."

Ian didn't parade it about in public, but his patronage of the Orphan Hospital in Canongate was no secret. He wondered if she knew this, for her words certainly had an accusatory tone to them. He was no idler, no vapid fop, no gambler, no womanizer who frittered away his family's fortune. But he was not a fool either, and she was directing her comments at him for a reason.

"It sounds as if you're suggesting I'm unaware of something that I've failed to do. Or worse," Ian said, feeling the heat rising beneath his collar. "Are you being critical of my character? Or my lack of civic responsibility?"

The carriage came to a stop, and the groom immediately appeared and opened the door.

Rather than correcting Ian, she began to get out. He put a hand on her arm.

"Whatever you're accusing me of, don't you think I deserve to know what it is? Don't I get a chance to speak in my own defense?"

"Outside," she said, turning a pleading glance his way. "If you please, let's speak outside."

Ian would have preferred they sit in the privacy of his carriage until he understood what she was implying, but he wasn't about to force her.

Stepping out, he offered her a hand and she took it. Telling his driver where to wait, he turned around to find Phoebe already moving at a good pace up the incline. Before Ian could wonder if he was going to have to run after her, she stopped abruptly and stood looking across the fields out at the palace.

"The Abbey," she said when he caught up to her. She motioned toward the roofless ruins of Holyrood Abbey, visible just beyond the royal residence.

Trying to keep up with her was a challenge, but he was determined to understand her.

"I think I should have taken sanctuary within those walls."

For centuries the abbey and surrounding grounds had provided a place of protection for petty criminals and debtors. These so-called "Abbey-lairds" could live in modest housing unmolested by authorities and creditors within the boundaries of church land.

"Why?" he asked. "Are you afraid of being prosecuted for some offense?"

She bent down and pulled a bluebell from a patch growing along the path. "I'm afraid that *you* will prosecute me for the things I say."

He smiled and shook his head.

"There will be no hiding for you," he warned. "I believe tradition holds that you will be free to leave the grounds on Sundays, but I'll be waiting right here, demanding answers."

Ian was surprised when she tossed away the flower, looped her arm into his, and started along the path.

"Could you please forget what I said?"

He walked with her. "No, I think not. I want you to finish what you began."

She raised her face to the sky and as she increased their pace, her foot slipped on the path. He took her hand and Phoebe's long fingers fit perfectly into his.

"My words were not an attack on you as a person. I was speaking against the establishment."

"I'm relieved, but I'm still not clear what establishment you're referring to."

The warm day and the bright sun had brought out other walkers. Small groups of young men were moving up the steady incline ahead of them. Her hurried steps and the grip of her hand indicated a battle she was fighting with herself. Ian walked along in silence, knowing that sooner or later she'd tell him what was on her mind.

Suddenly aware that they would soon catch up to the group immediately ahead, she drew him to the side of the path and stopped.

"*You* were the reason for my argument with Millie this morning."

"I see. She disapproves of me?"

"Hardly." Phoebe freed her hand and took a deep breath. "She feels I should be completely open with you and hold nothing back."

He approved of Millie's advice. "I agree."

Another painful sigh. She was certainly not acting. He couldn't imagine what could be causing her such agony. She paused as two couples passed them on their way down from the summit.

"Gaius Gracchus," she said finally when they were alone.

He stared at her, not fathoming how an ancient politician was connected with their discussion. Perhaps she was testing his knowledge of Roman history.

"Wait. I hope you're not fleeing to the temple of Diana to commit your life to her service."

She stepped toward him, her face tilted up. "That is the assumed name I use for my newspaper articles," she said in a low voice.

"I thought you were a novelist."

"I never said so. You only assumed it."

He thought back to their conversation in the garden. "I asked you if you were a novelist like your aunt Gwyneth," Ian reminded her. "You didn't deny it. That's the same to me."

In truth, he didn't care if she wrote novels or articles or epic poetry. Anything undertaken by a woman that smacked of intellectual prowess was frowned upon by society. Dr. Johnson famously said, after hearing of a Quaker woman speaking on a religious topic, that "a woman's preaching is like a dog's walking on his hind legs. It is not done well; but you are surprised to find it done at all." Unfortunately, many among the ton agreed with Johnson. Ian thought it was perhaps the most foolish thing the man ever said.

"Well, now you know the truth," she said, throwing her hands up. "I write articles under the name Gaius Gracchus that are published by the *Edinburgh Review*."

Ian was impressed. He knew Archibald Constable very well. He was also aware of the high standards the publisher and his editors adhered to. He decided not to share his congratulations quite yet, however, for there seemed to be more that she was anxious to share.

"Do you read that newspaper?" she asked.

"I do, fairly regularly."

"Have you read any of my articles?"

"I don't recall the name, but what were the topics?" he asked. "How long have you been writing for the paper?"

Phoebe turned around and paced a few steps away and came back. "Almost a year. I've written four pieces for them. And I think you would have recognized the name if you'd read them."

"Then perhaps not," he told her. "But tell me, what have you written about?"

Her restless nature wouldn't allow her to stand still. She turned her steps up the path, and he fell in beside her.

"I was quite deliberate in the name I chose."

"Then you must concern yourself with reform and the redistribution of the wealth."

"I expose corruption in those holding positions of power," she told him. "In the column I'm preparing now, I plan to address the conditions of the sickest of the poor in Edinburgh, and the ruthless way they're being treated in advance of the imminent arrival from London of the Select Committee on Poorhouses."

Ian put a hand on her arm and made her stop walking. This was a topic close to his heart. "I don't understand. Explain to me how our poor are being treated *ruthlessly* when we do things better here than they do in England.

That's what this commission is about. They're trying to learn from us."

"And they can, but only if we allow them to see we are not perfect. We have flaws too. Not everyone is healthy in our poorhouses. Not everyone is capable of working. Many are sick and dying. Many have spirits that have been crushed by their poverty."

Phoebe was an idealist. He could respect that. But there was more to what she was saying that he didn't understand.

"I do not disagree, but are you saying that our institutions are treating people worse *because* of this visit?"

She looked to her right and left. A group of noisy schoolboys was moving past them. There was nowhere for her to go.

"That is exactly what I'm saying. They're expelling the old and very sick. They're putting them on the streets rather than be seen as inefficient."

Arguments arose in him, but he decided to find out what she knew.

"What institutions are doing this?" he asked. "And by what authority?"

"I believe it is happening in every poorhouse and institution in the city that is to be visited. The Edinburgh Parish has already been meeting with individual charities and giving the instructions."

Ian's first thought was that she was mistaken. The Scottish people cared for their poor voluntarily. There was no compulsory tax or church tithe to help them. That was why it was essential for property owners and the wealthy to be involved and contribute. In Edinburgh, only the *legal* responsibility for the poor fell to the City Parish.

After Sarah's death, Ian searched for a worthwhile

cause to which he could devote time and money. He wanted a way that he could make a difference in the lives of at least a few unfortunate children. He'd not done enough for his sister, but perhaps he could make a positive change for some other young person. That was when his involvement with the Orphan Hospital began.

"How do you know this?" he asked.

"I cannot tell you the names of my sources."

He recalled that the attack on Phoebe happened near an opium den. And she'd been waiting in her carriage in the Grassmarket for Duncan to return. It all made sense. Desperate men would say anything. Do anything.

"Reliable sources?" His tone was sharp.

She nodded, her eyes flashing at him.

"And they have proof that *all* the institutions that are to be visited are following this same policy?"

"The directions from the Parish are alleged to be consistent across the city. But so far, I have proof for only one charity house," she told him. "The Orphan Hospital in Bailie Fife's Close."

"It's a lie," he said flatly.

"You are a director and a benefactor. You are not involved with the daily operations." She put a hand on his arm. "I know you're blameless in this."

"I don't believe it. This is either a terrible mistake or a horrible slander."

"I have seen the—"

"Have you *been* there?" he demanded. "Do you know what the inside of those charity institutions looks like? Do you have any comprehension of what it takes to manage one? Or who makes the decisions?"

"I've spent plenty of time in my sister's shelters, both in the Borders and here in the city."

"I give Lady Jo a great deal of credit for what she has accomplished. But her homes shelter how many?"

She struggled to come up with a number quickly.

"A hundred?" he asked, his impatience unleashed. "Two hundred?"

"I don't think this is relevant."

There was no explaining it to her. No point in trying to impress her with numbers. It was equally futile to describe the accomplishments of those children who'd lost their parents and had grown up inside these institutions. They'd been given skills and training that would prepare them for the world, and many had then gone on to live successful lives.

No, there was only one way to do this.

He took her arm and started down the hill. Ian was angry enough to drag her there if need be, but he was relieved when she didn't protest but went along willingly. If she wanted to pursue a career with her pen, then it was time someone taught her the importance of proper research.

"I see this is the end of our outing."

"Not at all," he said tersely. "We're only getting started. We're going to the Orphan Hospital."

$\maltese$ 8 $\maltese$

PHOEBE KNEW how to respond to loudly delivered lectures. She was a competent debater when she retained her composure. But Ian's unwavering silence after he'd given instructions to his driver, his refusal to speak to her or even acknowledge her, made his feelings clear. He was disappointed with her.

Her own reaction surprised Phoebe. He'd been abrupt on the hill, and her initial instinct was to withdraw. But he didn't give her any opportunity. They were going to the orphanage. Still, she'd restrained her natural instinct to refuse, fight back, and only do things on her own terms. She'd argued with herself that he needed a chance to get over what had to be a shock. Phoebe understood the strong loyalty he had to this particular charity.

So she forced herself to be patient. Not her strongest quality.

When the carriage stopped on High Street, just below Tron Church, he muttered something about waiting until he returned, and she watched him disappear down Bailie Fife's Close.

While arguing with Millie this morning, Phoebe had predicted this would happen. She'd wanted to let the sleeping dog lie and forego writing the article. But her sister had spoken about what Phoebe wanted to accomplish with this column. If she saw her writing as a moral duty to create change for the better, then it was "imperative" that she speak to the captain and share what she knew. She'd insisted that perhaps not by her pen but by his influence, a change could be made.

Phoebe had grudgingly accepted her sister's position . . . and look where it had gotten her. Abandoned in a carriage and scorned by the only man she'd ever been romantically drawn to.

"No self-pity," she chided herself. She was here to visit the oldest charity establishment in the city. If anything, this was an opportunity to learn. Perhaps she would gain knowledge that she could share with her sister Jo.

"Learn and be useful," she whispered under her breath.

"Excellent advice."

Startled, she shut her eyes for a moment and ordered her heart to restart its beating. He did this to her every time.

The captain handed her out of the carriage and introduced her to a Mr. Douglas, one of the managers of the orphanage, who was clearly enthusiastic about showing them around the facility.

The driver was sent away, and as Phoebe followed their guide, a cloak of sadness descended on her. The tall man walking beside her was acting like the distant

Captain Bell of her youth, who never noticed her in all the years of her friendship with his sister.

"Buildings have been added on to other buildings as the need for more places for children has been steadily increasing," Mr. Douglas told them. He went on to explain that they'd had a surge during the wars. The orphanage spread in every direction and was now crowded in by other buildings on every side.

"When the Orphan Hospital was originally opened here," the manager told Phoebe, "the neighborhood was rural. One wouldn't even guess it, to see the area now. The city has quite overwhelmed us, but we do the best we can."

As Mr. Douglas went ahead of them up the steps of the first building, Phoebe turned to her companion. "Please don't feel the need to accompany us, Captain Bell. I promise not to run away or offend anyone."

"On the contrary, I'm keen to see the place operating on a normal day, without any of the frills of a Directors' Visit."

If their guide had any inkling of the tension between his guests, he showed no indication of it and ushered them in.

"We've come a long way since our inception eighty-five years ago. We initially opened our doors to thirty orphans," Mr. Douglas explained. "Today we care for over two hundred fifty."

The face of Jock Rokeby came to her again, and she wondered if he was too old to find shelter in a place like this.

They moved from room to room, floor to floor, where boys and girls were busy with a multitude of tasks involving both books and trade. They all looked younger than Jock. And all of them looked healthy, but the allegations she'd passed on to Captain Bell were never too far from her mind.

"The great architect William Adam designed this hospital building two years after the Orphan Hospital opened," the manager informed them as they moved to the next building. "And that allowed us to house increasing numbers of abandoned children. Our charter is to care for all and bring them up to be healthy, God-fearing citizens. We don't take that charge lightly. We educate them and teach them a trade. We prepare them for the world, m'lady."

"I see," she replied.

She could feel Ian close behind her. He asked no questions and said nothing to her, but she knew she was being watched.

Suddenly, a dozen girls poured into the corridor they were passing along, bringing with them noise and liveliness appropriate to their age. One of the children stopped near Phoebe, curtsied, and stared up at her. Nothing said, only large, dark eyes studying her.

Phoebe crouched down to the child's level. "Good morning. What's your name?"

"Nylah."

Curly, dark hair struggled to escape the confines of a cap. The sprinkle of freckles on her button nose was endearing. "How old are you, Nylah?"

"Six . . . on my next birthday."

Phoebe thought of her brother Gregory and his adopted daughter, Ella. She too was an orphan, but fortunate to be blessed from birth with the love and devotion of her aunt Freya.

"Are you here to work in the sick room?"

The child's question drew Phoebe's attention. "No, I'm not."

"Too bad."

"Why do you ask?"

She shook her head and small brown fingers reached up and touched Phoebe's face. "Your eyes. They're nice. Like the women who care for us when we're sick."

Phoebe had no opportunity to ask anything more of the child, as she ran off to rejoin her group and disappeared down a set of stairs.

Phoebe started to straighten and found Ian's proffered hand. She took it and their gazes met as she stood up.

"Your eyes. They're nice," he whispered before letting go of her hand and stepping away.

He knew exactly how to knock her off her feet. She followed Mr. Douglas as he continued with his commentary about the building, but Phoebe's mind kept returning to Nylah and her words . . . and Ian's echo of them.

"About fifty years after the initial construction, the spire was built. The wings to the east and west were added soon afterward."

The faces of the children fascinated her. Despite the harshness of losing parents and the dire circumstances that led them here, they were alive, and their eyes shone with curiosity and hope. She understood Ian's interest, his passion to protect the institution that offered this young generation a future, unlike the disaster and danger that awaited boys like Jock.

"Six years ago, a large school room, the new wards for

the sick, and the wash house and laundry were constructed," Mr. Douglas announced.

Phoebe came to a stop and turned to the manager.
"The wards for the sick. Can you take us there?"

"Of course, that area is right on our way," he replied.
"We're quite fortunate in that we enjoy the support of the
medical college's directors. Our sick children are cared for
by doctors. And we have a group of matrons and older
orphans who see to the patients' needs."

Phoebe felt her cheeks go warm with the heat of
embarrassment. She was wrong. They were ignoring the
City Parish's orders.

The baseless nature of her accusations cut at her
conscience. Ian's strong objection to what she'd said to
him on their way to Arthur's Seat was justified. She hadn't
misread the minutes Leech had given her. There were
specific directives, but they'd been disregarded. This was
a possibility she'd never entertained.

Ian followed her closely on their tour. Always near, but
she felt the wall he'd erected between them. She wished
for a private moment to speak with him right now. There
was so much she wanted to say, to explain. But there was
no slowing the manager down.

"Here we are," Mr. Douglas announced when they
ascended stairs to a corridor where several intercon-
necting rooms housed the sick. "This morning, we have
nearly twenty children here because of fever, and that has
us worried."

Phoebe stood in the doorway. Rows of beds were filled
with sick children. Flushed faces peered up. Young
women dressed in plain homespun dresses and long
aprons carried bowls of water and fresh linens from bed
to bed. The visitors continued to the next room and the

next. It was all the same. The sick were being taken care of.

As they descended and went out into the courtyard where they started their tour, she turned to their guide.

"Thank you, Mr. Douglas, for allowing me to have such a thorough and educational look at your institution," she told him. "I'm very impressed."

The young manager beamed. "I am so happy to hear you say so, m'lady. We've always been entirely grateful for the generosity of Lord and Lady Aytoun in support of our efforts."

"My parents help out, you say?" she replied quietly.

"Indeed, as does the Lord Justice, your brother. A steadfast supporter of our efforts, he is. It's an honor to share what we are trying to do with any member of the Pennington family. I only wish we could have prepared for your visit."

A chill ran through her at the thought that while she'd been ready to write a scathing report on the Orphan Hospital, her own family was a staunch supporter of it.

"Thank you, but you could not have given me a more enlightening tour. And I do hope your patients mend quickly."

"As do I, m'lady," he replied, glancing up at the windows of the sick rooms.

Phoebe didn't want to look into Ian's face. She'd inferred that he was disappointed, and now she knew he had every right to be. As a director of the institution, he had to know about the involvement of her parents and brother here. How foolish he must think her for jumping so easily to the wrong conclusion.

Congratulating Mr. Douglas one last time for his

efforts, Phoebe left the captain speaking with the manager about charity business.

Ian's carriage waited on the street, but she bypassed it and turned up High Street. She needed to breathe, to think, to try to come to terms with what it was that she'd set out to do and where she'd gone wrong.

Phoebe passed through the intersection of High Street and South Bridge. Crowds of pedestrians, carts, and carriages filled the crossroads. Street vendors hawking their wares stood along the front of Tron Church.

She'd not walked twenty paces beyond when she felt the same sensation she'd had in the Grassmarket the other day. Someone was watching her.

Phoebe looked around her. Strange faces stared back. A shadow moved in a doorway across the street. A man jostled her as he passed. An idler leaning against a building flashed a knife, only to cut an apple. A chill washed along her skin, raising gooseflesh despite the warm sun. She could feel other eyes on her.

Phoebe bumped into a woman carrying a large basket of linens. A small lad with a dirty face and eyes the size of saucers trailed after her. Begging the woman's pardon for not watching where she was going, she glanced around to find the sensation gone.

The washerwoman and her boy moved off. For a brief moment, she imagined Jock's tall and lanky frame standing in the shadows of a doorway, watching after her. But she blinked again, and he was gone too.

Phoebe started up High Street again, her mind returning to the mess she'd narrowly avoided. Still, the poor on the streets were very real. The growing numbers of women and their wee ones in the shelters were not her imagination. And the rumors were everywhere about the poorhouses turning out the old and sick.

She recalled how she'd come upon Leech's name. An Edinburgh woman newly arrived at the Tower House at Baronsford. She'd related to Phoebe that she had friends in the city who'd mentioned a clerk for the City Parish who had proof of the rumors. When she pursued it, he'd been willing to sell his information for a price.

That was her first mistake. She'd too readily believed him. She'd done nothing to corroborate what he offered her.

"How foolish of me!"

"You're far from foolish."

She whirled around and found herself face-to-face with Captain Bell.

"Why are you so intent on frightening me out of my wits time after time?"

As she tried to calm the swirling mix of emotions within her, Phoebe realized it didn't matter. He was here. He'd come after her.

"You're not foolish," he repeated, taking her by the arm. "But we need to talk."

She couldn't agree more. They walked back to his carriage, where he climbed in after her.

Phoebe needed to say what was on her mind while she still had some control over her emotions. Grace's advice. Millie's words. But none of it applied. Today wasn't about compromise, but rather about her arrogance in thinking she had enough knowledge on an issue. She'd made a mistake. A premature assumption. And she had thankfully been given the opportunity to learn more before she dug a hole large enough to bury herself and the entire *Edinburgh Review*.

"I'm glad you brought me here. I needed to see this place for myself. I was foolish . . ." She stopped herself, seeing his frown. "I was too quick in jumping to conclusions. I'm heartily sorry for my wrongful attack on the orphanage."

It was difficult to say those words, but Phoebe knew she'd decided on the tone and direction of the article without giving any thought to the possibility that the individual institutions would decide for themselves how to proceed. The minutes of the meeting proved nothing.

"An idealistic person has a view of the world as it should be," he said. "And there is so much confusion and corruption in evidence everywhere that it's hard not to see fault where none exists. But that only makes the duty of the person who wields the pen so much greater. He . . . or she must be relentlessly thorough in the search for the truth."

Phoebe recognized the power of the press and thought she understood the responsibility that went with that power. But she'd learned she had some distance to travel in that regard.

"May I share a story with you?"

"Please do," she said, happy that he wasn't going to insist on her groveling. Although, if groveling eased her current feeling of guilt, she might be willing to eat humble pie for days.

"Eight years ago, a similarly unwarranted attack was made on the Orphan Hospital. The charges were made in an article that appeared in the *Scots Magazine.*"

She hadn't heard of the article, but she now better understood Ian's reaction. "What were the charges?"

"The writer relayed the accusations of a German aristocrat who'd been in Edinburgh on a prolonged visit. In the column, the magazine printed the traveler's insinuations, based largely on secondhand reports, that the Orphan Hospital had seen a dramatic decline in order and management."

Phoebe thought of the papers she received from Leech and how easily she'd assumed the worst.

"I take it the writer who penned the article never visited the facility," she said.

"I believe that to be the case. But that's not the end of the story." Even now, Ian could not hide his irritation.

"While the managers of the Orphan Hospital knew the accusations were groundlessness, they also knew the dangerous effects of such a report," he explained. "They invited the Principal of Edinburgh University, a noted professor of divinity, the presidents of the Royal Colleges of Physicians and Surgeons, and the Lord Provost of the City to conduct an immediate and thorough investigation into the institution."

"What happened?"

"The libelous defamation was refuted. A full report was issued and printed in the same magazine, with an editorial apology."

And the writer had been discredited, she thought. This could just as easily have happened to her. And in Phoebe's case, she'd have the wrath of her family on top of it too.

"But none of what I said describes the true damage," he continued. "With the publication of the article, false rumors spread word-of-mouth, adding to the poison. Before the results of the investigations could be published, financial support of the Orphan Hospital decreased substantially."

The implications of his words were sinking in.

Damage to a charity had been immediate, and the children being brought up there were surely the ones who suffered from it.

"How long did it take for support of the orphanage to recover?"

He shrugged. "The fall is swift, but the climb back requires strength and patience and time."

Phoebe tugged at the ribbon of her bonnet and yanked it off her head. Damnation. The impulse to rush ahead without considering consequences was indeed a great flaw. And she recognized it in herself.

How close she'd come to causing a disaster for this charity.

"Before coming out with you today, I'd already decided not to write the article I told you about." She jammed her reticule in her bonnet and put it on the seat. "However, my decision had been based on knowing you were involved with the Orphan Hospital. But now I find myself far more knowledgeable. I'm ashamed I even brought up such allegations."

"In bringing you to the orphanage, I knew what you'd find. And I'm not saying that our system of caring for the poor in Scotland is perfect. But what we have is far better than they have in England," he asserted, holding her gaze.

He leaned forward and planted his elbows on his knees, swallowing up the space in between them.

"If directives are being issued regarding this visit from London, I suspect they are intended to flaunt Scottish superiority rather than to injure those who are injured already. What red-blooded Scot doesn't want to be better than an Englishman in everything? But if other institutions are wrongheaded enough to be putting their sick out on the street, we can assert pressure to stop it."

"Stopping it is what is most important," she told him.

"I shall write today to the contacts I have in those places, as well as to their directors," he replied. "And if you like, I can arrange for you to visit every poorhouse in Edinburgh and Glasgow that you care to see."

Phoebe didn't know what to say to him. Regardless of their disagreement, he had behaved in the most generous manner imaginable, and her heart ached with gratitude. She so much wanted to reciprocate in some way. She wanted to do something for him. Truth be told, she wanted to do something for the two of them. Phoebe desperately needed to know if he still considered her a friend or if she'd forever lost his respect.

She brushed her fingers against his, drawing his attention. "There is a visit I want to make. One that is long overdue."

"Where is it you'd like to go?"

"Would you very much mind if Millie and I were to pay a visit to your mother at Bellhorne?"

He had two lives. Two worlds in which he moved.

Standing on the rocky shore, he stared out at the wall of fog that covered the grey-green waters of the Firth of Forth. He could feel them coming.

Since the beginning of time, wild-eyed sailors, drinking hard to forget, would tell tales of sharks and sea monsters that could tear a man in half with a single bite. And of kraken and leviathan that would hunt a ship for a fortnight and then demolish it in a single moment, leaving only splinters and corpses to float upon the sea.

Men lived in one world. Monsters lived in another.

He stared out at the water. The worlds were separated by the thinnest gauze. By a hair's breadth of mist.

He'd heard the captain say a monster hunted in the city, killing the innocent.

It wasn't true. He was no monster. He was indeed a hunter.

Beyond the grey waters, beyond the mist, he hunted when the voices came. Time to avenge once again. Find the prey. Execute them. Mark them.

Yes, he lived in two worlds.

There in the city, he knew the dark places where the foolhardy ventured out. There he hunted.

But when it was over, when the blood had been washed clean, he made his way back across the water. He returned here to his lair.

To Bellhorne.

❧   *9*   ☙

STANDING on the new pier at Queensferry and waiting to board their ferry for the crossing, Phoebe gazed around her at the small boats moving busily about and at the green shore to the north. Beyond the distant point of land jutting out into the Firth of Forth to the east, a large three-masted ship was moving steadily toward the port at Leith. The whole world seemed connected, and she only wished she had a way of bridging the gap with the man standing behind her.

She and the captain had established a connection, only to lose it. She thought they'd resolved their disagreement the day he'd taken her to visit the Orphan Hospital, after their conversation in his carriage. She'd owned up to the mistake she very nearly made. And he'd been accepting of her writing, so long as she understood the responsibilities. But then something within him shut down.

At first, Phoebe sensed the change in him when she

suggested visiting Bellhorne. But after considering it, he'd put her mind at ease by saying a visit from them would be a pleasant change of pace for his mother. They'd set the date for Saturday. He would pick them up, travel together to Fife, and he would convey them back to Edinburgh on Monday.

And then . . . nothing.

She didn't understand the change in him. Their parting that day had been civil, but hardly affable. She told him that Hugh and Grace would be in Edinburgh overnight, but he declined her invitation to dine. And during the carriage ride today, Ian had again been largely silent in her company. He didn't look at Phoebe as he had done before. In fact, he avoided looking at her at all. There was a severity in his demeanor that made her think all that had been gained between them was lost.

The road from Edinburgh had been slippery and wet from the rain, but there were breaks in the clouds now, and the skies over Fife on the far shore looked promising.

Phoebe stepped away from her sister and the captain, walking to the edge of the pier and pretending to look down at a fishing boat that was tied up at the foot of some stone steps. She hazarded a glance back at Ian. He was holding his hat and cane in one hand and studying the activities of the ferrymen preparing for them to board.

His hair looked rumpled, but it fell in handsome waves across his brow. She itched to approach and run her fingers through the thick locks, pushing them off his eyes. He had a manner of standing that was striking. He was balanced and relaxed, and yet he had the coiled feline energy of a man ready at any moment to spring into action. The wind riffled his black greatcoat, flapping it around his booted legs. As she watched him, Phoebe realized he was even more handsome now than he'd been in those heady days of youth.

She was treading on emotionally vulnerable ground, so she forced her attention away from the man, focusing on their surroundings instead.

The recent additions to the piers they were standing on had enclosed the harbor and provided more dock space for the busiest ferry crossing in Scotland. But this was a regular travel route for Captain Bell. He knew where to go, whom to see, when the tides were in. As a result, they were soon onboard and underway.

Before long, Queensferry was behind them, but their destination across the water to Fife seemed quite far away. Millie, occupied with the excitement of being on a boat, wandered toward the bow.

The wind caused the ferry to sail far out in the Firth of Forth before tacking back toward the north shore, and Phoebe smiled at an old sailor murmuring the lines of the Scots ballad as he passed.

"The king sits in Dunfermline town, drinking the blood-red wine. 'O where will I get a good sailor, to sail this ship of mine?'"

Left alone with Ian, Phoebe seized her chance to try and draw him out. "Is the water fifty fathoms deep here, Captain?"

"I don't know," he answered, glancing at the grey-green firth. "Why do you ask?"

"Half o'er, half o'er, to Aberdour, it's fifty fathoms deep." She smiled, continuing the poem she'd overheard. "And there lies good Sir Patrick Spens—"

"With the Scots lords at his feet," he finished. "A good question."

His dark eyes met hers, and instantly her cheeks warmed. She was helpless when it came to her reaction to the man.

Ian moved to the railing. The spray from the white caps sparkled around him as the wide boat rose and dropped on the rolling swells.

"I wonder, Captain Bell, if you'd consider doing what you've encouraged me to do several times in the past."

He struck the shroud with the head of his walking stick. "What would that be?"

"I wish you'd tell me what's troubling you."

He hesitated, his attention on the passing water. But before Phoebe could press him, he straightened up and faced her.

"It's my mother."

"Oh, I see . . ."

He squeezed the brim of his hat and tapped it against his thigh. "Outside of the small circle of friends and acquaintances who live near us, she hasn't received any visitors since Sarah's death."

Rumors had circulated that Fiona Bell had become a recluse after Sarah's death. But that didn't excuse everyone else's negligence. Whatever guilt Phoebe harbored for not taking this trip sooner, increased.

"I must apologize for my family, but especially for myself. I should have reached out to her."

He stopped her. "That isn't necessary. When my sister disappeared, she received many letters. Many came from friends who wanted to visit her at Bellhorne, and often she was invited to go to them. She turned them down."

And Phoebe had been lacking in even that simplest of gestures. No offer to visit, no invitation to Baronsford. She'd left the matter totally in her mother's hands. Her grief, however, did not excuse her from doing what was proper. Embarrassed by her negligence, she tried to summon a reasonable explanation, but she had none.

Phoebe untied the ribbon holding her bonnet and pulled it off before a wind gust tore it from her head. She felt ill. And here she'd practically forced herself and Millie on the hospitality of his family. No wonder he was unhappy.

"How does she feel about us visiting today?"

"She doesn't know," he replied. "I thought it would be best for her if you arrived unannounced."

The hat ribbon twisted around and around her fingers. She would need to have a proper apology ready for when they arrived at Bellhorne. Her lack of correspondence with Mrs. Bell was an insult that she'd never intended.

How much damage is done in the world unintentionally, she pondered.

"This way there will be no panic, no needless distress in advance."

"That is quite sensible," she said quietly. "Our sole purpose for this visit was to provide her with some company and a sympathetic ear if she desires it. Nothing more. We didn't mean to impose. And we certainly didn't want to cause either of you trouble."

Ian steered her toward the outside of the cabin where the wall blocked the wind. *Always alert, always thoughtful,* she thought.

"Does she like to talk about Sarah? Is she still grieving?"

For a prolonged moment he looked into her eyes, and she sensed there were things he wanted to say. The thought occurred to her that perhaps he was uncomfortable sharing family confidences. From what he'd seen of her as a writer, she might not be trustworthy. When his attention seemed to fix on a gull that flew up, hung in the air near them, and then drifted back toward the stern, she put a hand on his arm.

"Please, Captain. Tell me," she asked again. A lock of her hair had come undone in the wind, and it whipped across her eyes. "If you're concerned at all, Millie and I can board the next ferry heading back. We don't want to complicate your life or add to your mother's sorrows."

His touch resembled a caress when he caught the errant lock of hair, held it for a moment, and then let it loose again to dance around her face.

"Life at Bellhorne," he said finally, "is a carefully contrived charade to keep my mother happy. The housekeeper, Mrs. Hume, keeps my sister's rooms clean and ready for when Sarah . . . when Sarah returns. Every day, the cook prepares my sister's favorite pastries and serves them at breakfast. The grooms exercise her mare and have it ready. The butler, the house staff, the gardeners, and even the tenants that my mother might come in contact with are a part of this imaginary world in which Sarah is still alive. They're all committed to the game. My cousin Alice Young, who came from Maryland to be my mother's companion, the physician who sees to her health, even the minister."

He stopped and ran a hand through his hair.

"My mother believes that Sarah has been on an extended visit to America, where she's staying with family in Maryland."

Phoebe thought back to the first news that came of Sarah's disappearance. Her friend was there one day and the next she'd vanished. She wondered how Mrs. Bell could have accepted Sarah's sudden absence. And what about now? Three years, Phoebe thought in disbelief. Three years in which a mother never questions such a lengthy absence? She was no expert on the workings of the human mind, however. Her sister Jo had been separated for sixteen years from Wynne Melfort, but when those two met again in the Highlands, it was as if they'd never been apart.

"This story of Sarah traveling to America . . ." She had to know the truth. "When was your mother told this?"

"Right after my sister disappeared." Ian tapped the cabin wall with the head of his stick. Two lines furrowed his forehead. "Before we knew for certain what happened to her. The lie was kinder than all the ugly rumors that were beginning to circulate."

Phoebe had vehemently defended her friend when the stories and gossip spread of Sarah running away with a phantom lover. They were all lies. She knew her friend. There was no one she cared for enough to leave her family that way.

"My mother has always been attached to her children, but to Sarah especially. And she hasn't been well for years. Since my father died, she's become frailer and frailer, and her heart is weak. I never doubted Sarah's character or judgment, and I feared the worst may have happened to her. I didn't think my mother could handle the uncertainty . . . or the tragedy."

Phoebe's heart ached for them all. From the first moment of hearing the distressing news, she'd suspected there had to be foul play involved. And she'd been right.

"And she believed it all?"

"Her memory is not what it once was." He shrugged. "With enough help, anyone can build a castle of lies."

"So she never heard that you discovered Sarah's remains?"

He shook his head. "I couldn't. I wouldn't. No parent should ever be exposed to that kind of horror."

Her brother Hugh's face came to her mind. How shattered he'd been after losing his son and his first wife.

"That was why the funeral was held in Edinburgh. That's why your mother was absent. She didn't even know."

Ian leaned a shoulder against the cabin, his lips a hard, thin line. The pain he'd endured!

"Afterwards, I brought Sarah's casket back here and laid her to rest in the church crypt."

She understood his reasons for deciding it had to be this way. Still, the idealist in Phoebe wanted to say it was a mother's right to know. *She* would want to know. But she wasn't Fiona Bell. She wasn't married. She had no children. She had never loved a daughter, only to lose her so horribly.

She also tried to imagine herself in Ian's position. How do you convey such tragic news to your own mother, knowing she was not strong to begin with? She couldn't.

"What do you want Millie and me to say?" she asked. "We were friends of Sarah's. I . . . I loved her like a sister. Should we even ask about her?"

Relief flickered in his dark eyes as his hand reached for hers. Her fingers slid into his as if they'd always belonged there.

"She'll bring it up on her own. Sarah is her favorite topic. And it doesn't matter that you've been to Bellhorne so often and that you already know our family history," he told her. "She'll show you the roses she planted for Sarah. She'll take out my sister's favorite books and share memories of their walks. And you'll hear the same stories several times over the next two days."

Phoebe wished she could wrap him in her arms and hold him and try to soothe the sadness that weighed him down. Mrs. Bell dwelled in a fortress of dreams. What worried Phoebe now was a son's heartache.

She looked down at their joined hands instead. "I won't disappoint you, Captain. My sister and I will be everything your mother needs us to be during our visit."

Ian had sent word ahead from Edinburgh, and a carriage was waiting for them at the ferry dock.

He sat across from Phoebe for the sixteen-mile journey to Bellhorne. Before they climbed into the carriage, he'd overheard bits and pieces of her telling Millie what lay ahead. Ian did not worry that these two would be true to their promise. He also was certain that his mother would be happy to see them. These young women, especially Phoebe, were reminders of the days when Bellhorne pulsed with life and friendships.

The carriage rolled past Inverkeithing Bay, and Ian looked out at the retreating tide. He'd told Phoebe he'd built a castle of lies, but he knew it rested on a foundation of sand. It was only a matter of time before it all came crashing down.

Everything about what he was doing went against the grain of his integrity, against his very character. The perpetual fabrications about Sarah's well-being, the news from fictitious letters, and the false assertions of her adventures constantly ate away at him. And now he'd promised his mother he would write and convince his sister to come home for a visit.

Lies and more lies.

Telling Phoebe the truth did nothing to ease his guilt, but he felt the link between them grow stronger. He knew her secret, and now she knew his.

They were not a half hour from the ferry when Millie laid her head on her sister's shoulder and dropped off to sleep.

Ian's knee brushed against Phoebe's skirts. She hadn't bothered to put her hat back on after the crossing, and he admired the dance of dark curls around her face. He liked to watch her, and he wondered if she knew how plainly her moods were reflected in the arch of an eyebrow, or the blush on her cheeks, or the tilt of her rebellious bottom lip. Her attention was on the passing countryside, but he sensed her mind was on him, as well. Every now and again, she glanced back at him, and their gazes locked.

He was attracted to her. There was no denying it. And she was drawn to him. The spark between them was unmistakable, but this week had been a trying one. Between the lecture he'd given her after their visit to the Orphan Hospital and telling her today about his mother's condition, Ian would hardly win any prizes as a suitor.

As a suitor. He'd never thought of himself in those terms before. But it was the truth.

Millie started in her sleep, then nestled her head into a more comfortable position against her sister's shoulder. Her breathing soon became deeper.

The tenderness on Phoebe's face as she looked over at the younger woman was endearing. The Pennington bond.

He knew of no other family that had such a strong sense of devotion amongst its siblings.

"Were the Viscount and Lady Greysteil offended I didn't come for dinner last evening?" he asked quietly.

"No, they were only in Edinburgh for one night, and they understood that my invitation was made at the last moment."

"I hope *you* weren't offended."

"Not offended, but disappointed that you declined." She unbuttoned the top of her traveling coat. "I thought I'd already lost your good opinion of me."

Her reaction two days ago when he'd relayed the history of the hospital's troubles had only increased his respect for her character.

"Quite the contrary. But I hope you know that all the things I said after our visit to the Orphan Hospital were made as suggestions, not demands. My intention was not to force my opinion on you. I only wanted you to be aware of the tenuous position of charities with regard to their supporters."

"I understand," she said softly. "But I would be very happy to let the topic rest, at least for now, until I have an opportunity to learn more."

He couldn't ask anything else of her.

Phoebe Pennington was smart, beautiful, talented, and in a position to do as she pleased when it came to writing her article. But after their talk, he realized she wasn't after accolades; she wanted positive change. He admired her for it.

Yesterday, he sent over to the *Edinburgh Review*'s offices for the past issues containing Gaius Gracchus's articles. Last night, he read them. As he'd expected, she was well-read and projected an attitude in which principle took precedence over self-interest, and pragmatism had little value in governance. He had no interest in arguing with Phoebe right now about political compromise and what it took to run a city such as Edinburgh. But someday he sensed they would have some lively discussions.

She had more to say. But instead, she picked up her kid gloves from the seat, smoothed them on her lap, folded them, and put them back.

"You've changed," she said finally. "Or perhaps I had the wrong impression of you when I was younger."

"At the risk of sounding vain, I'd be interested in what your impression was then," he replied. "And even more interested in how it's different now."

"You're patient and understanding of other's positions now. Of mine, for example."

Her compliment was soothing as a gentle breeze. He understood her nature. It was defined by her passion. He would be very unhappy if she decided to abandon their relationship because of differences in their opinions.

"And that was unexpected," she continued. "For if my memory serves me correctly, you had a reputation of being overly protective and insistent on having the final say."

"That sounds like my sister's perception of me."

A shadow of sadness clouded Phoebe's expression. She nodded.

Sarah's complaints echoed in his memory to this day. She'd rebelled against his demands that she report where she went, and with whom, or when she would return. So many times she'd accused him of taking the responsibility of her guardianship far too seriously. He was only her brother, she'd say, and he was ruining their friendship with his "draconian strictness." And then she'd laugh and do what she wanted anyway. No wonder she and Phoebe had been such good friends.

"How far apart in age are you and your brothers?" he asked.

"Hugh is nine years older. Gregory, three years."

"Are they protective of you?"

"Too protective. In fact, most times they're impossible," she asserted. Realizing she might have been too loud, she checked on her sister before continuing. "Of course, I'm speaking of my brother Hugh primarily. But Gregory is no better if he thinks no one else is supervising my every move."

She glanced at her sister's sleeping form again. "And I do mean *my* every move," she repeated. "They're far more trusting of Millie."

Ian understood why they might worry more about Phoebe, but he decided to make no comment.

"They're like a pair of mastiffs taking turns guarding a bone. My father expects it of them too. I'm certain of it."

Regardless of all their protectiveness, Ian knew how much trouble Phoebe could have found herself in if he hadn't been patrolling the Vaults the night of her attack.

"Fathers and daughters. Brothers and sisters," she said a moment later. "I take your point."

He wouldn't say it to Phoebe, but his biggest regret in life was not being *more* protective of his sister. But how could he have stopped what happened to her? He was not about to keep her locked away like some fairy tale princess. The truth was that no matter what one did, it was never enough.

Ian contemplated the rolling hills rising to the north. The mystery of the night Sarah was murdered continued to gnaw at his mind. The senseless nature of the violence did nothing to explain her actions.

"Have you gone back to the Vaults since that night I . . ." Phoebe paused and the words hung in the air between them, drawing Ian's attention back to her. "Since the night you came across me there."

"I have gone back," he admitted.

"Many times?"

He didn't want to tell her that he rarely slept well at night. Roaming the city streets and hunting through the Vaults beneath South Bridge was an act of necessity. Finding someone to help or frightening a would-be attacker off with his presence seemed to give him a kind of reprieve from the ghosts that haunted him. Until the next sleepless night.

"Do you go every night when you are in the city?" she pressed, not giving up.

He shrugged. "I don't pay much attention. I go when I feel the need."

Phoebe started to say something but then seemed to decide against it. She stared out the window. But that didn't last long. Her eyes were stormy when she looked back at him.

"Do you always go down there alone?"

"I do."

"Why?" she asked. "Why not take a footman? Or Mr. Crawford, your valet? You could even hire a bodyguard like Duncan Turner. Or a company of guards."

Another man might have been amused by her suggestions, but he wasn't. He knew her concerns were legitimate. She'd faced a dangerous assailant down there. Her encounter was far more perilous than any he'd ever had. Still, he thought better than to make light of her fears.

"You're seriously asking me to hire a small militia to accompany me when I go down there?"

"Why not."

"What you are saying is preposterous."

"I worry for you."

The words were a mere whisper, but they pierced him and encircled his heart. He reached out for Phoebe's hand and took her fingers in his own.

"I'm always armed. I'm always careful."

He wanted to remind her that he'd faced far more dangerous opponents while fighting in the war than he was likely to meet down there. But he doubted anything he said would lessen her fears. She again started to say something but stopped and glanced first at her sister. Millie was still sleeping peacefully.

"Have there been any other . . . ?" Her free hand fisted on her lap.

He knew what she was talking about. Killings.

"None that the authorities know about." Ian had enough paid informants among the constables to know that no dead bodies had been newly discovered.

"The killer," she whispered. "You said he's consistent in *how* he leaves his victims. Is there any consistency in *when* he attacks his victims? Perhaps at the full moon?"

"No, you're not doing this. This is not a topic for your writing," he warned, squeezing her hand before letting go. "Gaius Gracchus writes about politics and corruption. You are *not* getting involved in this."

He must have been too loud as Millie stirred and opened her eyes.

"You're not getting involved in what?" she asked, stifling a yawn.

Neither of them answered, and she looked from Ian to her sister.

"Nothing," Phoebe said, adjusting herself in her seat. "I'm not getting involved, so there's nothing to talk about."

❧ 10 ❧

SARAH WAS a mature sixteen-year-old the first time Phoebe met her. But the similarity of their likes and dislikes and their temperaments were such that they immediately became fast friends. And that was the start of the many crossings of the Firth of Forth as Sarah came to Baronsford and Phoebe traveled to Bellhorne, sometimes with Millie, but often alone.

As the carriage turned off the main road and started up the long drive to Bellhorne Castle, the memories tossed and churned like rushing water following the curve of a river. Phoebe recalled the conversations they shared, the stories they told, the quiet havens they escaped to.

She stared out the carriage window and remembered how often the two of them stole away and walked to the top of the highest hill on the estate, a favorite place to sit in the grass. They'd look out at the Firth of Forth for the white sails of ships and talk about their dreams of traveling to faraway places. From there, they could see the ancient oak where

Sarah's father had proposed to her mother after he returned from the colonies in America. One time, they'd seen the smoke of a cooking fire rising from a camp of Romani travelers, and she told Phoebe about a wedding the passing nomads once held there. The romantic music of the fiddles and tambourines had drifted across the fields till near dawn.

Their visits to the stony shore were frequent too. Phoebe recalled a wet and misty day they'd spent looking for perfectly matched shells they could each save. It was the first time she came to Bellhorne. Sarah had told her about the handsome minister in the village, and then grown somber, relating the news from Ian's latest letters about the battles on the continent.

But when the lightning and thunder of Fife's summer storms flashed and raged outside, they would go at night into the west tower in search of the ghost of a dashing Jacobite rebel that her friend claimed roamed through the castle in search of lost treasure.

Once he'd returned to Bellhorne from the wars, however, the only specter that interested Phoebe was Captain Bell, who might appear unexpectedly, show his handsome face, greet them sternly, and then go as suddenly as he came. A hero in the fight against Napoleon, he was now master of Bellhorne, its fishing village with the stone kirk, and the rolling lands that went on for miles and miles. But to Phoebe, he was a wounded knight errant, returned to the towers of his grey stone fortress, awaiting the arrival of his true love.

Many times when she came to see her friend, Phoebe tried to get the brother to notice her at dinner, the only time he joined the family for any extended period. On the journey home from each visit, she let herself imagine that next time, he'd discover she was witty and engaging and worthy of pursuing.

And now she was here, at Bellhorne, escorted by the only man she'd ever yearned for. She was happy about that, of course, but Bellhorne itself would never be the same. All those golden afternoons, all their adventures, all their heart-to-heart talks were a thing of the past. A past she could never reclaim. Sarah was gone. Her friend was lost. Stolen away and brutally murdered. It was a fate her sweet friend did not deserve. And there was an empty space in her own life that would never be filled.

The lump in Phoebe's chest burned painfully. But there was nothing she could do to bring Sarah back.

"Here we are," Ian said. His eyes and his gentle tone made her think he knew where her mind had wandered. He seemed to understand the sadness that visiting Bell-horne would summon in Phoebe. He shared in that loss, and she knew Sarah's absence haunted him.

Whatever sorrow Phoebe was feeling, however, she needed to hide it deep inside of her, for there to greet them as the carriage door opened was Mrs. Bell, her face shining with joy at the sight of the visitors. She met them with the same effusive warmth and affection she'd always greeted them with when her daughter was still alive.

"Lady Phoebe! Lady Millie! You do indeed brighten our quiet corner of the world, coming to see us here. My dears!" She sighed happily as Ian bent to kiss her cheek. "So many precious memories."

Before the introductions and greetings could continue, the older woman faced Phoebe, thin cool fingers cradling her face. She touched her cheek and caressed her hair, showering her with the affection of a mother. "You, my dear. My sweet girl. I'm so glad you are here."

Words struggled to emerge, apologies for not coming sooner, regrets for not writing to her. Condolences that she couldn't voice. She bit her lip, and when her eyes burned, Phoebe hugged Mrs. Bell before she could discover the runaway tears.

When the two of them pulled apart, Ian was standing beside her. There was a tender touch on the small of her back, almost a caress, as he introduced her and Millie to his cousin, Mrs. Young, and continued on with good-natured grumbling about how he was hungry enough to eat an ox.

As they all headed toward the house, Mrs. Bell walked between Phoebe and Millie and ordered a late luncheon to be served.

"We'll eat in the garden by Sarah's roses, shall we?" she suggested, pointing the way with her cane. "As we always did when the sun peeked out."

As they strolled around the castle and entered the gardens through the archway, Phoebe detached herself from the other two and paused to look out at a distant hill, rising from a thick of oak trees. Sarah once told her the story of a relative hiding in that forest for an entire summer following Culloden.

Phoebe was recognized as a storyteller by everyone who knew her from the time she could hold a pencil to paper and string words together. Sarah took great joy in telling her the legends and ghost stories and gossip that permeated the grey stones of the thirteenth-century castle. *You'll rival Mrs. Radcliffe with your stories*, she'd say with a laugh, *and make her sorry she ever took up a pen*. She wondered what her friend would think of the new direction her writing was headed now. To create fiction or report facts. Phoebe was certain she had the answer a month ago, but now she wasn't too sure.

Ian moved beside her. "The Rebel Oaks," he said, following her gaze.

"I've always wondered if a tale Sarah told me about it was truth or legend."

"Quite true," he replied. "The man spent nearly two months in a burnt-out tree trunk."

Taking her hand, he put it on his arm, and Phoebe felt the warmth of his body as they trailed after the others.

"Thank you for bringing us to Bellhorne," she said in a low voice.

"I wanted you to see the place again. To see my mother." He paused. "I wanted you to come."

Phoebe blushed, not at all certain if she had any right to entertain the hope warming in her heart regarding his intentions.

The maids had already set up the luncheon before a lattice wall of flowering clematis. The gardens spread out around them.

"Shall I send a message to Dr. Thornton and Mr. Garioch, and ask them not to come to dinner tonight?" Mrs. Young asked as they arranged themselves around the table.

"Not at all. Not at all. I want them here," Mrs. Bell told her companion before addressing the guests. "You know my doctor and the rector. It will be delightful to reunite such old friends."

Phoebe exchanged a look with Ian. She'd heard both men's names mentioned on her prior visits, but she had met neither of them. There was no purpose in saying so. From what she'd seen and heard so far, it wasn't Mrs.

Bell's memory that concerned her as much as the older woman's fragile state of health. Walking to the garden, they'd made several stops for her to catch her breath.

"Tell me about your dear mother," Mrs. Bell asked as they ate lunch. "And do your parents still divide their time between the Borders and Hertfordshire?"

While Millie brought their hostess up to date with all the news of their parents and siblings and marriages and additions to their growing family, Phoebe's mind turned again to her lost friend.

The grassy lanes and garden beds were brilliantly colored with the fondest memories. The scent of roses evoked a very different time in her life. Many nights during a visit, Phoebe and Sarah would sit together on the bed and share stories until dawn, while the night fragrances of the garden wafted in on the summer breeze.

Phoebe remembered her last time here. Sarah had been adamant that she was hearing footsteps in one of the spiral staircases. A fortnight before, she said, her red slippers had gone missing, only to be found two days later at the foot of the same staircase. Long before, she'd told Phoebe the tale of a young woman named Anne Erskine who lived over a century ago in the castle. The details were unclear, but somehow she fell to her death from a window at the top of the west tower, and now haunted the castle. Sarah believed the footsteps and the theft of the slippers meant the lonely spirit was trying to reach out and befriend her.

Bellhorne was already home to at least one ghost. Even though Sarah died in Edinburgh, her earthly remains had been brought back to the home she loved. Phoebe wondered if her friend's spirit would find the way back here where she could haunt the stairwells with Anne Erskine.

Suddenly she noticed the table had grown silent. A question had been directed at her. She discreetly glanced at Millie for help, but her sister only directed her gaze toward Ian's cousin.

"I'm sorry, Mrs. Young. I was distracted for a moment. Did you ask me something?"

"I've found volumes of your aunt's novels in the library and—"

Mrs. Bell held up a hand, hushing her. Her dark-eyed gaze rested gently on Phoebe's face.

"I know she's not here with us, but you feel her presence too, don't you?"

Phoebe tried to swallow the sudden lump in her throat. Sarah was indeed with them, in memory, in spirit, in the brush of the breeze over the leaves and the flower petals. She struggled. No answer she could give came to her. The conversation she had with Ian on the ferry about his mother not knowing of Sarah's death, the promise she'd made to him of not destroying the pretense, all rushed back. But at this very moment, looking into the clear, intelligent eyes of their hostess, Phoebe could not help but wonder if she knew.

"How can we not think of Sarah while we sit here breathing in the sweet fragrance of all those roses that were planted in her honor?" Ian asked, putting an end to the prolonged silence. He laid his napkin on the table. "Unfortunately, I need to meet with Mr. Raeburn this afternoon, if you ladies can do without me for a few hours. Mother, do you want to rest before dinner?"

Thin fingers stretched out toward the son. "Indeed. Indeed, I should. And Alice, would you be kind enough to make sure Lady Phoebe and Lady Millie are settled in their room? Have Mrs. Hume assign maids to see to each of them."

"I'll take care of it."

As the servants cleared away the luncheon, Ian escorted his mother to her rooms while Phoebe and Millie were ushered in by his cousin.

"I'm sure it must be very difficult—as old friends of Sarah's—to carry on this pretense," Mrs. Young said in a low voice once they were out of hearing range of their hostess.

Phoebe watched the woman lead them across the great hall toward the stairs. From the information Ian offered on their journey here, she gathered Mrs. Bell's companion was in her mid-thirties. She'd been married to a clergyman in Maryland and widowed about a year before coming at Ian's request to Bellhorne.

Maybe it was because she'd read so many novels in her youth, or because she herself had strong feelings for Captain Bell, but the thought had crossed Phoebe's mind that perhaps Mrs. Young entertained a romantic interest toward her cousin. But meeting her in person now, she perceived no such attraction. Kind, reserved, and matter-of-fact, Ian's cousin appeared to be a person grounded in the practicalities of life. And her attention was focused entirely on Mrs. Bell.

"Did you and Sarah ever meet?" Millie asked the woman as they walked through the upper-floor gallery. Family portraits covered the high walls.

"Sadly, I never had the chance. She was born in Fife, and I in Baltimore. We're cousins through her father and my mother," she explained. "I only knew her through our letters. But the way this house has been maintained,

Sarah's presence is—as Mrs. Bell mentioned at the table —undeniable."

Midday light spilling through the windows illuminated the handsome Persian rugs and the huge paintings of family members and stern-faced ancestors. Phoebe had walked through this gallery many times, and she now paused by one of her favorite portraits. Ian and Sarah. She was an adorable seven-year-old, and he was a fresh-faced version of the handsome man he was today. Dressed in his military uniform of the Coldstream Guards, the young man stared ahead with eagerness at the adventures lying before him. But Sarah's eyes were on their joined hands. Small fingers held her brother's larger ones. She wasn't ready to let him go.

Phoebe thought of her conversation with Ian about continually returning to the Vaults. Three years after Sarah was taken, *he* was not ready to let her go. And she understood the sentiment.

They were waiting for her in the doorway at the end of the gallery, and she hurried to catch up.

"I was told to put you in the room across from Sarah's," Mrs. Young said as they reached their destination. "I hope that suits you."

"It's perfect," Millie assured her. "We often stayed in this room when we visited Bellhorne."

As soon as Ian's cousin left, Phoebe walked to the windows and pushed them open wide. From the first moment they'd arrived, her emotions had been working like a riptide, draining the sandy foundation from beneath her feet. Little by little, she was sinking deeper and becoming less secure. The timing of Ian's interruption at lunch was perfect. She wouldn't have been able to answer his mother's question rationally.

"What do you think is worse?" Millie asked softly. "To know your child is dead, or to believe she's become estranged because of some injury you've inflicted but can't recall?"

Phoebe turned to her sister. Millie was not waiting for a maid. She already had their traveling trunk open and dresses laid out on the bed.

"What makes you think Mrs. Bell believes Sarah's absence is the result of something she did?"

Millie shook her head. "During the luncheon, I know you weren't paying attention to much of what was being said."

"What did she say?"

"Mrs. Bell said *twice* that all the news of her daughter comes from her son," Millie explained. "And just like a mother, she immediately made excuses about her eyesight and how Sarah knows she needs help to read or write her own letters. And how happy she is that the brother and sister are so close."

"None of what you say makes me think she blames herself for Sarah's absence."

"Mothers always take the blame for their children's actions," her sister told her. "And for their bad temperaments and their sicknesses and their ill-conceived marriages and whatever else there is to take responsibility for."

Wrapping her arms around her middle, Phoebe considered her sister's words and thought about their own mother. From what she recalled, every troubled day Millicent Pennington endured could be traced to some worry or some real catastrophe pertaining to her children.

Motherhood. She knew next to nothing about it. She

couldn't even imagine what kind of mother she'd be herself.

Phoebe hung their dresses in the wardrobe and wandered to the window as her thoughts drifted in another direction. To the same place they'd been since the night she met him again.

Ian.

At least it seemed she hadn't lost his good opinion of her. Their conversation in the carriage drifted back to her. His attention, the words he'd spoken, and every touch was cherished and etched in her mind.

The kiss they'd shared in the garden at Baronsford felt as if it happened an eon ago, but it was still very alive in her memory. She touched her lips.

Phoebe worried about him. About where he went and what danger he was putting himself in with his nocturnal trips into the city's netherworld.

Strength, confidence, and training were meaningless when a knife came out of the darkness. The man she'd fought with was committing murder. She'd escaped death, as had young Jock Rokeby. But thinking of Ian as a potential victim of this killer sent a shaft of hot steel straight into her heart.

Suddenly, she couldn't breathe. Voices came at her. Faces. Sarah's. Jock's. A dark-cloaked man running through the passages of the Vaults.

The greenery and the sunlight outside their window called to her. Phoebe turned toward the door. She needed room to move and air to breathe if she was ever going to clear her mind and be a tolerable companion to their host for the limited time they were visiting.

"I'm going for a walk."

"Give me a few moments to arrange our things and I'll come with you."

She couldn't wait. She didn't want company. She needed to think.

"Look for me in the rose garden," she told her sister, picking up her bonnet and going out.

The hallway was empty, and Phoebe paused and stared at Sarah's door. Ian's words came to her of how the rooms had been kept ready for his sister's imminent arrival. She couldn't go in there. She needed no reminders. Her friend was already with her in spirit.

"Sarah," she whispered, pressing her palm against the door before hurrying down the corridor.

Passing through the gallery, Phoebe felt the eyes of Ian's predecessors staring down at her. Hurrying down the steps, she heard the ordinary sounds of the household, and it occurred to her that they should have been more comforting. But beyond the familiar, she felt a strange presence. She couldn't identify it. A ghost, witnessing her every move. She paused on a step and looked up at the landing leading to the gallery. A shadow moved behind a column. She stood perfectly still for a dozen heartbeats, waiting, but there was nothing.

She made her way down the great hall. Weapons arranged on the walls between tapestries gleamed dully. The uneasiness that had edged under her skin caused her to shiver as she walked, and then ran, and then walked again toward the sunshine outdoors.

No one was in the rose garden, and that suited Phoebe perfectly. She moved along the row of roses, and the sweet scent filled her head. Ian and Sarah had both grown up here. This was as much home to them as Baronsford was to her.

She touched a white flower on a rose bush. The petals shivered and fell at her feet.

Sarah. Beautiful Sarah. Intelligent and wise Sarah, who complained about her brother's rigidity, not knowing he'd never lost his confidence in her. Sarah, who for all her talk of rebellion, was the most cautious of people.

Phoebe followed the well-trodden paths of the garden to the old wall. The smell of newly cut hay lying in the fields drenched her senses. She passed through a gate beneath an arch and kept walking, trying to empty her mind of sadness and recall the happier times at Bellhorne. Perhaps this was how Mrs. Bell had come to terms with her daughter's absence.

She followed the lane past the meadows, dotted with bundles of hay that had been gathered and stacked.

She wandered on for a while, and suddenly she knew where her feet were taking her.

Nobody from Bellhorne went there, Sarah said, but on summer days when Phoebe was visiting and the weather was particularly fine, the two of them would steal away past the high walls that contained Mrs. Bell's beautiful gardens. Running through the fields and the empty nomad's camp and along the burbling brook above the loch, they'd come to the Auld Grove, a wild forested park that Sarah loved dearly.

Phoebe followed the path now, cutting across the fields until she reached the track that led along the bracken-lined brook. She knew this way so well, and soon the cool shade of the ancient grove enclosed her.

A rustle of branches behind her drew Phoebe's attention. Still carrying her hat, she shielded her eyes with her hand and looked back. She startled when a half-dozen birds took flight noisily a few yards away. She waited, expecting to find someone emerge from the undergrowth. But no one appeared. There were no more sounds.

"Druids," she whispered.

Phoebe recalled exploring the woods and ruins of ancient buildings and the stone circle in the glen by the waterfall. Sarah told her the standing stones were still visited by witches and sorcerers who performed ancient rituals on moonlit nights, and they came from all over Scotland. Phoebe never saw any, but she believed her friend.

She reached the waterfall and stopped on a grassy spot. Patches of bluebells nodded their heads in the breeze. One sunny day, the two of them sat right here amid the purple-blue flowers, looking up at the passing clouds, and Sarah told her she had a scandalous secret to share. One of the lads from the village had kissed her under the oak tree where her parents had agreed to marry. *He was handsome and strong. He smelled of salt and sea winds,* adding with her mischievous laugh, *and herring.*

Phoebe smiled at the recollection. The family referred to the rose garden as Sarah's, but this grove of wildflowers was the place her friend loved the most.

The path soon brought her to another clearing. Phoebe recognized the ruins of several huts that were being overtaken by the encroaching woods.

A summer afternoon, not much different from this one, edged into her memory. Sarah shared stories of Ian since he'd returned from war. She worried about her brother. He was hurting. And her friend told her that she knew Phoebe was carrying a torch for him.

Phoebe moved through the high grass toward the crumbling buildings, and her throat tightened as she recalled all they'd talked about. Love. Marriage. Family.

Her eyes burned with unshed tears. Things Sarah wanted but would never know. Never have.

Pushing through a clump of bushes, Phoebe suddenly found herself standing at the edge of a well. She stared down into the black void and thought of the Vaults in Edinburgh.

"Why did you go down there, Sarah? What happened to you?"

Phoebe heard no footsteps, no warning that she wasn't alone. But the hand that shoved her from behind belonged to no ghostly presence. And before she could turn, or grab for a branch, or even cry out, she was falling through the darkness, tumbling like a stone toward the center of the earth.

He stared down into the hole. Silence.

She'd fallen for some time. That was good, though the dull, hard splash at the end surprised him. But no sound followed. Also, good. She was gone.

Her hat lay like a downed wood pigeon in the tall grass. He picked it up and tossed it into the well.

He'd stalked her from the moment she came down the stairs, looking for his chance. And she led him here. It was perfect. So isolated. So silent.

This was his home. His lair. He'd never before hunted here. Bellhorne was his home. He hunted in the city. It was clean. The prey was plentiful. And it was safer.

This one, though, this Phoebe Pennington, had come face-to-face with him. That was enough reason for her to die.

But more, she'd struck him, attacked him. And in

meddling, she'd caused him to lose his chosen prey. She started this blood feud, and she had to pay the price.

And she had paid. If they ever found her body, they would never suspect foul play. He was a skilled hunter. Gifted. He'd made the clean kill.

It was done. She would bear no witness against him.

No one would hinder him now. No one would interfere with his pursuit of destiny. No one would stop him from doing what he was chosen to accomplish. He could hear the whispers beginning. The voices growing louder and more insistent. He'd feel their fingers scraping along his skin, and then pressing until, finally, they delved into his flesh and reached into his soul.

The time was nearly upon him. A few days. A week. He knew the hour was almost here. He would go back to Edinburgh. Destiny awaited. The power awaited. The reward awaited.

Nothing was going to stop him.

❧ 11 ❧

TIME SLOWED TO A NEAR STANDSTILL, and Phoebe floated downward. Darkness enclosed her, and an endless void yawned below. Her arms and legs were not hers to command, and they flailed ineffectually around her. But when her hand struck a stone protruding from the wall, she felt the sharp pain in her shoulder and then spun like a top as she plummeted to the bottom. A scream formed in her throat but never emerged, for an instant later she hit the water at the bottom, and the impact knocked the air from her lungs.

As Phoebe sank into the blackness, no sense of up or down existed. Suddenly the realization cut through to her stunned mind that she was about to drown. She fought off the paralyzing panic. The will to live took charge.

She kicked her feet, one hand clawing at what felt like a wall of stone, and then her body began to move upward. She broke through the surface into air nearly as cold as the water, but still could not draw breath.

No. No. No. You will not die.

Trying to move her hands and feet to keep herself afloat, she found she had no feeling in her left shoulder. Her arm floated uselessly, as if it had become detached from her body. Her chest was locked in a painful spasm that would admit no air. She grabbed her arm and shoulder, and a sharp pain radiated across her back. She felt a jolt of air enter her lungs, and she tried to think.

Another breath. She looked up. Stone walls stretched straight up for an ungodly distance. A well. She'd fallen into a well.

The water was very cold, and her dress was weighing her down. Another breath seeped in. She looked up again and the distance to the top seemed to stretch even farther.

She started to call for help but immediately stopped. Her hat came fluttering down the shaft.

The memory returned. Fear formed a tight knot in her stomach. Someone had pushed her. And this same someone was standing at the top now.

The hat landed on the water beside her.

She tried to move her left arm again and the sharp pain caused her to stop kicking. Her chin dipped beneath the surface. Phoebe swallowed a mouthful of foul-tasting water and she gagged. Retching and gasping for air, she scratched at the wall, slippery with moss, desperate for something to hold onto. Her fingers found a narrow lip of stone.

She looked up again once the retching subsided. Someone at Bellhorne wanted her dead.

. . .

"I'll be going to Edinburgh myself next week," Dr. Thornton said. "I'll see to it that the doctor from the medical college comes back with me. Have no fear, Captain."

Ian wished he could remain as composed as the doctor. He'd been away from Bellhorne less than a week, and yet upon his return, his mother appeared even paler and weaker. Getting a specialist here to see her was beginning to feel critical, and he told the man his concern.

"I understand your thinking," the doctor agreed. "When I arrived earlier, I stopped up to see her before coming to your office. Whatever decline you're seeing now may be temporary. But I must tell you the change may very well have been caused by the excitement of this unexpected company."

"She was quite happy to greet them." The welcome his mother gave Phoebe had touched Ian the most. The way she took Phoebe into her arms brought back more memories of Sarah. She'd touch her daughter's face and look into her eyes as if she could discern, with that simple gesture, everything that was right and wrong.

The doctor shook his head. "It may have appeared so to you, but she thought the household wasn't prepared to receive the daughters of an earl. The cook is all at sixes and sevens apparently, and the housekeeper is in a panic shuffling staff about to tend to these young ladies. I had to hear her every worry. If you care for her health, you'll spare her this type of agitation."

Ian knew it was in the man's character to speak his mind regardless of whom he was addressing, but he felt his temper rising. Most days, he would allow the doctor to say his peace and let it go. But suggesting that Phoebe should not be welcome at Bellhorne was exceeding the bounds of his position.

"I do care for her health, Thornton," he said sharply. "And I'll address any confusion in the household, starting with Cook and Mrs. Hume. But to be clear, Lady Phoebe and her sister are welcome guests at Bellhorne, as they always have been and always will be. Once you meet them, you'll realize their presence will have a positive impact on my mother's . . ." A soft knock at the door stopped Ian momentarily. " . . . on my mother's health."

As Ian went to open the door, Dr. Thornton grumbled something under his breath and turned to the window. He'd half expected it to be Phoebe and was surprised to find Millie waiting outside. She looked pale and out of breath. He noticed bits of hay caught at the bottom of her skirts as if she'd been walking through the fields.

"Lady Millie, what's wrong?"

"I am sorry to interrupt, Captain, but I was hoping you might know where my sister has disappeared to."

"What do you mean 'disappeared'?" he asked, unease clenching his stomach in a tight grip.

"She left our room soon after our luncheon with your mother. I was to meet her in the garden. But I've looked everywhere, and she's nowhere to be found."

He reminded himself to stay calm despite his tendency these days to imagine the worst. Phoebe was a frequent visitor to Bellhorne while Millie joined her sister only on occasion. The older sister was more familiar with the castle and the grounds.

"Where *exactly* have you looked?" he asked as he ushered her toward the great hall with Thornton on their heels.

"The garden. The orchards. I checked with the

grooms in the stables, thinking Phoebe might have decided to go for a ride. But no one saw her, and no horses are missing."

A footman appeared.

"Get Mr. Singer now," Ian ordered, sending the man running for the butler. He turned back to Millie. "Could she be up with my mother?"

"She's not. I asked Mrs. Young to check. She said your mother is resting, and Phoebe has not been to see her."

The butler rushed into the hall. Ian gave directions to organize a search. "Get Mr. Raeburn here as well."

The household was already stirring because of the urgency of his calls. The housekeeper appeared. "What is it, Captain?"

"We can't find Lady Phoebe. Have the servants look for her. Look everywhere."

As Mrs. Hume hurried out, Ian turned to Millie again. "Did you look in Sarah's room?"

"When she wasn't in the garden, that was the first place I looked," she answered. "She's not there."

He tried to think of all the places where Sarah liked to take her friends. Bellhorne was a large house with extensive grounds, and Phoebe was no stranger to it. Running footsteps could be heard now, as well as doors opening and closing.

Millie suddenly looked somewhat embarrassed by the upheaval she'd set in motion.

"Perhaps I've overreacted, and my worry is for nothing. I know my sister. I know she has an adventurous nature. Perhaps she's simply off on her own and will be back by dinner."

Nothing would make Ian happier than to have that be

so, but wishing it did not make the worry diminish. He wouldn't rest until they found her.

———

Phoebe had little strength left in her legs to kick and keep herself afloat. She'd found a slippery, narrow lip protruding on the stonework, and she clung to it for her life. Her fingers were growing numb, however, and she kept losing her hold. Each time, she sank deep into the water. But she wasn't giving up, and each time she thrashed her way to the surface.

She had no voice left to call for help. The only sound in the well was the clicking chatter of her teeth and the hollow lapping of the water around her.

The feeling in her left side had returned, but the cold and exhaustion rendered the arm useless. Her body felt more and more like dead weight, and she knew it was only a matter of time before she lost her handhold and sank to the bottom.

Time. She didn't know how long she'd been down here except that the sky far above was taking on a darker shade of blue. Whoever pushed her in had to be gone. Nothing else rained down on her. No boulders. No branches. There was no attempt to cover the top. Perhaps he thought the fall had killed her.

She had no doubt they'd have realized by now she was missing. Millie would go looking when she didn't find her in the rose garden. Phoebe wasn't giving up, but the chances were poor that anyone would search the Auld Grove. And even if they did, how would they find her at the bottom of a forgotten well?

Phoebe closed her eyes and rested her face against the

slippery wall. She couldn't lose hope. She couldn't die. No. Not here. Not at Bellhorne. Ian's face formed in her mind's eye. He'd already suffered too much. He held himself responsible for what happened to Sarah. She couldn't add to his guilt.

"I'm waiting for you, Ian," she murmured. "But find me."

Bellhorne and the estate grounds were in complete turmoil. Every member of the staff was looking for Phoebe, and the tenants had now joined in.

Fearing additional upset for his mother, Ian decided he needed to remove her from the center of the commotion. The minister, Mr. Garioch, stepped in and invited the older woman to join him in the village for dinner. The carriage was brought around, and Alice Young accompanied her to the rectory. Millie, however, would go nowhere until her sister was found.

The house was searched again with care, room by room. The dogs had been taken out of the kennels, and field hands and grooms were combing the fields.

Ian was about to lose his mind. He could not fathom where Phoebe might have gone. They'd arrived here in his carriage. She'd taken no horses from the stables. There was only so far she could have walked in a few hours on foot. But in which direction would she go?

As soon as the search was well underway, he rode to the village to query the fishermen laying out their catch to dry along the shore. Worry topped worry. What if she had been taken against her will? Everyone he questioned answered the same. No one had seen a woman matching her description. No strangers had traveled through. No one had seen her. All Ian was able to accomplish there was to enlist the help of more men to expand the search up and down the shoreline.

He didn't want to think it. There was no parallel between Sarah's disappearance and what was happening now. They were at Bellhorne. They were not in Edinburgh. No dangerous netherworld of crime existed out here. He trusted his tenants and the villagers, everyone that she might have come in contact with.

Riding hard back to Bellhorne, he prayed she'd be waiting there with Millie. But what if she wasn't? Dread washed down his spine, and he spurred his horse on.

Ian tried to put himself in Phoebe's place. He knew she was upset while they were having lunch in the rose garden. His first thought on hearing of her disappearance was that she might have revisited places she'd gone with Sarah. But they'd already searched all the spots he could think of, and she was not to be found.

Evening was drawing near. Soon the dark of night would overtake them. Ian felt the tension straining his every limb. He could hardly think with the knot of pain throbbing in his head.

"Where are you, Phoebe?" he called out into the wind. No answer came back.

Put yourself in her place. The words echoed again and again in his mind. How could she disappear? Where would she go? And why?

He knew her. He'd witnessed her courage, her willingness to face danger.

Ian had almost reached Bellhorne, and he saw his men and their dogs stretched out in lines across the fields. Raeburn was directing them. She hadn't been found yet.

"Where did you go, Phoebe?"

The image of her unconscious body landing at his feet in the Vaults came to his mind. Few people he knew—man or woman—had her heart, her courage.

The realization was slow in coming, but to solve any puzzle one needed to assemble the first pieces. And he had them.

He'd found Phoebe wearing men's clothing for her sojourn into the Vaults, the most dangerous place in Edinburgh for anyone. He'd followed her through the streets of Edinburgh, only to catch up to her by Greyfriars Kirkyard, where headless ghosts of Covenanters rose from their graves. She wanted to climb to the top of Arthur's Seat where Bonnie Prince Charlie stood and surveyed the capital he'd come to fight for. She was drawn to the dangerous, to the untamed.

The Auld Grove. No one went there anymore, except the travelers who camped nearby later in the summer. Like a fool, he'd shown his sister the standing stones once, and then, thinking better on it, he tried to warn her off with stories of witches and blood rituals. He thought he'd succeeded, but now he wondered if Sarah had taken Phoebe there during her visits.

And if he was right and something happened to Phoebe out there, then he had one more reason for burning in hell.

Phoebe stared at the pale hand clinging to the mossy rock. The bloodless fingers didn't belong to her. A vague indifference was clouding her brain, and she found she no longer worried about the cold, for she could hardly feel her legs. The chattering of her teeth continued, but she only occasionally heard it. Her panting breaths were not taking in enough air. But she didn't care about that, either. All she wanted to do was sleep.

She rubbed her cheek against a slick rock and thought of her regrets.

"Reg . . . rets." She struggled to get the words past her lips. The sound bounced around her head. Or was it echoing off the walls? She didn't know.

Regrets.

She was a good daughter, even though she caused her father to lose his temper every other time they argued. She was also a good sister. And if Hugh and Gregory claimed that she'd given them the grey patches beginning to show in their hair, it was a lie. Millie and Jo loved her, tolerated her without their brothers' meddlesome theatrics. And she was socially aware of the problems facing the poor. She had used her gift of writing for their welfare.

She had no regrets.

"Another lie," she breathed.

Closing her eyes, she saw Ian's face. *He* was her regret. Not going after him. He'd always been the one. The only one.

She was twenty-seven years old, and their few moments alone—and his kiss—were all she thought of.

"Ian," she whispered.

She had secured a place for herself as a writer, despite the difficulties presented because she was a woman. She was writing columns for the *Edinburgh Review*. It was a great accomplishment. But what of the other things that could bring her happiness?

Marriage. Children. Sex. It occurred to her that the order was muddled, but what did it matter? She'd missed all of it. She'd missed the passion that went with giving a man all of herself, body and soul. She was dying in a hole dug centuries ago in a forgotten grove . . . and she had not yet experienced life.

"Let me go," she said as one hand slipped off the rock. It would be so easy to let the other one go too.

Her body begged to be allowed to sink to the bottom. Easy. Phoebe stared at the slippery hold keeping her afloat. All she had to do was release each finger.

"Ian." His face. He wouldn't let her be.

So, she had regrets. But what of his? she wondered. His sister was dead, and after three years he was no closer to resolving his feelings of guilt. And what about her? He'd saved her in the Vaults. He worried about her, lectured her, but treated her like an intelligent, feeling human being. And then he brought her to Bellhorne. He would feel responsible for her death. She had no doubt of it.

Death. The grave. What did it matter if it was a casket in a kirkyard or the water at the bottom of a well? She stared again at the obstinate fingers clutching the rock.

"Ian," she cried out with all the breath she had.

Ian would never have heard it if he'd not followed the broken branches and trampled clumps of bracken and tall grass. The faint cry came from the bottom of the well, nearly hidden by the overgrown shrubs.

As he led a group of men to the Auld Grove, he'd been worried that if Phoebe had ventured out here alone, she might have twisted an ankle. Much worse, she might have been attacked by a vagrant passing through. But the well? It had never occurred to him.

"Blast me," he cursed.

As he scrambled to get to her, he nearly went in himself. Staring down into the darkness, Ian shouted orders to his men to bring ropes and a lantern.

Going down on his hands and knees, he leaned into the well and heard the sound of a splash at the bottom.

Relief at finding her and worry over how badly she might be injured battled in his brain.

"Phoebe!" he called down to her. For a moment panic hit him that perhaps he'd imagined it. He'd wanted to hear her voice so badly that he'd conjured it up. "Talk to me, Phoebe."

"No."

The single word reverberated up along the stone walls, and relief swept through him.

"That's the spirit," he said.

A lantern was lit and lowered into the well. Ian could see her upturned face. Her wet hair was pushed back, her skin as pale as the dead. Tired eyes flashed in the flickering light.

"I'm coming," he said. "Hold on."

Ian quickly tied a large loop at the end of a second rope and went down into the well. As he descended, his heart almost broke. Wet and shivering, she clung to the moss-covered wall.

When he'd nearly reached her, she stretched her arm out to grab the rope, but her fingers wouldn't close over it and her body sank out of sight. Letting go, he knifed into the water, praying he wouldn't drop on top of her.

The water was black and cold, but he found her immediately. Wrapping his arm around her waist, he propelled them both quickly to the surface.

He wanted to kiss her senseless.

"Phoebe," he breathed her name. Her face had taken on a masklike grey hue. Her skin was like ice, and she was shivering uncontrollably.

Bloody hell, he thought. How long had she been in here?

Sitting her in the loop, he tried to get her to wrap her hands around the rope. He wanted to get her out of the water, but she clung to his neck and was not letting go. He understood her response. He wanted to do the same.

"Phoebe, you need to let me go. We can only get out one at a time."

She shook her head and held on tighter to his neck.

"There's a warm blanket waiting for you. Dry clothes. A bed."

"No."

"I promise to hold you, sweetheart. I will never let you go once we're out of here."

She still was hesitant. Forcibly removing her arms from around his neck, he then wrapped them around the rope. He kissed her lips and shouted to the men above to pull her up slowly.

"Hold on, my love."

Her eyes looked into his as they began to lift her. She was alive, he told himself. Alive. She'd survived the fall into this well. An absolute miracle. He commanded the worry carping at him to be silent. He hadn't lost her.

"No regrets," she said through chattering teeth. "I want no regrets."

She continued to watch him as she ascended, and he never took his eyes off her.

Delirium can make a person say strange things, he thought, but Phoebe didn't sound delirious.

No regrets.

As he waited for the rope to come back down the well, Ian wondered what she meant.

❧ 12 ❦

WEAK WITH EXHAUSTION, emotional, and chilled to the bone, Phoebe felt she'd gained a new chance at life once they pulled her out and sat her beside the well. Ian found her and saved her, but she knew she had enough life left in her to limp to the house on her own two feet.

But he wouldn't allow it. Wrapping his coat around her, he then picked her up and carried her, holding her to his chest as if he would keep her there forever, just as he'd promised.

As they crossed the gardens at Bellhorne, servants ran from every direction to meet them. It was a spectacle, to be sure. Shouts rang out. Millie appeared and burst into tears before they reached the house. She acted as if her sister had been dead and was now brought back to life.

Phoebe didn't want to think how close she'd come to giving up.

Everything around her was a blur, and the excitement moved her, but she wanted nothing more than to sink deeper into Ian's embrace. His name was what she'd continuously intoned during those moments when all hope seemed lost.

All good things must come to an end, however. Once he carried her upstairs, her hero was pushed out of the room. In what seemed like an instant, Mrs. Hume and several maids stripped her out of her clothes, bathed her with warm water, dried her carefully, and tucked her into bed in a nightgown with a hot drink. Millie stayed with her, supervising and fussing over her every second. She was so weary and cold. She couldn't warm up.

"The doctor will be coming up," the housekeeper told them as she and the others went out.

"Mrs. Bell?" Phoebe asked her sister when they were alone. She could only imagine how upsetting the news of her disappearance could be to the woman. "I hope no one told her I was missing."

"She and Mrs. Young were taken to the rectory." Millie looked out the window at the early evening sky. "I don't know what story Captain Bell came up with to send his mother away, but it was all arranged quickly and efficiently. I don't believe she knows."

Phoebe was relieved, but she had no more time to speak privately with her sister as there came a sharp knock at the door. Millie admitted a man who introduced himself as Dr. Thornton.

"So she's alive," he began, scowling at Phoebe from the darkening shadows by the door. "The instigator of this ruckus."

Even if she knew the doctor well, his rudeness would not have been easily overlooked. Of average height, he carried himself like a man ready to do battle at any moment. His face was pockmarked and showed a number of whitish scars that stood out on his ruddy skin, but beyond that, there was nothing distinctive about his features. Phoebe knew for certain she'd never met him. But the way he paused when he entered, staring at her before coming into the candlelight by the bed, made her wonder if they might indeed have been introduced before. Perhaps when Sarah was still alive, she thought.

Millie introduced the two of them, and the coolness in her tone indicated that she too was taken aback by the man's behavior. The doctor, however, showed no awareness of how he was being perceived.

"I know well enough who you are." He scowled at Phoebe as he checked her pulse and bent to inspect her face and eyes. "You're guests here, and I don't mind telling you that no good comes of taking liberties when you're a stranger."

She was no stranger to this house, not to the gardens and the grounds, and she was *not* taking any liberties. But as Phoebe began to reply to his impertinence, he picked up her hand, raised her elbow, and then proceeded to bend her arm in every possible manner until she gasped in pain. Apparently satisfied, he released it without ceremony. Turning to Millie—who hovered like a nervous mother and watched everything he did—he announced that nothing was broken, so far as he could tell, the heart was still beating, and her breathing was perfectly fine.

"I won't know how badly the shoulder is bruised until the swelling recedes. Perhaps tomorrow or the next day, we'll have a better idea."

Phoebe stretched her left arm and flexed her shoulder. It hurt more now after his abuse, but she wouldn't complain to this man if the limb fell off and dropped onto the floor.

"So," he said, looking at Phoebe, "in bringing chaos to

the house, upsetting your hosts, and raising an uproar that caused men from two counties to leave their farms and join the search, the consequences of your irresponsible behavior are a few scratches on the side of your face."

She was good at deflecting reprimands, but this man had a way of delivering a sharp jab, and he caught her off guard.

He shifted his attention again to Millie. "And the scratches will heal soon enough and leave no scars."

"Doctor," Millie began curtly, "I hope you know that my sister—"

"I know that being where she doesn't belong and wandering alone in unfamiliar places are dangerous pastimes," he said, cutting her off sharply and glaring at Phoebe. "If you saw the anguish you caused Captain Bell, after all he's been through."

"I didn't . . ." Phoebe said through gritted teeth. "I didn't go into that well . . ."

"No?" He turned on his heel. "Watch for bouts of hysteria in her," he ordered Millie. "Forgetfulness, fever, confusion, or memory loss."

None of which would be as disagreeable as enduring this man's manner for even a moment longer.

The doctor started for the door. "Have Captain Bell send for me if any of those symptoms appear." He stopped with his hand on the knob and frowned at Phoebe. "You're lucky to be alive, young lady. Cherish this moment. Next time, no one may come around to save you."

The physician's words rang a warning bell. The push from behind. The way she'd been left. Whoever had done it assumed no one would ever find her, never mind save her.

The bedroom door closed behind Dr. Thornton, and Millie looked back at her with utter disbelief. "Have you ever known anyone more disagreeable?"

She had. Their father could be fairly disagreeable after one of their arguments. But the earl's temper was generally justified.

Millie came to the side of the bed, fussing with the sheets and blankets. "You're still shivering, and you're very pale. You should try to eat something and then sleep. I'm going to ask Mrs. Hume to send up some light supper. Would that be all right?"

Phoebe took her sister's fluttering fingers in hers. She looked into grey eyes still red-rimmed from earlier tears. "I know you were frightened. I'm sorry." She placed a kiss on the fingers. She hated seeing her younger sister upset like this.

"What happened to you?" Millie sat on the bed. "You're adventurous but not clumsy. How is it possible you fell into a well? This is so unlike you."

It was one thing to share her adventures and successes with her sister. It was quite something else to divulge the dangers. Just as she could not tell her what happened in the Vaults, Phoebe remained silent now.

"We'll talk about it later," she replied. "But would you ask Captain Bell to come and see me?"

"Of course." She stood slowly. "I'll fetch him now."

Phoebe waited until her sister was at the door. "And Millie, if you please, I need to speak with him alone."

"You have no reason to worry, Captain. Her ladyship is hearty enough. What's a wee dunking to a lass her age?"

Standing in the gallery, Ian frowned at the doctor. Thornton was working at being his most disagreeable tonight. If this was the way the man spoke to Phoebe, he decided, they'd better lock every door to the castle to keep her from running back to Edinburgh tonight.

"What about her fall? Her face is bruised. Her shoulder was injured."

He waved a hand unconcernedly. "She'll recover from her bumps and scratches in a day or two. I spoke to the sister about complications to look for, though I don't see much possibility of anything developing."

Ian walked him to the staircase and watched the doctor descend to the great hall. On occasions like this, he wondered if Thornton was worth the aggravation he left in his wake. Perhaps it was time to find a replacement for him. He shook his head. He couldn't. Not after what he'd heard tonight.

His mother had returned from the rectory only minutes after he'd carried Phoebe back to the house. Thankfully, she'd gone straight to bed, unaware of the chaos that had taken place. Not long after, however, Ian had overheard bits and pieces of an argument in the great hall between Thornton and Alice.

It had been nearly three years since Alice arrived from Maryland, but Ian realized tonight he barely knew the woman. He'd been completely blind to the romantic triangle which had developed right under his nose. Thornton's angry words were louder than Alice's, but it was clear that his cousin had developed an unrequited affection for the minister while the doctor had been pursuing her to no avail.

Little wonder Thornton was more prickly and short-tempered than usual this evening.

Shaking off thoughts of other people's problems, he made his way toward Phoebe's room. The doctor's assurance meant nothing. Ian found her in the well, and he saw how fragile and helpless she was while clutching his neck. He needed to see her himself and make sure she'd recovered as swiftly as Thornton seemed to think.

Millie appeared at the end of the hallway as he reached it. "Captain, I was coming to find you. My sister would very much like to speak with you, if you would."

He had so much he wanted to say to her too. Those hours when she was missing had wreaked havoc in his mind. With every tick of the clock, Ian had imagined worse and worse things befalling her. He gestured for Millie to lead the way, but the young woman hesitated.

"I should like to visit your library and choose a book, if you don't mind."

"Of course not. Please help yourself."

"And after I find something to read," she said, "I need to go down and ask Mrs. Hume to have a supper tray sent up for my sister."

Ian started to ask if he could send someone to the kitchens for her when she stopped him.

"I know I've thanked you for saving my sister, but I cannot express to you the gratitude my family—"

"Please," he said. "There is no need. I'm just so relieved this has all turned out as it has."

Millie twisted a kerchief in her hands and disappeared in the direction of the library.

A few moments alone with Phoebe. He would not compromise her honor, but propriety was all but meaningless right now, considering the circumstances. Ian went swiftly down the corridor and knocked once. Hearing her reply, he stepped in, leaving the door ajar behind him.

Ian paused inside. Phoebe lay on the bed, propped up with pillows, blankets pulled up nearly to her chin. Waves of glorious dark hair spread out around her face. He silently cursed the doctor. Any fool could see from the pallid skin and bruised cheek, she'd been hurt.

"I know I must look a fright, but I feel quite well," she whispered, freeing a hand from under the bedclothes and stretching it toward him.

Ian took one step, two . . . and then he couldn't hold back, regardless of everything he'd ever been taught about gentlemanly behavior. He reached her side in an instant, and she sat up, opening her arms to him.

"Hold me, please. I cannot warm up."

He was a lost man. Sitting on the edge of the bed, he gathered her to his chest. Her left side had been bruised, and he was cautious of it. She pressed her face against his heart, and Ian caressed the silky softness of her hair. One hand moved down her back, and he rubbed the night-gown along her spine, trying to create warmth. She moved closer to him, and he felt her shivering.

"You don't appear well. I'm sending for another doctor. We can get someone here from Dunfermline by dawn."

"Hush," she whispered, lifting her face before he could move. Her uninjured hand slipped around his neck, and she tugged at his hair. "You are what I need. No one else."

The warmth bloomed on her cheek. Their lips were a breath apart. Ian swam in the azure depths of her eyes, and her words dangled alluringly between them.

She no longer looked unwell to him. She looked alive. Very much alive.

At this moment, right now, he would have liked nothing better than to lift her onto his lap and hold her until the sun rose high in the sky. As thin as it was, that nightgown was a barrier, keeping him from the pale skin he wanted to warm with the touch of his hands and his lips. If he could, he would pull the string knot and kiss her throat, her shoulders, her breasts, and those dark hard nipples showing through the material so enticingly.

Ian wanted to make love to her. His blood was hot, he was growing hard, and this was the woman he wanted. But he was a scoundrel for even thinking it, considering everything she'd gone through today.

He tried to pull back, but she stopped him.

"No regrets," she whispered, looking into his eyes.

The meaning of the words she'd spoken earlier came to him. No regrets. No regrets about the two of them. During her direst moments in the well, Phoebe had been thinking about him. And while she was missing, he was going mad with the thought that she was lost to him forever.

Ian could think no more. He lowered his head to taste her lips. Phoebe's mouth parted, and her sigh of pleasure was his undoing. He deepened the kiss, and her mouth battled back, giving and taking. Quickly their play of passion became a battle of wills. He captured the back of her head to hold her still and drank from her giving mouth. She was driving him to lose control, to live in the moment without thinking of anything but the heat building between them.

She pushed back what remained of the bedclothes and move one leg over him. Instantly, she was straddling his lap, and Ian gave in to her eager mouth. He battled the urge to roll her back onto the sheets and tear away the damned nightgown. He wanted to run his tongue over every inch of her silky skin. He wanted to hear her cry out his name with pleasure. His hand slid along her shapely legs. He couldn't tell if the sigh was hers or his when his palms possessed her heart-shaped bottom. He pressed her against his hardened cock, and her breath caught in her chest. She lifted her head. Stormy eyes looked into his, understanding his needs.

"Phoebe," he whispered. Words tumbled over each other in his frenzied brain. Words he wanted to say. He wanted her. Body. Soul. Heart. He wanted her for today. He wanted her forever.

She laid a hand on his chest, burning a brand through his linen shirt clear to his heart.

A noise outside the door startled them. He'd left the door partly open. Anyone could walk in on them at any moment. Ian shifted her off his lap and rolled her back onto the bed, covering her with the bedclothes. Her face was flushed, but she was not afraid of anything or anyone. He almost laughed and leaned close to her.

"You're jeopardizing my reputation, Lady Phoebe," he whispered against her lips, pulling the blankets to her chin.

Before he could step back, she caught his wrist. "Don't go. There's something I need to tell you."

<hr>

She'd asked Millie to get Ian for the purpose of telling him what happened in the Auld Grove. But once he came into the room, her body battled with her mind. After the traumatic shock of being nearly murdered today, all she wanted was to feel the dizzying whirl of passion in his embrace.

Improper. Indecorous. Wicked. Unladylike. Phoebe

knew how her fierce desire for him could be construed. But she almost died. *Died*. And when he entered, looking so concerned for her, all she wanted was to feel his hands on her skin. To feel his lips on her throat, on her breast.

A blushing heat flamed from the collar of the nightgown to the top of her scalp as she thought about how she'd attacked him and climbed onto his lap. Given another moment, she would have torn the clothes off both of them.

He brought a chair close to the bed, but still at a respectable distance. He was giving them both some space. Carrying Phoebe back from the Auld Grove, he'd wrapped his coat around her, and the warm manly scent of him had enveloped her, comforted her.

He'd changed out of his wet clothes, but he hadn't dressed completely. He wore boots with the buckskin trousers that hugged his muscular legs, and the white linen shirt was immaculate beneath his deep brown waistcoat, though he'd not bothered to don either coat or cravat. As he sat down, she could not help but notice the pronounced bulge in his breeches. She'd felt it pressing against her a moment ago. She wanted to feel it again.

"I'm glad to see that you're afraid of me."

"Afraid *for* you is not the same as afraid *of* you." He smiled and glanced at the door. "Another time, another place, under more appropriate circumstances, and I'll show you who is afraid of whom."

She lay her hands flat on her belly, feeling the heat emanating from her body now. "I'll hold you to that promise, Captain Bell."

"I'm counting on it."

As much as she would have liked it, Phoebe couldn't lie here and flirt with him all night. She'd asked Millie to give them a little time to talk privately. She had no doubt her sister would be back shortly.

"I want to tell you what happened in the Auld Grove." The ache in her shoulder had returned now that she wasn't distracted by Ian's closeness. Carefully, she pulled her bruised arm from beneath the blankets and rested it on top. "I didn't want to speak of this to anyone but you. And I'd prefer that you don't even mention it to my sister."

Immediately, his expression became serious. Ian leaned forward, his elbows on his knees, and waited for her to say more.

"I went there because that's where Sarah and I used to escape to during my visits," Phoebe told him. "I don't believe anyone followed me from the house. At least, I didn't see anyone. And once I was there, I saw no sign of any vagrants in the camp by the waterfall."

He raked a hand through his hair and his expression grew dark. "I should have covered that well long before now. It's dangerous to have—"

"I didn't fall in, Ian." She inched up on the pillows. "It wasn't an accident. I saw the well. I was standing and looking into it when someone pushed me."

"Pushed?" His boots hit the floor and he was on his feet.

Phoebe recalled the hand between her shoulders. "Yes. Someone pushed me in and then threw my hat in after me. He or she, whoever it was, wanted to make sure I'd never be found."

A cat has nine lives, they say. For three, she plays. For three, she strays. And for three, she stays. But Phoebe Pennington was no cat. She would die.

She'd started this feud between them that night in the Vaults. And since then, she'd become a worm in his flesh, a disease eating at his brain. She tormented him in his sleep. She was a distraction. Instead of focusing on what he'd been called to do, he was thinking of how to destroy her. She was feeding off of him. Tearing his thoughts from his true calling. Dividing him against himself.

He stood in the darkness as the frothy fingers of the black firth reached toward the world of sleeping men. The voices were coming closer. The cold fingers were on his flesh.

But oh, how this unnatural chit plagued him!

The creature had escaped death twice, but that did not give her nine lives. She'd used up all she would ever have.

Nine lives. It was all a lie. He'd seen cats go in the mill pond. They never returned.

❧ 13 ❧

Phoebe awakened in the morning to find her sister dressed and preparing to go down to breakfast.

As she swung her feet over the side of the bed, Phoebe realized she had more use of her arm than she expected. Her shoulder was stiff, but the ache in her left side seemed to center on the bruise. Looking in the mirror, she was happy to see the scratches on her face were not nearly as bad as the ones she'd come home with after the fight in the Vaults.

There was no reason to see the horrible Dr. Thornton again, and Millie agreed. As far as Phoebe was concerned, it would be best to minimize any attention to her and the incident until they left Bellhorne tomorrow.

As a maid helped her dress, Phoebe felt the events of yesterday quickly receding into a vague and dreamlike realm. The grove. The meadows filled with bluebells. The ancient, ruined huts. The drop through the darkness. The endless time in the frigid water. The feeling of imminent doom. And then Ian, like an angel, descending from above, coming to her rescue.

She took a deep breath, recalling the moments of passion in his arms later. She hadn't even noticed the injuries while his hands glided over her body, while desire set them both ablaze.

And then she'd told him about the well.

Immediately, he had been like a great hound unleashed. Angry and impatient to leave, he'd vowed to find whoever had attacked her. Later, from the maid who came up to take away her dinner tray, Phoebe learned that Captain Bell had taken a group of men back out to the Auld Grove. Equipped with lanterns and dogs, they went searching for something or someone.

Phoebe tried to stay awake and succeeded for a while. With every noise, she sat bolt upright, wondering if he had returned. Finally, exhaustion claimed her, but she spent the night tossing and turning. During the few times when sleep came to her, Phoebe dreamed of running through crypts while skeletons and monsters clutched at her. Sarah appeared, wrapped in a shroud, and carried by an unseen power to the hilltop overlooking the firth. She dreamed of falling through darkness and landing not in the icy water of the well, but in the stone catacombs of the Vaults. Ian was trapped. She searched desperately for him, but every labyrinthine passage led nowhere. The dank smell of death oozed from arched niches. Walls of stone closed in on her. And no matter how hard she ran, she couldn't find him.

She woke up, soaked in sweat, relieved to see the sunlight.

She was dressed when Millie came back from break-fast with news of Captain Bell and the search. They'd returned just after dawn, but they'd found nothing. He was absent at breakfast and was not accompanying his mother to church for the Sunday service.

All of this, Ian's worry and his quest to find whoever pushed her into the well, troubled her. Bellhorne was his home. A sanctuary for his mother. A safe haven. It could easily have been a vagrant passing through the Grove. Fearful of prosecution for trespassing, he'd responded badly.

Phoebe needed to see Ian and beg him to let this go. She'd never completely related to him everything that happened in the Vaults. She should have saved him from specific details this time too. She never should have mentioned her hat being thrown down the well after her.

She waited until Mrs. Bell and Mrs. Young left for church. She wanted to resolve this while they were gone.

The breeze coming in the window pushed at a napkin on the breakfast tray that had been brought up for her. Millie crossed the room and draped a shawl over her shoulders.

"I'm going to need a few minutes with the captain in private," she pleaded as they were getting ready to leave the room. "I'll meet you in the garden after I speak with him."

Millie put her back against the door. "I am not making that mistake again. Yesterday you made the same promise and look what happened. You meet with Captain Bell, and I'll wait outside the door to his office."

"Honestly, Millie."

"Stop." The gentle command sounded so much like their mother's.

The quiet strength behind the words resonated with echoes of Millicent Wentworth, the abused wife of a slave-owning squire who rose like a sapling from the charred fields of his cruelty and became an oak tree for many who suffered under his lash. Millicent, who in a moment of destitution, married again with a promise to care for the broken Earl of Aytoun. Millicent, their mother, was the bond that held the Pennington family together.

And Millie was so much like her.

"You think you're protecting me, but I know you too well. You are far too surefooted to fall into any well. Someone pushed you. That's why Captain Bell went back out there."

Millie was too smart not to realize what was going on. And considering Ian's reaction, Phoebe wondered who at Bellhorne, other than Mrs. Bell, wouldn't know.

"I love you, little mother." She linked arms with her sister as they left the room.

"I know you do."

A breeze whistled down the corridor, and Phoebe stopped by Sarah's door. Thoughts of Sarah's mother, her own mother, and the twists and turns of their relationships hung in the air. The foolishness of youthful complaints nagged at her. Phoebe wondered if her friend knew how Fiona Bell suffered because of those meaningless final words.

"I miss her."

"She was your best friend," Millie said.

Her hand raised with the recollection of how Sarah would burst through the door before she could even knock, always ready for a new adventure.

"I always had to compete with her."

"Compete with her?" Phoebe drew her hand back and pulled the shawl tighter around her.

"For your attention. For the joy of doing things with you. For the pleasure of hearing and reading your stories. For your trust in sharing the trouble you always seemed to find. For your friendship."

For a moment Phoebe couldn't breathe, the truth in her sister's statement squeezing her heart.

"Oh, Millie."

"I know . . . I know you've always loved me as a sister. But when Sarah became your friend, I was no longer your confidante. I wasn't the one you'd run to when you had a secret to share or when you wanted to talk about your most recent heartache or when you just needed a shoulder to cry on."

Phoebe batted away a tear and wrapped her arms around her sister, hugging her tightly. "You never said a word."

"I never resented your feeling for her. I understood. But after she died, I thought we might regain what we always had. And we have. But only up to a certain point."

She wanted to deny all of this, but Millie's words were like a surgeon's scalpel, peeling away the lie and exposing the truth. In her relationship with Sarah, there was no sibling conflict, no petty arguments over ribbons or shoes, and no worry about setting a bad example as the older sister. With Sarah, she could be herself. Millie was so astute. It was only after her friend was gone that Phoebe rediscovered the treasure of friendship with her younger sister.

"I'm sorry, Millie. I'm sorry for every moment of pain I've caused through my neglect of you. No one has been as unfailingly true to me as you."

"I should never have said any of this." She drew back.

"The truth is you've changed and matured so much in these last three years."

Phoebe laughed, but tears rolling down her cheek betrayed her emotions. "Matured? Hardly!"

Millie brushed away the droplets. "Now I feel guilty for having upset you. Yesterday, when I thought I'd lost you, I was undone. Lost. And now . . . someone tried to hurt you."

"I am *too* much trouble." She took her sister's arm, and the two of them started for the stairs. She'd not wanted to upset anyone and somehow managed to get everyone riled up. "I've been to Bellhorne many times, and I know no one who might have a grudge against me. I've done no harm to anyone. What happened was surely a random act by someone passing through."

Phoebe wanted to say exactly this to Ian. Everyone needed to stop worrying. She'd heard from the housekeeper that on Sundays, Mrs. Bell liked to have guests from the village join the family for an early dinner. She didn't want to disrupt the family's routines any more than she already had.

When they came to Bellhorne, Phoebe hoped they could be helpful. But she'd failed. Passing through the gallery, she felt the eyes of the ancestors glaring down at her.

The sisters descended to the great hall, and a flurry of activity in an entry foyer arrested their progress. The outside door stood open, and Mrs. Bell hurried in with Mrs. Young at her heels.

Shafts of light from windows above the galleries encircling the great hall did little to illuminate the spacious dark-paneled room. Standing in the shadow of a tall column at the base of the stairwell, the two hesitated.

"Oh, no," Millie whispered. "They're back from the service too early."

"I hope she's not unwell."

Mrs. Bell was hastily removing her hat and coat, and her voice carried to them. "Find her for me, will you, Alice?"

The cousin came into the great hall and spotted Phoebe and Millie. Looking first over her shoulder and finding Mrs. Bell questioning the housekeeper, she immediately hurried over to them.

"She knows what happened yesterday," Alice said softly to Phoebe.

"How?" Millie asked.

"No sooner had we arrived and were entering the church, several of the parishioners approached us and expressed their relief that our guest had been found alive."

Phoebe had heard from the maid helping her dress this morning that everyone at the estate and nearly the entire village had helped out with the search yesterday afternoon. "As exciting as the Lammas Fair, it was," the girl told her, adding with a blush, "when you were found, I mean."

Alice took Phoebe's hand. "Once Mrs. Bell heard the news, she was adamant about leaving that very moment. She's sick with worry about you. She wouldn't believe me when I told her you were safe and well."

There was no point in considering what to say or not say with their hostess only a few steps away. "I'll put her mind at ease."

Phoebe left her sister and Alice and walked to the foyer where the housekeeper looked greatly relieved to see her approaching.

"Mrs. Bell," she called out. "Good morning."

Phoebe had no chance to get into formalities, as the older woman whirled at the sound of her voice and burst into tears.

"You're alive," she cried. "You're here. Thank heavens."

Phoebe closed the distance between them, wrapping her arm around her. This was the drama she was hoping to avoid. "Of course I'm alive. Nothing to fear. Nothing. I'm right here."

"When they told me . . ." She clutched Phoebe's hand. "They wouldn't . . . I didn't . . ." She couldn't finish her sentences.

"Mrs. Bell. You can see I'm perfectly well. Hale and hearty." Phoebe worried about the ailing woman. Her breaths were becoming short and labored. She looked helplessly at Mrs. Young. "I'm right here with you."

"But to simply go like that . . . taking you away from here . . . I couldn't bear it . . . in the well . . . gone . . . never to come back to me . . . never."

Tears streamed down the wrinkled face. The words continued to come in fragmented spurts. She didn't seem to hear anything Phoebe said. Alice and Millie appeared beside them. Millie was offering her a handkerchief, Alice opening the door just down the corridor.

Tears of her own burned in Phoebe's eyes. Witnessing the grief in Ian's mother squeezed her heart. She wondered if Mrs. Bell was thinking about her or if some of this anguish had to do with her missing daughter.

"Come into the morning room where you can sit for a moment," Alice suggested. "The sun is shining bright in there, and we'll open the garden doors, just as you like."

"I can't. Not without you," she protested, clinging to Phoebe's hand. "I can't."

"I'll come with you. We'll go together." Phoebe motioned to her sister to take the other arm of the woman.

Alice murmured to her that she was sending the carriage for Dr. Thornton.

The family certainly trusted this doctor, Phoebe thought, deciding he must be more dependable than she was giving him credit for.

Guiding her, encouraging her to put one foot in front of the other, the two sisters shepherded the aging woman to the morning room, where she collapsed on the nearest sofa, clutching her cane with one hand and Phoebe with the other.

Searching for a distraction, Phoebe turned to her sister. "Perhaps Mrs. Hume could have some tea sent in." With a nod, Millie hurried out.

"All is well. Try to catch your breath," she said soothingly. She propped a pillow behind the older woman.

"Your face. My dear, look at your face. The horror you must have endured."

A cool, frail hand caressed the scratches and bruises on Phoebe's face. The dark eyes brimmed again, and droplets followed the paths the others had marked.

"Please be assured that I'm perfectly well. Fully recovered." She took Mrs. Bell's hand and placed a kiss on her palm. "Thankfully, your son found me and brought me back."

"My Ian," she whispered. "He brought you back."

"He did indeed. And the scratches you see are the worst of it. And by tomorrow we'll hardly notice them."

"Ian brought you back. What happened to all the dresses?"

Phoebe smiled weakly, realizing the mother's mind was once again drifting elsewhere. The lace curtains by the open windows swayed to the whispers of the wind, and Mrs. Bell's head turned in that direction as if expecting someone else to enter.

"I asked him, you know. I begged him. But he won't bring her back."

Words in Ian's defense struggled to burst from Phoebe. She wanted to tell her that what he did was not by choice. But she couldn't, so she remained silent, respecting his confidence.

"I know he can't force her. He wouldn't be able to. And I wouldn't want it. No matter how much he tries, or how desperate I get. It's beyond his control." She rested her hand on Phoebe's. "But now you're here. We can plant a rosebush together."

Phoebe held the fragile fingers between her own. Ian's mother hovered between two worlds, two conversations, two periods of time. It was difficult to guess from one moment to the next where her attention might shift. It appeared that thoughts of her and Sarah became muddled at times.

Phoebe still had no idea of how Sarah's initial disappearance had been explained to the mother. A trip to America took preparation, months of planning. She never recalled Sarah talking of it. And without doubt, she would have done so. How Mrs. Bell could accept something so preposterous was puzzling.

"It was my fault she went to Edinburgh," she told her, her breath catching.

Releasing Phoebe's hands, she absently picked up her

cane, which was leaning against her leg. The head of the stick was made of ivory, with intricately carved leaves culminating with a large, partially opened rosebud.

"My stubbornness drove her to it."

The pain in the older woman's voice cut into her. She knew this much from Sarah's letters, the last of which arrived just before the disappearance. Phoebe was in Hertfordshire with her parents at the time. Her friend had been complaining that her mother was insisting she go to London for the season. Sarah didn't want to go. She didn't need to travel so far to find a husband. She was happy in Fife. But Fiona wouldn't listen, and they'd quarreled. So though her heart wasn't in it, she wrote in her final letter, she'd come to Edinburgh to shop and be fitted for dresses. Sarah signed off the letter, *Blast the ton!* Phoebe remembered laughing as she read it.

But she hadn't laughed for very long. The news came soon enough that her friend had gone missing. And then the rumors began.

Mrs. Bell's attention was drawn to the windows again. This time she focused on the breeze ruffling the leaves on the roses in a vase. "She visits me, you know. Quite often. In my dreams. Sometimes, right here in this room."

Yesterday, Phoebe experienced the same sensation. Everywhere she walked, memories of Sarah were with her. And she felt alive in them.

"I drove her off, but she has already returned. Her favorite place is among the roses out in the garden." Ian's mother smiled sadly.

She held the ivory rosebud to her lips, kissed it, and Phoebe felt a lump the size of a fist forming in her chest.

"I know Ian can never bring her back, but she is with me here. That's why I hate to leave."

Awareness formed and descended like a heavy cloak over Phoebe. She stared at the woman's thin frame, at the lined face, and at the eyes that constantly searched the room for Sarah's presence.

This mother, burdened by the guilt of pushing Sarah away, felt responsible for her daughter going away and never returning. A terrible burden to bear.

But how much did Mrs. Bell know? And what did she mean, Sarah had already returned to her? Questions piled on top of each other, daring Phoebe to speak, but she forced them to remain unasked.

"It's not really a deception if one willingly believes it."

Phoebe wanted to ask her directly what she meant by 'deception'. She peered at her closely.

"Today, when all those people in the kirkyard began saying things. Asking about you. Wanting to know what happened to you." Her dark eyes were wide, but she wasn't looking at Phoebe. She continued to study the walking stick as if the answer to some profound secret could be found in the delicate curves of the leaves and petals. "I didn't think my heart could take it. Not you. Not again."

This was exactly what she'd feared last night and this morning. Phoebe didn't want to add more worry and more unhappiness to this woman's life.

"Ian. My Ian would never recover if something happened to you." She patted Phoebe's hand. "You're different. How he feels about you is different."

She opened her mouth to reply, but words were lost as her heart soared.

"You're the one, you know. Sarah always thought so. As did I."

Phoebe had come here to offer assurances and calm an

agitated mother. But their positions had somehow become reversed. Tears no longer lay on the older woman's cheek; they were now coursing down her own. Ian's mother was giving her blessing.

And what about Sarah? Mrs. Bell was calmer now, but the earlier confusion in her mind weighed on Phoebe. What did she mean about willingly believing?

"Why did you say that Sarah is with you here?" she managed to croak, wiping her face.

A gentle breeze blew in, lifting the curtain.

Phoebe glanced up at the window as a warm, invisible hand descended on her shoulder. Fingers pressed gently as they trailed across her back, distinct and undeniable. The tingling remained on her skin like the kiss of sunlight on one's face in the spring. And then, unexpectedly, a sense of peace slipped into her heart.

Sarah was here.

Mrs. Bell caressed the carved rosebud. "I think you know why. But I'm very tired, my dear."

"Please, let me help." Phoebe asked, recovering her composure, "Do you wish to go up to your rooms? Should I call for someone?"

The older woman leaned against Phoebe's shoulder. She rested for a few moments before she spoke. "It must stop."

"What must stop?" she asked, not daring to make any assumptions.

Fiona drew back and took a deep, shaking breath.

"The pretending. Tell him I know Sarah is dead. Tell Ian I'm ready to grieve for my lost girl."

❧ 14 ❧

STARTING with the nomad's camp, Ian and his men had combed through the Auld Grove so thoroughly that a three-legged rat wouldn't have escaped them. They'd gone out looking for vagrants, poachers, Highland Travelers, anyone who might have camped or passed through in the last couple of days. But there was no one. Early this morning, Ian and Raeburn had gathered another group of men and searched again. In daylight, the outcome was the same. Nothing. Whoever pushed Phoebe into the well had disappeared without a trace.

"I suspect a poacher," Raeburn told him as they walked back across the fields. "The neighbors have been complaining of vagrants coming through from Kirkcaldy, and a man on the road with a chorred cock-pheasant can be a dangerous creature. If getting caught means the noose or transporting, I have no doubt he'd give her a push and be off like a rabbit. Lass or lady, it'd make no difference."

Ian hated to think that anyone walking through the

fields and farms of Bellhorne was not safe, whether it be Phoebe or one of his tenants. But the same was happening in towns and cities all over Britain. The poor were getting poorer, and a hungry man—especially one with a family to feed—would take great risks even for a meager meal.

His thoughts went to Phoebe's articles about the unequal distribution of wealth in Scotland. Less poverty led to less crime, she argued. But whoever pushed her had to know she would die in that well. During the war, Ian had never killed because he was hungry, but many a man had died by his hand in the fight for survival. Men do what they must to live. Still, if he got hold of this one, the rogue would be sorry he was ever born.

He raked tired fingers through his hair. Phoebe was safe. She'd survived the fall. That's what was most important.

And while his tenants and workers would need to be more vigilant in the future, some improvements could make the place safer for all. Things like covering that blasted well and perhaps fixing up the old cottages in the grove to provide shelter to families traveling through. He couldn't feed every vagrant coming out of the Highlands, but if those who ended up on his land felt more welcome, perhaps there'd be less need for committing a crime.

Arriving back at the castle, he was surprised to encounter Dr. Thornton stalking stiff-legged across the courtyard to the carriage. The physician hadn't been expected here until dinner. Worry immediately darkened his mood. Phoebe? Or his mother?

"It's a curious thing, Captain, to have a carriage come stop by my door and interrupt my Sunday morning to deliver me out here on urgent business," the doctor said with a perfunctory bow when Ian reached him. "But when I arrive, no one cares to see me."

From all reports this morning, Phoebe was improving, and his mother should have been at Sunday's service with Alice.

"Who sent for you?"

"I never did get a clear answer to that question. Not at my door and not out here," he grouched, dropping his bag into the carriage. "But what *was* clear was that I wasn't wanted. Mrs. Hume told me your mother has barricaded herself in the morning room with Lady Phoebe, that they're both in fine health, and they didn't care to be disturbed. Though I'm sure I don't know who *does* care to be disturbed on a Sunday morning . . . in the middle of his breakfast!"

Ian didn't try to hide his relief. He'd tried to protect his mother from hearing that Phoebe had gone missing yesterday, but it was inevitable that she'd find out. And it didn't matter much, in any event, since she was back safe and on the mend.

The feel of her body on his lap last night, the heat of their kiss, and the silkiness of her skin all came back to him now, reaffirming that she would recover from the fall and the time in the well. He glanced at the house.

"Then," the doctor snapped, forcing Ian to pay attention to him, "I go searching for Mrs. Young, assuming she may have been the one who sent the carriage."

Thornton slapped the side of the vehicle, startling the horses.

"And . . . ?" Ian encouraged, wanting to be done with this conversation.

"And she doesn't wish to speak with me either." The

man cast a disparaging look at the castle. "Wasted an entire morning."

Ian considered the scraps he'd heard of the argument between his cousin and Thornton. The heated tone of conversation made him think the doctor was feeling a bit slighted by Alice's unwillingness to give him a satisfactory answer to something.

"You and Mrs. Young . . ." he started, kicking himself as soon as he said the words.

Suddenly, the brusque, grumbling professional man was gone, replaced by a wounded, lovelorn schoolboy. With a sad, downturned mouth, Thornton sent a longing look at an upstairs window, then scuffed at the gravel and stared at the stones skipping away. The transformation was stunning.

The doctor tossed the tails of his coat back and clasped his hands behind him. "I've been meaning to speak with you about a matter of delicacy."

Now Ian was more than sorry he'd broached the topic. All he wanted was to see Phoebe. But the doctor was not to be stopped.

"I hope, Captain, you don't think I've overstepped my position in making a formal proposal of marriage to Mrs. Young before consulting with you."

"You've proposed to her?" Ian asked, surprised. He was not offended at all. Alice was certainly young enough to marry again. He'd always thought the arrangement for her to be a companion to his mother was a temporary one.

"Indeed. And it's been two months I've been awaiting a damned . . . awaiting an answer. She hasn't rejected me, mind you. Every deuced time I bring it up, she says that she's much obliged and still considering my offer."

Ian didn't particularly like Thornton's disagreeable nature, but he imagined the man's temperament could only improve if he were married to the mild-mannered Alice. A union between the two would also keep his cousin near Bellhorne, so his mother wouldn't lose the younger woman's companionship completely.

The doctor was grousing about the "indecisiveness of women," but Ian wasn't listening. Thornton's talk of marriage brought to mind a proposal that had been slowly evolving since the day he and Phoebe went to the Orphan Hospital. The idea had crystalized for him yesterday. But before he asked Lord Aytoun's permission, he wanted to ask her first. Phoebe was proud of her independence. Perhaps she wouldn't take him. He didn't think she'd toy with his affections the same way Alice appeared to be treating Thornton.

Phoebe was a passionate woman. They'd come quite close to tossing propriety out the window last night. No, he needed to ask her soon and settle on their future, or he'd be fighting duels with every blasted male in the Pennington family.

"I understand that she's a widow, and she has responsibilities here at Bellhorne." The doctor's words cut into the path of Ian's thoughts again. "But I've given her as much time as any woman should need to decide."

Ian rubbed the back of his neck. Why the devil did he start this conversation?

"And while I wait, I need to stand by and watch her flit and flutter about, acting like a woman half her age, whenever our handsome Reverend Garioch is anywhere in the vicinity."

Ian was definitely not interested in the direction this was heading.

"Garioch is a penniless parish minister, except for the living you've given him," Thornton fumed. "All he does is conduct his service on Sunday and traipse around the country the rest of the time, researching his deuced liturgical history book that no one will read. I tell you, Bell, the man is angling to land some woman of fortune. He has no interest in marrying Mrs. Young. I am certain of it. I've heard him say it."

Ian had opened the door. Now, he clearly was to bear the punishment.

"I know I'm not much to brag about. I'm just a country doctor. But I'm a decent, educated, plain-speaking man. I'll treat the woman as she should be treated. Unlike that smiling, pretty-faced, smooth-talking—"

"Ah, there is Mr. Singer," Ian interrupted, never so happy to see the butler emerge from the house. "I believe he's looking for me. We'll see you at dinner, Thornton. And my apologies for the inconvenience this morning."

He was not a dozen steps away when he heard the door of the carriage slam shut and the driver's "Walk on" to his horses. But Ian was no longer thinking of Thornton. He was formulating his own plan for proposing marriage to Phoebe.

Waving off the butler, he started around to the gardens.

Ian was thirty-three years old, and for the first time in his life, he was driven by the desire to marry. But it was not simply marriage he wanted. And not any wife. Only Phoebe. He wanted her and no one else. But she was a writer, a storyteller, a master of words. He couldn't just walk up to her and say, "Marry me," or "By the way, when I found you missing yesterday, I realized exactly how much I love you and, since I'm on the subject, marry me." No none of that would do.

Would it?

"Captain Bell."

She sprouted in his path like a vision, and he would have liked nothing better than to lift her in his arms and kiss her.

The sweet scent of blooming roses registered in his brain. He'd been oblivious to where his steps were taking him. But he saw now, they were standing in the gardens with Sarah's roses around them.

All the words he'd been trying out and rejecting were now ready to spill from his lips. He wanted her to know his intentions. By the devil, he was ready to propose. But servants were setting a table for lunch just a few steps away, so he bowed instead as she curtsied. He almost laughed at the formality.

Beneath the deep maroon dress with its thin stripes of golden thread, the long curves of Phoebe's body were hidden from him, but their perfection was branded in his memory. The nightgown she wore last night did little to keep his eyes and his hands from learning the contours of her feminine form. The shawl she held over her breasts was superfluous ornamentation.

"I saw you pacing out here from the morning room," she said, motioning to the open window.

He was about to ask about her injuries, but he saw the red-rimmed eyes. She'd been crying.

"What's wrong?" He took her by the elbow. "You must sit down. The doctor is not far. I'll send a man to fetch him. After my treatment of him, we may need to hold a pistol to his head, but I'll bring him—"

"No. Please." She took his hand and stopped him. "No. I'm perfectly well. I just left your mother."

Thornton said the two of them had been speaking together and were not to be disturbed.

"And all is well? I'm guessing my mother knows what happened to you yesterday?"

"Most of it. I put her mind at ease."

He held her hand, knowing there was more. Phoebe sent another look in the direction of the windows before her somber face came back to him.

"She wants to see you. She'd like to speak to you now, if you can manage it."

"Of course." Whenever Ian was at Bellhorne, his mother was in the habit of asking his opinion on all matters small and large. This morning, he hadn't been available to her before she went off to the church in the village. "Will you wait for me here until I get back?"

She gave a quick nod and looked away. "I'll be here."

"In the rose garden," he stressed. "No going off anywhere else."

Watching her, he wasn't convinced she totally understood the importance of waiting for him. So, he ignored her questioning looks and led her to a stone bench by one of the arbors.

"My mother's questions never take long. Please," he said, motioning to the seat. She sat down. "I'll be back shortly."

Ian never recalled feeling as impatient as he was now. Perhaps it was because of his talk with Thornton. Maybe it was because of what happened between Phoebe and him in her bedroom last night. Tomorrow they'd be traveling back to Edinburgh; it was essential that he ask her today.

He turned toward the house, but her voice stopped him.

"She wants to speak with you about Sarah."

He looked back at her.

"She knows, Ian. She's always known."

A large, carved alabaster icon of a mother and daughter smiled down from above the mantle. Ian's father had commissioned the work from a painting of Fiona and Sarah. Looking at the mischievous expression on his sister's face now, Ian felt the same poignant feeling of love and loss that pierced his heart every time he entered this room.

This was his mother's favorite, and he knew why. Bright and airy in the good months, warmed by the sun and a log fire when it was cold and wet outside. Ian held her hand now as he sat beside her.

A wild mix of emotions battered his brain.

Relief. Guilt. Responsibility. Satisfaction. Worry. At times as he and his mother spoke, it felt as if a cannon blast had stunned him, leaving him listening to the muffled echoes of her voice.

In one sense a huge weight had been lifted off his shoulders, but he also feared that in accepting the tragedy of Sarah's death, she'd give up and succumb to the frailty of her afflictions.

Before he left Phoebe in the garden, she'd suggested that he let his mother ask her questions. And then he should answer them without holding back. They had years of misunderstanding to work through.

He'd done exactly that. He explained every fabricated

detail. From Sarah's trip to London when she'd first gone missing to her travels through the continent to her journey to America. He laid out for her all the elaborate fictions and showed her how they'd grown more transparent and less believable as the months and years went by.

Ian had imagined this day so many times over the past three years, but he'd always pictured tears of anger at his failure and his deceit. He was wrong. She was more than forgiving.

"I knew when she was taken from us," Fiona said finally, leaning against him as her gaze fixed on the swaying curtain by the open window. "She died six days after she left Bellhorne."

He'd begun the search for Sarah the same day her friend arrived at his townhouse in Edinburgh. Despite her hysteria, he'd understood his sister had disappeared. Months later, when he'd finally pried open the notes of the anatomists at the university, he learned that Sarah had most certainly died that very day.

"It was painful to remain silent." She twisted her handkerchief around thin fingers. "All those rumors. All the senseless chatter that my daughter had eloped with an imaginary lover."

"I'm sorry, Mother." He'd so hoped the gossip would never reach her. The letters were supposed to be screened by the housekeeper and later by Alice when she arrived at Bellhorne. The visitors were turned away unless Ian had previously sent word ahead of time to the butler. "I tried to protect you from it."

She waved a hand as if it were insignificant.

"There is no antidote for that kind of poison. You couldn't possibly control it. No one could," she said. "A friend of a friend, stopping for something to eat at the village inn on their way to Stirling. Cousins of a neighbor, walking in the kirkyard after Sunday service and running into me. I wasn't accepting visitors here, but somehow they still found me. And they couldn't help themselves. Whispers were everywhere, but I knew the truth. I knew Sarah was dead."

During those horrible months, Ian had imagined the worst, but he wasn't certain of what happened to Sarah. Not until later. "How could you be so sure?"

She didn't answer at first. Her gaze followed the path of a breeze riffling everything in its way from the window to the door and then settled on an empty chair across the room. The chair his sister like to sit in with her sewing or her books.

"A mother's intuition," she said finally, squeezing Ian's arm. "The clenched stomach that warns us tragedy has occurred. The cold sweat, the dread, the urgent need to weep when nothing calls for it. And then later, something more. The whispers of her voice behind me in the gardens, or the sweet smell of roses in the gallery."

He would be a fool to deny anything his mother said.

"When you had gone off to fight the French, I knew when you suffered but—unlike your father, who despaired when everyone thought you were dead—I knew you weren't. But when Sarah left . . ."

She stopped, her voice choked by the breaths trapped in her chest. She wiped away her tears.

He put an arm around her and drew her fragile frame closer to his side. This was the woman who brought him into this world. The one who raised him, reproached him, taught him, and cherished him. He loved her, and it broke his heart to see her grieve. As hard as he tried, Ian had been unable to protect her from the tragedy of Sarah's death.

She used her handkerchief and wiped away her eyes and cleared her voice. "I knew Sarah was dead. She was gone from us the entire time you were away from here, searching for her."

Ian thought he'd go mad when she first went missing. During those early months, he did abandon his mother as he searched in Edinburgh and beyond. He followed every shred of news, every rumor. He crossed Britain from one end to the other. Gretna Green. London. Bath. The Highlands. He went anywhere his sister had a friend, even Baronsford. When he couldn't go himself, he'd sent a clerk. He had no mother's intuition to guide him. In his heart, he knew the rumors were wrong, but he couldn't stop himself from pursuing every possibility.

"And then you came back to me with that elaborate story of your sister's plans. Travel, visiting your father's family. The great adventure she'd never spoken about."

Ian watched a wistful expression cross her face. Her eyes clouded with memories of a different time.

"I surprised myself when I realized I could accept what you were telling me. Your story was kind and gentle. It had hope. While deep in my heart, I knew it was untrue, it made me want to fold reason away in the cedar press with Sarah's things. It was a happier existence, believing the possibility of it."

Her easy acceptance of the fictions had shocked him at the time, but he'd overlooked it. Now he understood why. Three years ago, he had been desperate to protect her, and her response was a relief.

"Sarah's funeral." The soft breeze from the window

ruffled the back of his hair. "I'm sorry I left you out of it. I robbed you of the chance to grieve her death."

"I don't blame you for that." His mother caressed the rosebud handle of the cane that leaned against her leg. "What help would it have been to be surrounded by the condolences of others in such circumstances? For the life of me, I don't know how a mother, faced with such shocking news, prepares herself. I wasn't ready."

Ian recalled Phoebe's words about how alone and unapproachable he'd been that day. He was mourning Sarah, but he was also lamenting the fabricated tales he had no intention of ever denying.

"You spared me substantial pain. My grief, often hidden even from myself, has been going on for a long while."

Ian raked his fingers through his hair and gazed up at the carved depiction of his sister. Just a wee lass leaning against her mother's knee, looking away. In the painted original Sarah was laughing at a kitten playing with a ball of yarn she'd tossed in its direction.

"I also knew when you brought your sister back to Bellhorne and put her in the family crypt."

"How? Did the minister tell you?"

"No, Mr. Garioch has kept your confidence. So have Dr. Thornton and Alice. Everyone in this house has been true to their promise to you." She shook her head, wiping away the last of the tears on her face. "I visit your father every so often. I saw the crypt had been disturbed. A new family member had been added to the old bones of the departed. There was no mention of her there, but I knew it must be Sarah."

She gazed at the windows and the rose garden beyond again. If he didn't know better, it would have been easy to imagine his sister was standing there, watching them.

"My dear sweet Sarah. I felt the loss of her then, to be sure."

Years of warning those coming anywhere near Bellhorne to be sensitive to her fragility. Ian thought of all the guilt, all the battles he'd fought inwardly about telling her the truth. Some of them had been very recent.

"Last week, you asked me to write to her and have her come home, even though you knew it was impossible." He kept his tone gentle, but it stunned him how he'd believed she was unaware of the truth. "You cried over her roses dying in the garden."

Eyes as dark as his own challenged him. "You built a make-believe world, and I've lived in it. It's only right that you should live with my confusion."

He couldn't argue with her.

"And more and more, that is exactly what it's been like for me of late. Confusion. Puzzlement. I've been living in two worlds." A pale hand waved in the air, indicating everything around her. "One that is real and one that is made of dreams. And as more time has passed, I've become more and more attached to my imaginary world."

He'd done this to her. All blame lay with him.

"Sometimes there are moments when I forget which is real and which is invented. When I found one of the rose bushes dying, I was lost. I didn't know. For a short time, I believed you could bring Sarah back. I wanted to believe it. But that's behind us now."

Whatever she did to give him a taste of his own bitter medicine, he deserved it. Her confusion was his fault too.

"You're a good son, Ian." She placed a hand on his, drawing his attention. "And I know that everything you've done to protect me has brought no relief for you. I know you've suffered. I know you're still suffering. But I want you to consider that perhaps . . . perhaps you'll never be able to avenge your sister's death."

He didn't want to talk about vengeance or *his* suffering. He didn't want his mother to know that since his search for Sarah started, he'd seen another side of life. Every time he descended into that netherworld of the city, he'd seen with his own eyes the tragic conditions in which people were forced to live. The crippling poverty of farmers forced from their land and scratching desperately for food and shelter in the squalid rookeries of Edinburgh. The opium addicts, throwing away productive lives for an hour of oblivion. The drunken dock men, giving away a week's pay with one throw of the dice. He'd held the hands of starving children, standing beside a mother's lifeless body.

Sarah's death had changed him in every way. Yes, he still spent sleepless nights in search of her killer, but he also found that in his waking hours, he could do something to help those who suffered.

"Why now?" he asked. "Why did you decide to put an end to all of this?"

His mother's attention again moved to the open window.

"Phoebe."

Beyond the curtains, sitting on some bench in the garden, Ian had asked Phoebe to wait for him. His Phoebe.

"When I heard this morning that she'd gone missing yesterday and that she was injured, my imaginary world folded and burned to tinder in an instant. Suddenly, the past was repeating itself, and I could no longer live in a dream."

Ian felt the same urgency yesterday while he searched for her. He'd been a man possessed.

"She was Sarah's closest friend," he said. "From the moment she arrived at Bellhorne, your response to her presence here—"

She put a hand on his arm, interrupting him. "My reaction when I heard she'd been hurt wasn't because of Sarah's relationship with her, but yours. You, Ian. The man who has sacrificed so much of his life for this family, for me . . . I couldn't fathom losing our Lady Phoebe. I know how much she means to you."

Losing Phoebe would have meant the end of his sanity, the end of him. He stared at the furnishings of the room, at the alabaster icon on the wall, at the mementos of his and Sarah's youth scattered around him. But everywhere he looked, there was only Phoebe. She was alive in his thoughts of today, in his dreams of tomorrow, in his hopes for happiness in the future.

He turned to his mother. "How do you know what she means to me? We've spent so little time together in your company."

She smiled.

"A mother's intuition."

He had no mother.

He was found at the river. No basket of bulrushes had been woven for him. No pharaoh's daughter standing by. No one called him *prophet*.

But those who found him, raised him, and scorned him always had a word for him.

Trouble. Ghoul. Accursed. Disaster. Barghest. Pain monger. Chain rattler. Blight. Satan's hall-boy.

They never let up on him. He was always the cause of every evil.

The rain's come in . . . The barley's withering . . . The barn is flooded . . . The milk is soured . . . The rats bit the old man . . . The new calf froze . . .

'Tis the boy!

And when the old couple grew tired of searching for names or crimes to hang on him, he was . . . he was . . . nothing.

How many years? How many years?

Then the voices came, whispering, murmuring. *Chosen.* Snatches first, then louder, clearer. *Avenge Us.* He couldn't ignore them. They were speaking to him. Coaxing. Prodding. Screaming. *Kill.*

He had no mother. But then the voices came. *You have been Chosen. You above all others. Avenge us.*

And on that day he was born.

❧ 15 ❧

Phoebe stood by the sundial in the garden, urging the shadows to move. Some promises were surely not meant to be kept, she thought, eyeing the bright sun, which had apparently come to a standstill in the sky.

"And waiting on a bench for more than a few minutes is one of those unenforceable promises," she assured herself, thinking of what she'd told Ian. "But at least I'm still waiting in the garden. That should count for something."

She wandered along one of the grassy lanes where she could keep an eye on the door Ian had used to go into the house. She'd tried for a while to remain near the bench where Ian left her, but her restlessness had soon turned to worry. And by the time a full hour had passed, she'd made several trips back and forth to the sundial.

It was difficult to believe they'd arrived only yesterday. So much had happened. Both bad and good, Phoebe thought, breathing in the garden smells. The scents and colors of the roses and azaleas, wildflowers and herbs

213

invigorated her. The bright blue sky and the clear, clean air offered such a contrast to Edinburgh, though she did truly love the city too. Still, here one could almost forget about the world's troubles. Almost. But she understood how, living here, Mrs. Bell had been able to pull the blinders over her eyes and shut out the harsh reality of her daughter's death.

Phoebe had completed several more circuits of the garden when the door opened. It wasn't Ian, but she was delighted to see her sister coming out and carrying a book.

"I saw you out here waiting, so I brought something to read to you to help pass the time." Millie held up the volume. "*Frankenstein; or, A Modern Prometheus*. It's new."

"I've read it." Phoebe knew the book. It had caught her eye because it was published anonymously. And once she read it, she guessed the writer had to be a woman. "It was one of the books that came from London this spring for the library in Hertfordshire."

"Oh." Millie wrinkled up her nose. "I must have missed it."

"It's interesting enough. The so-called hero is a scientist who creates life in his laboratory, thereby leaving women out of the process entirely. You'll see how well that works out for his motherless monster and for him."

For a while the two of them sat on the bench where Ian had asked her to wait, chatting about books, Mrs. Bell, and the events of the visit. But soon, having left the book on the bench, they were circling the rose garden and then stretching their travels into the orchards and the long rows of berries.

Moving along the raspberry bushes, Phoebe thought again about how staying busy with the grapevines and fruit and flowers could provide a shield for a broken heart against the arrows of hurtful rumor and gossip.

Millie was browsing amongst the flowers in the bushes for berries that might have ripened early. "As abrupt as Mrs. Bell's admission sounded to you today, I think it's very encouraging news. The captain must be relieved."

Only moments ago, Phoebe had shared the conversation she had with Ian's mother in the morning room. Still, as logical as Millie's statement sounded, she was worried. An end to the pretense at Bellhorne of Sarah being alive didn't put an end to Ian's hunt. The mother could finally mourn her daughter's death. But what about Ian? When would he be able to lay his sister to rest?

"I imagine his life will be a little easier now that his mother knows," Phoebe finally answered.

At the end of the orchard, they decided not to venture out into the fields, though the smell of cut hay was enticing. Arm in arm, the sisters started back toward the gardens.

"Are you ready to go back to the city tomorrow?" Millie asked as they moved through the arched opening in the wall.

"I have to be, don't I?"

"I don't know." The two of them stopped by an arbor where the vines of red and white roses climbed and twisted and became inseparably entwined. "I see the way you look at things. The trees in the orchards, the fields, the sky, the gardens, the house. We haven't even left yet, but I believe you're already missing Bellhorne."

Phoebe was about to use Sarah as reason enough for her attachment to this place, but she couldn't. It was no longer true. Yesterday had been about remembering her friend. But today . . . now . . . especially after the talk with

Mrs. Bell and her words of encouragement, she was seeing Bellhorne differently.

She recalled what Ian said as he helped her out of the well: *I will never let you go.* And his words when he'd put an end to their moments of passion: *Another time, another place, under more appropriate circumstances . . .* Could it be? Was it possible that one day she'd call this house her home?

"I am right. Admit it," Millie teased. "I can see you now, sitting in the rose garden on a sunny morning with your pen and paper, writing your stories or your articles. Later, you'll have a bite to eat with Mrs. Bell or an early dinner when your husband comes back after his rounds with Mr. Raeburn."

"Don't do this to me," Phoebe protested.

Her husband. Her face caught fire with the excitement of the possibility, remote as it might be. But for her part, Millie was too close to the truth.

"Do what?"

Phoebe was already sorry she'd told Millie about Mrs. Bell's giving her blessing. "Make me want things I may never have."

"Make you want what, for example?"

"Stop it, Millie," she ordered. "I'm not going to pour out my heart."

"You don't have to say anything. I see it in your face."

"No, you don't." Phoebe plucked a red petal from the climbing roses and held it to her lips. The fragrance of the flower was almost intoxicating. "I'm already guilty of spending too much time with my head in the clouds. Don't make it worse by encouraging me."

"I'm your sister. Why shouldn't I encourage you to

pursue what makes you happy? To pursue all of your passions?"

"My passion." Phoebe held the rose petal up in her open palm and then blew it away. For so long, her passion had been her writing, and she always assumed that would be enough. To spin out onto a page the threads of stories and the poems and the arguments, and see the web of thoughts adhere and form a coherent shape had been a wonder. It had always been satisfying enough to forego marriage, children, a husband . . . but no longer. "I don't know that I want to pursue one passion when it means I must forfeit another. Why can't women have it all?"

Millie quirked the corner of her mouth and arched an eyebrow. It was their mother's famous *you can do better than that* look. She shook her head. "I'm sure I don't know what you're talking about because *my* sister would never accept less than all."

Phoebe stamped a foot and frowned. Millie was supposed to be her voice of reason. The calm, the rational, the conventional-thinking sister who encouraged caution and careful consideration before taking action of any sort. She didn't know this stranger standing before her.

"Having it all would include someone this tall and this broad across the shoulders," Phoebe said, holding her arms out to show the height and breadth of Ian. "But that particular man—whom we happen to be waiting for right now—is not so pliable that I can simply bend him to my fancy. So my only option is to wait, and wait, and wait until he is ready to pursue me."

"Until *he* is ready to pursue you."

She nodded, recalling the promise she'd made to allow herself no regrets. The words were simple enough but last night, after Ian had left her bedroom, she'd been morti-fied by what she'd done. Well, maybe not mortified, but slightly embarrassed, in any event.

"Do you love him, Phoebe?"

"What kind of question is that?" Now *she* was the one with hands on her hips, glaring at her sister.

"It's a simple question. For my own peace of mind. Do you love him?"

"Of course I love him."

She let out a frustrated breath and tipped her head back, staring at the sky as memories of her youth rushed back. Walking these same garden lanes. Following Sarah through the house in search of ghosts. And then Ian. One look from him was enough to melt Phoebe in her tracks. A few friendly words and she might have swooned. But those days were gone. What she felt for him now was the love of a woman.

"I've never loved anyone else. I know there will never be another. Ian Bell has always been my one true love."

Millie smiled, turned, and hurried away.

"Where are you going?" Phoebe called after her.

She took a step and picked up her skirts with the intention of running the troublesome creature to ground, but a hand on Phoebe's shoulder stopped her.

She didn't have to look to know it was him. She recog-nized the warmth of his strong fingers, the tantalizing pressure.

Finally, she found her voice, though it sounded more like the strangled honk of a goose. "How long have you been standing behind me?"

"Long enough."

"Why do you do this to me?"

. . .

Considering everything they'd been through in the last twenty-four hours, Ian thought, the day was improving by the minute.

"Because I can't stay away," he said, gently pulling Phoebe around.

A blush was blooming on her cheeks, and her blue eyes slowly lifted to his as he drew her into his embrace.

"Because I've been blind for much of my life," he continued. "But now that my eyes are opened, I can't get enough of you."

She bit her lip, watching him closely, and he brought her closer, his arms tightening around her. Whether it was her drumming heart or his that he could feel, it made no difference, they'd become one.

Her words, the admission she'd made to her sister about loving him was the most precious gift he'd ever received in this life.

"I'm a flawed man. My body is scarred. I'm tormented by guilt. I don't know that I'll ever be content until I find out what happened to Sarah." He traced the line of her high cheekbone, her jaw, her chin. "But I love you."

He held her face and looked into her eyes as his words registered. He could have swum in their blue depths.

"You love me?"

"I do."

Ian was about to say everything he'd intended. The conversation he'd overheard a moment earlier between Phoebe and her sister meant something. He wanted her to write and create. He wanted them to have a family. He wanted her to have it all.

"But I can't ask you to marry me," he said.

She stiffened in his arms, but he held tight.

"I can't ask you to marry me because it's become clear to me that *you* should be doing the asking."

Her eyes narrowed, and her lips thinned. The blush on Phoebe's cheeks turned a few shades darker.

"Are you making fun of me?" she asked tensely. "Has it occurred to you, Captain Bell, that this is supposed to be a romantic moment?"

If there was one thing he wanted, it would be to sweep her up and carry her off to some enchanted place of romance, where warm sea breezes bathed them with the sweet fragrance of tropical flowers. Where wines and exotic fruits from faraway places lay always within their reach. Where the azure sea dazzled the eye, and the sun kissed every inch of her glorious skin. Where every night was filled with the sounds of distant music. Where he would make love to her until the dawn glowed on a distant horizon.

"I'm afraid I know very little about romance. But at the risk of sounding even more unromantic, two issues face us. First, you are an earl's daughter. Second, you've been propositioning me for years with your beauty, your wit, your intelligence—"

"You're mocking me."

"I'm not. I was a blind man for years, but now I see everything clearly. That's why I think it's only right that you should ask me, considering the importance of the matter."

"Ian, you are not only being unromantic, you are also being ungentlemanly."

He smiled. "If I recall, last night a certain party had no interest in my gentlemanly qualities."

"Now you're determined to embarrass me."

He feared that perhaps his attempt at humor had gone

too far. But she wasn't trying to escape him, so he held her tight, his nose touching hers, his lips stealing a kiss, and then another. A moment later, she sighed and kissed him back, her body becoming soft in his arms. She opened her lips, and he deepened the kiss and heard a moan in the back of her throat.

He drew back slightly, and her blue eyes opened.

"I am not as tall nor as broad as you think. And you don't need to force me. Last night, you told me 'no regrets,'" he reminded her. "I love you, Phoebe. I'm yours for the asking."

She pressed her fisted hands against his chest. "You had better say yes, or I'll strangle you right here in this garden."

"Well, that's a very romantic start to a proposal."

"I mean it." She was glaring at him, but he could see the sparkle of amusement in her eyes.

"More threats. More propositions. I'm mad about you."

"And my family thinks *I* am overly dramatic." She sighed. "Very well. Captain Bell, will you . . . ?"

"Wait. Have you brought a ring to seal our betrothal?"

"You know that I haven't, Captain. And I suggest you refrain from interrupting me again."

Ian smiled. "I'll not interrupt you again. If the sky suddenly fills with angels blowing their horns and announcing some glorious event for mankind, I'll tell them to wait."

Phoebe took a deep breath and began again.

"Will you do me the honor, Captain Bell, of being my husband?"

"Yes, Lady Phoebe. I would be honored."

He kissed her, and she kissed him back. The press of

her body against his, the softness and the scent of her hair, and the warmth of her skin all spoke to him of a lifetime of romance that lay ahead of them.

Breaking off the kiss, he drew back and dropped to one knee.

"Phoebe, you know who I am. You know the jagged scars of my past. You know the shadows that I chase."

"Ian, there's no need—"

"But know this too: I shall love you until every star plunges from the firmament. I shall cherish you until the moon melts into the sun. I promise that you will have the life you want . . . with all of the independence you require and all the support I can give. I'm yours, my love, now and forever. And I seal that vow with this."

Ian drew from his pocket the ring his mother had given him, a family heirloom that had graced the hands of Bell family brides for generations. The large diamond, mounted in an intricate gold setting at the center of a bed of rose petals, surrounded by small leaves of emerald. And now it would grace Phoebe's slender hand.

Standing, he slipped it onto her finger.

The surprised smile and the tear running down her cheek told him all he needed to know. As she threw her arms around him, Ian kissed her and lifted her in the air, whirling her around before setting her down.

"So you're finally to make an honest man of me."

Phoebe wished she could grow wings. She wanted to share her news with her sister that very instant.

A dozen measured steps, a half-dozen running, again a restrained pace as she passed a middle-aged couple walking arm in arm in their Sunday best. Phoebe smiled and tried to look composed and demure as they greeted her. But as soon as she passed them, she was running again.

She could no longer control her excitement as she flew down the lane after her sister. Millie hadn't gone far, and Phoebe saw her waiting under an oak tree at the edge of the fields.

"Millie," she shouted, waving as she ran.

Her sister turned around and the smile on her face told Phoebe she knew the cause of her excitement.

"He proposed?" she squealed as Phoebe collided with her in the eagerness of the moment.

Arms wrapped around each other. Laughter filled the air. For a few moments they were not mature adults; they were once again youngsters, holding each other's hands and dancing in a happy circle.

"We're to be married." Phoebe kissed her sister on each cheek and hugged her tightly again. She held out her hand so Millie could inspect the ring. "He gave me this."

"So beautiful!" she gasped. "You said yes! Of course, you said yes!"

"I did, but he had to make it difficult. First, he made me do the asking, and after he said yes, he offered me the ring with a proposal of his own."

The giggle in her sister's chest rose to full-blown laughter, and she pulled back to look at the ring again.

"He's the right man for our family. Never boring."

Ian had always been perfect for her. She'd known it long before he realized it himself.

"But you set me up," Phoebe scowled. "All the questions of whether I love him or not, and how I should pursue my passions. You gave him all the ammunition he needed."

Millie smiled, pushed the hair out of Phoebe's face, and tucked it behind her ear. "I can't tell you how happy I am."

She wanted to dance. She wanted to sing. She wanted to shout out and share her news.

Phoebe once again pulled the younger woman into her embrace, but this time they held on to each other, neither in a hurry to let go. Sisters and friends. She was so glad that Millie was the first person she could share her joy with.

Ian had gone back to tell his mother there would indeed be a wedding. Phoebe knew there were formalities they had to attend to once they returned to Edinburgh. Ian wished to speak to the earl and properly ask his and the countess's permission. She doubted anyone in her family would have any objection. In many ways, she guessed they'd be quite relieved.

"Jo and Wynne and Cuffe leave for Jamaica in less than a week," Millie reminded her. "She'll not go if it means missing your wedding."

"We can get around that. We'll plan to have the wedding after she gets back." Phoebe took her sister's hand as they started walking back along the lane toward the house. "The last thing I want is to disrupt any of their plans or take away attention from them."

Jo had endured sixteen years of waiting before she and Wynne Melfort found each other again. Their older sister deserved to savor her long overdue moments of joy.

"Perhaps you and Captain Bell could plan to hold your wedding at Christmas. It seems that it has already become a tradition to have a wedding around either the Summer Ball or the Christmas Assembly."

Millie was right. Hugh and Grace married a year ago,

the week of the Summer Ball. Gregory and Freya married last Christmas, and Jo and Wynne exchanged their vows less than a month ago.

She shrugged. "I'd be happy to run away to Gretna Green, if that's what Ian wants."

"Phoebe," Millie responded, a note of warning in her voice. "You will not ruin the occasion for Mother. Nor for me. Nor for Jo."

"I know. I know. I know. I'll be agreeable. I promise."

When they reached the castle, a maid was waiting in the entry foyer with Phoebe's spencer jacket, gloves, a bonnet, and the message that the carriage was in the courtyard.

"Where are you going?" Millie asked. As Phoebe buttoned the short jacket, she arranged the bonnet for her.

"I asked Ian if he and I could go to the village." Phoebe glanced at the door as Ian entered and came toward them. "Do I look respectable?"

"Perfectly," her sister replied. "But why are you going to the village?"

"I wanted to share . . . *we* wanted to share our news with Sarah."

❧ 16 ☙

THE CHURCH of brown and grey stone with its squat, square steeple sat on a promontory at the edge of the village, overlooking the choppy waters of the firth. Crossing a stone bridge, the carriage wound its way through a tidy kirkyard, where a half-dozen sheep were grazing between gravestones.

The sunny skies of this morning had gradually filled with clouds as the day progressed. By the time they stepped out of the carriage, a soft rain was falling, and a fog was rolling in along the coast.

"Why don't you wait inside for me while I run up to the rectory for a quick word with Mr. Garioch," Ian said, escorting Phoebe up the steps of the church. "I think the minister may be relieved to hear my mother has decided to forego having company in for dinner tonight. He was very accommodating in entertaining her while we were searching for you yesterday."

On the way into the village, Ian told her Mrs. Bell was both elated and exhausted after everything that had happened. She wanted to be surrounded only by family today. And Phoebe was happy with this arrangement as well. She didn't completely trust her ability to sit across the table from Dr. Thornton at dinner and refrain from making one or two snide comments. She told Ian how she felt about the man's manner, and he told her what he'd learned of the doctor's affection for Alice.

Poor man. Or perhaps, poor Alice. Phoebe decided it was not for her to judge either of them over a matter of the heart. In any event, she would try to think of the doctor in more favorable terms, considering Ian's cousin was allegedly contemplating his offer of marriage. It was difficult to imagine a woman not rejecting him outright, but perhaps Dr. Thornton had some redeemable qualities Phoebe hadn't been fortunate enough to experience.

"You can wait for me in here, out of the rain," Ian said, pulling Phoebe into his arms as they stepped into the small, empty vestibule of the church.

"Where would I go?" She smiled up into his face, still reeling with the happiness of knowing this man was going to be her husband.

"No walking in the kirkyard, no going back over the bridge, no strolling in the fields." He placed a kiss on her nose, her chin, and her lips, emphasizing every place he didn't want her to go.

"If you're going to make your points so enticingly," she murmured, sliding her hands up over his broad chest before slipping them around his neck. "I can think of at least a dozen more places I might wander off to that you haven't mentioned."

He guided her back into the shadows of the antechamber until she was pressed against a dark, paneled wall. Phoebe's breath caught in her chest as he wrapped her tightly in his arms and crushed her lips beneath his own.

Heat spread through her. This was exactly what she wanted. The time, the place, why they'd come here, all of that disappeared from her thoughts. She was only conscious of the excitement racing through her veins.

Her hands seemed to move of their own accord, exploring beneath his coat, feeling the muscular lines of his back. He groaned his approval. Powerful arms gathered her closer to his body, pressing her to him until there was nothing left between their two hearts, pounding wildly as one.

The embers of passion she'd felt last night were back, fanned by his embrace.

He kissed her deeply, and she responded to him. She felt his tongue searching, tasting. As he pressed her back against the wall, his body warmed every inch of her with his heat. His hands glided down over her body—touching, possessing.

"Phoebe." He tore his mouth from her lips. "A wedding at Christmas is too far away."

It took a few moments to gather her wits and find her voice.

"I agree," she whispered against his throat. He smelled good, tasted good. "My brother Gregory and my sister Jo have both set the precedent of marrying privately first and having a public second ceremony later."

"This gives me another thing to talk to the minister about." He smiled. "Perhaps we can have him marry us here."

"There's always the blacksmith at Gretna Green to do the honors."

"I believe you may be on to something."

She was still tickled inside as Ian left her to go and speak with Mr. Garioch. Here they were—two adults, of age, independent, and free of impediments—talking about running away to Gretna Green.

Trailing her fingers along the paneled wall, Phoebe stepped past the vestibule and into the back of the church. She felt like a traveler bathing in a fresh, clear lake after a dusty and arduous journey. Like a child seeing a rainbow after a flood. Like a writer hearing her poem recited for the first time. It was almost inconceivable that a night of horror in the Vaults should have led her down the road to today, to this happiness.

Phoebe stopped beside the last pew. The wood was cool and smooth to her touch. The church was in darkness with only a few shafts of light stretching across the deep brown wood of the pews and the grey stone floor of the nave. The three tall, arched windows behind the altar and pulpit at the far end of the building had certainly held stained glass at one time, she surmised, but now they were filled with panels of the same dark wood that enclosed the bottom third of the interior walls. No decoration was visible anywhere, except for the carved stonework on the thick heavy pillars and the round arches that supported the roof.

Phoebe made her way down the center aisle. Everything about the kirk reflected the somber seriousness of religious observance, including the vague scent of liturgical candles. The Firth of Forth—with its salty scent and tidal sounds not thirty yards away—might as well have been thirty miles from here; Phoebe could discover no hint of it inside. The silence was broken only by the scratch of her soles on the worn stones. When she reached the transept, she saw a small alcove at the far end consisting of wide stone stairs leading downward.

The crypt.

As Phoebe moved through the murky light to the stairs, the cloak of happiness she'd been wearing around her shoulders slipped and fell away. Her memories of Sarah were back. Her friend had wished for her brother and Phoebe to come together. "Then we'll be sisters for life," she used to say. "Inseparable."

Phoebe fought back the sadness burning in her throat and thought of Mrs. Bell's words about Sarah being with them. If that were true, she'd know about the engagement. She'd be happy for them.

As her eyes adjusted to the darkness, Phoebe could see a hint of light at the foot of the stairs. Holding to the wall, Phoebe descended, and at the bottom, she found an iron gate that swung open with an unexpected screech that made her jump when she put her hand to it. A few more steps and she was standing in the crypt.

The space down here was darker than the church above, for only three tiny windows admitted any light. Still, she could see two arched alcoves on either side of the bisecting aisle. In the center, carved stone effigies of a knight and his lady lay side by side—likenesses, no doubt, of the inhabitants beneath—staring up for eternity at the black, barrel-roofed ceiling.

The alcoves to the right and left held stone sarcophagi with heraldic emblems and names of family members displayed, but it was too dark for Phoebe to read any of them.

She already knew from Ian that Sarah's name had been left off to keep his mother from learning the truth. But now, with Mrs. Bell openly aware of all that had occurred, a beloved name would be added.

The musty smell of death permeated the place, but she'd been in such places before and had been expecting it.

Standing in the dark chamber, Phoebe knew she had to wait for Ian to come and show her where Sarah's body lay. But for the time being, she shut her eyes and tried to close off her senses of touch and sound and smell, and open her mind to her friend's presence.

In the rose garden, Sarah was there. As she was in the morning room. But here in the crypt, Phoebe felt no sign of her friend. And then, suddenly, a pall she hadn't expected descended over her, a chill so icy that Phoebe shivered and wrapped her arms around her body. Images of lost souls, weeping and bereft of hope, ran through her mind's eye. The endless gloom of a bottomless pit yawned before her. A sensation of evil permeated the air, so close and so distinct that she opened her eyes and stared at each stone sarcophagus, half expecting them to burst open one by one and spew their contents of fragmented bone onto the shadowy floor.

The low sound, barely more than a breath, made her whirl around. There, on the bottom stair, a man stood.

Framed by the dim light coming from the church above, he was a statue, motionless as carved stone, a creature of death, risen from the murky recesses of the crypt itself.

Panic clutched her by the throat. She'd stepped into a nightmare. There was nowhere to go. Nowhere to hide. There was only one way out.

"Mr. Garioch." Ian's voice rang down the stairwell. "I've been looking for you."

The minister hadn't been in the rectory, and there was no sign of his housekeeper, which was to be expected, today being Sunday. Upon returning to the kirk, Ian found that Phoebe wasn't where he'd left her, but he wasn't surprised. A lamp flickered near the top of the stairs leading down to the crypt. Guessing she might have gone down ahead of him, he was happy to find Garioch with her.

Apparently, she'd given the minister a start.

"I must say I wasn't expecting anyone in the crypt this afternoon," the minister said as they all made their way back up into the church. "I thought I was in the company of a ghost."

Phoebe clung to Ian's arm. Her face was pale when they came into the light of the lamp at the top of the stairs. She too had been frightened by the unexpected encounter.

"Of course, I should not use the word '*ghost*' without added clarification," Garioch said.

He never seemed to lose the suave, composed manner of speaking that drove Dr. Thornton mad, Ian thought. Even seeing a ghost was not enough.

"Recent scholars of scripture tell us that the human consciousness doesn't cease to exist when our bodies die," he explained smoothly. "Lazarus, for example, retained his consciousness and responded when Christ called him from the grave."

"Yes, that is logical," Ian said, gently trying to cut him off.

"Therefore," Garioch continued, "this permanent existence, in the presence of God, must manifest itself in a form fuller and richer than our current physical state. And yes, we believe too that some people choose to live in a manner that separates them from God's goodness, a condition that continues for all eternity. That, my friends, is called *Hell*."

"Thank you, Mr. Garioch," Ian interrupted, "for the clarification," He really did not want to hear the sermon in its entirety.

The minister appeared to pick up on Ian's desire to change the subject. "But my alarm in the crypt just now stems from other sources. We're seeing all sorts of people hugging the coastline as they travel down from the Highlands." Garioch drew a kerchief from his pocket and ran it over his forehead and upper lip. "I've been thinking I may need to start locking the doors. I don't want to find a family of vagrants here or in the crypts some morning."

Ian knew when Phoebe was over the worst of her scare. Her hand dropped from his arm, and her back straightened. He was relieved to see she'd regained some color in her face. She was also paying close attention to Garioch's lecture.

"Pardon me," he said. "But you haven't been introduced. Lady Phoebe Pennington, may I present the Reverend Peter Garioch."

"I'm honored, Lady Phoebe." There was a polite bow and the famous smile that Thornton blamed for ruining every female from Edinburgh to St. Andrews. "I recall hearing you praised so often by the late Miss Bell. She was quite fond of you." He hesitated, and then scontinued, "And I can't tell you how happy I am to see you in such good health after . . . after your adventure yesterday."

This was as good a time as any to tell the minister the truth, Ian decided.

"One reason for coming in here today was to tell you

my mother knows about my sister's death. She's known all along, apparently, but preferred to remain silent. Today . . ." He paused and took Phoebe's hand in his. He still became emotional thinking of his conversation with her in the morning room. "Today, she told Lady Phoebe. Later, she spoke with me about it. The charade is over."

The minister opened his mouth to speak, but then stopped. Ian guessed this might have been the first time he ever saw the man at a loss for words.

"As you are her spiritual advisor, I'm certain she'll want to speak to you in more detail sometime soon. But for now, she sends her apologies and begs to withdraw your invitation to dinner tonight."

"Yes. Yes. Of course. She must be quite overwhelmed by the changes."

Ian had asked Alice to send a message to Dr. Thornton, as well, canceling his dinner invitation but asking him to stop by the house tomorrow morning. He needed to speak to the doctor before they left for Edinburgh. Using the announcement of their engagement to entice her, Phoebe had convinced his mother to travel back to the city with them. And since Thornton was going to Edinburgh himself this week, Ian wanted him to arrange a consultation with the specialist he knew at the university.

"I was planning to show Lady Phoebe where Sarah's remains lie," Ian said, deciding that whatever else he needed to say to the minister about his mother's condition, it could wait until after they returned.

"Of course." The cleric bowed, picked up the lamp, and handed it to Ian. "I shall leave you, then."

"Thank you. But I would like you to arrange for the stone mason to come and engrave my sister's name with the others."

"I'll see to it," he said cordially before turning to Phoebe. "And I hope you enjoy the rest of your visit here at Bellhorne."

"Thank you," she replied. "But I'm curious, Mr. Garioch. Is it possible that we've met before?"

"No, m'lady. I can assure you, we never have."

"Well, in that case . . ." She shook her head as if trying to clear it.

Ian took her hand and was surprised to find it ice cold. He turned to the minister.

"The good news, Mr. Garioch, is that you'll be seeing a great deal of Lady Phoebe in the future. She is to be mistress of Bellhorne."

Trapped. She had nowhere to go.

She thought she was so clever, coming here. Taunting him in his lair. She had no idea.

He could have had her here. Killed her. Finished it. It was so close. Before the captain came, he'd been about to wrap his fingers around her throat. Squeezing and squeezing until her face grew red and swollen, and her eyes bulged from her stupid head.

In an hour, or tomorrow, people would say it was a vagrant. Someone from outside. Others. Intruders, invading our safe little village. Bringing their dirty, violent ways with them.

He could feel her pulsing flesh beneath his thumbs even now.

Afterward, she looked into the very face of Death, and she didn't recognize him. She was blind. A fool. He might have let her live if she went away. If she disappeared forever.

But married. Married. Married. She was to stay, here in *his* lair. Taunting him. Staring at him. Condescending to speak with him. Safe in her castle. In her plush bed. With the litter of brats she'd bring into this world. Mistress of Bellhorne.

No. That would never do.

Phoebe Pennington must die.

❧ 17 ☙

SHE COULD LIVE HERE, Phoebe thought happily as she prepared for bed.

No day of her life compared to this one. Ian's proposal —or her proposal, whatever way one wanted to look at it —changed everything. It would certainly change both of their lives forever. And their conversations with Mrs. Bell and dinner with her tonight had also served to relieve some of the worry in Ian about his mother and her state of mind. She never mentioned anything of the fantasy world she'd been living in.

Tomorrow. A wave of joyful celebrations was sure to begin when they reached Edinburgh and shared their news with her family.

Regardless of the excitement still coursing through her, once Phoebe climbed into bed, she dropped off to sleep.

The dreams began immediately. The nightmares were so vivid and real. She was running in the dark. All the faces. But he was after her. She could feel his claws grip her arm. Feel the hot breath of the monster in her ear. Feel his merciless fangs on her neck.

Sweating and gasping for breath, she sat bolt upright in the bed.

"Millie?" she whispered in the direction of her sister's partially closed door.

Phoebe climbed out of bed and crossed the room. Peering in, she could see her sleeping peacefully, the candle by her bed snuffed out. She had no idea if she'd gone to bed five minutes ago or five hours. Phoebe went to her window and looked out. Clouds covered the moon, and the gardens below were dark.

Phoebe's hands were shaking as she shoved them into the sleeves of her robe and tightened the belt. She ran her hand over the place on her neck where she'd felt the monster's teeth. No marks, no blood . . . other than what remained of the small cut she'd received in her skirmish in the Vaults. Still, her skin tingled, and her heart was racing from the urgency of the nightmare.

A few moments later, as Phoebe was hurrying through the gallery, she noticed she'd forgotten her slippers. But she didn't care. The household slept, the sounds and lights of Bellhorne had been extinguished for the night.

She knew where to go. Ian's rooms were located in the attached tower. Years ago, she'd passed by his door many times in Sarah's company, always imagining herself brave enough to raise a hand and knock.

Tonight, there was no hesitation. She lifted a fist and rapped on the wood.

Silence was her only answer. Where was he? Out roaming the grounds as he stalked killers in the Vaults? She lifted a fist again, knocking harder. Nothing.

"What are you doing out of bed at this hour?"

Phoebe gasped and spun around. One hand went to her hammering heart, the other clutched at the wall. Ian strode down the hall toward her.

He was George, the dragon slayer. Hercules, the hydra killer. Bellerophon, the destroyer of monsters.

Phoebe stretched a hand toward him and he took it, pulling her tightly into his arms.

"You're cold. And you're shaking. What's wrong?"

He caressed her hair, holding her, and she welcomed his warmth, his strength, the silent vow that she wasn't facing any monster alone.

"Tell me, my love. What happened?"

My love. My love. The words echoed in her mind, and a beam of light dispelled the darkness and the horror that had plagued her sleep.

"I have something I need to tell you," she whispered, lifting her face off his chest. "It's important."

He looked back down the hallway, in the direction he'd come, but she pulled on his hand, opening the door behind her.

"Phoebe."

"I know you're a gentleman," she told him, pulling him inside. "And I promise to tear apart anyone who dares to speak poorly of your reputation."

"My lioness," he whispered as they went in. "Give me a moment."

Phoebe pressed her back against the door and waited as Ian went around the room. A candle flickered on the mantle, and he used it to light other candles. Moving to the hearth, he lit the fire. It was summer, but she knew he did it to warm her. A large bed took up the far side of the room, and around the fireplace two chairs, a sofa, and a writing desk had been arranged. An open door beyond the bed led to dressing rooms.

It thrilled her to think of a day not far in the future when she'd be sharing these rooms with him. Sharing this bed. Ian was to be her husband. It was a dream she'd had so long ago.

But the nightmarish creatures of her current dreams were interfering with the joy of being here with him now.

"Come." Ian padded back to her and took her hand, leading her to the chair by the fire.

She decided against a chair and sat on a sofa instead, pulling Ian down beside her.

His arm wrapped around her, pulling her close, and she leaned against him. She breathed in the comforting masculine smell of tobacco and whiskey, and he placed a kiss on her brow.

"Tell me," he said in a low voice. "Talk to me."

The nightmare was as alive now as it was the moment she opened her eyes, but she didn't want to repeat every horrifying step through crypts and through the Vaults' murky passageways. She didn't want to try to describe the faces that came out of the dripping walls, their features changing before her eyes. She didn't want to think about the sharp teeth on her throat.

She took a deep breath. "Have you ever considered that perhaps Sarah knew her killer?"

Phoebe felt every muscle in Ian's body instantly grow tense.

"I have. I still think it is a strong possibility. But I can imagine no one who knew her who would do such a thing," he said. "This is what frustrates me. You went down into the Vaults with a purpose. But she had no reason to go, even if she knew the killer. And whoever it was, they couldn't have dragged her against her will off a busy street in broad daylight. Someone would have noticed it and raised an alarm."

Phoebe knew many of Sarah's friends and acquaintances, and she couldn't imagine any of them being a murderer either. Images from her nightmare continued to parade through her head. Faces appearing . . . and then changing.

Different people.

She sat up straight and shifted her position on the sofa. Tucking one foot under her, she faced him. "What if there were two people?"

His dark eyes narrowed. "Tell me what you're thinking."

Truth. Lies. Bits and pieces of what had taken place that first night in the Vaults. She'd never told him the whole story, and that nagged at her. Young Jock Rokeby was in her dream last night, as well. Phoebe was holding Sarah's hand, and they were running through the dark after the boy. And then the faces, men changing into monsters. Sarah was gone then, and Phoebe was running. He was after her.

Phoebe didn't know where to start or end, but she couldn't help but think there was meaning in the madness of this dream. Perhaps her friend was trying to tell her things.

"What if Sarah saw someone she knew? A young man, an acquaintance, someone within the social circle of the family. A person she considered harmless." Phoebe decided to say what came to mind. The ideas were vague and disordered, but they needed to be put out in the light if they were ever going to be considered and dismissed. "And let's assume the man's purpose was not to hurt her, but to take advantage of a moment in a dark alley for . . . I don't know . . . something not completely honorable. A kiss, even. But Sarah quickly realized the man's intent and walked away, leaving him. That's when she was confronted by the real killer."

"And the blasted rogue decided to stay quiet about it when Sarah disappeared."

"Of course. What else was he going to do, knowing you'd kill him if you ever learned any of this?"

"I would kill him. Slowly and painfully. He'd die a thousand deaths before he breathed his last. For every moment of fear or pain she endured, I would make him suffer."

The time had come when she needed to tell him the rest. Phoebe inched back on the sofa.

"I believe the murderer, the one you told me about, chooses his victims randomly. He wouldn't have gone up out of the Vaults into the busy shops of the South Bridge to lure Sarah down."

That is, she finished silently, if Sarah's killer and the one committing all the other murders were the same man.

"The night you found me in the Vaults." She paused and waited until she had his full attention. "I haven't told you everything. I want you to know exactly what happened. The killer didn't come after me. I went after him."

If their positions were reversed, Phoebe knew she'd be shouting at him for not being forthright, for not trusting her with the truth. But she was already accustomed to Ian and his menacing silence. He was staring at her, looking like a great cat about to pounce, but taking his time.

There was no point in delaying the inevitable. No point in asking for forgiveness for her omissions. She told him, step-by-step, as clearly as she remembered, everything that occurred in the Vaults that night. She told him about Jock and how she'd come to learn his name when he approached her and Duncan in her carriage at Greyfriars Kirkyard near the Grassmarket. In just a few moments, the facts lay bare before him.

Still, he remained silent.

"I don't know if the man I fought is the same one responsible for Sarah's murder, but that night I witnessed it with my own eyes. He goes after anyone he happens upon. That's why I think two people—"

He moved too fast. One moment, she was sitting a safe distance away from him on the sofa, the next she was lying across his lap, looking up into a face inches away from hers. His expression was lethal.

"Reckless. Mad. You could have been killed down there," he shouted. "Killed!"

She flinched, fearing that everyone in Bellhorne Castle had heard him.

"What made you think you could possibly stop a murderer, unarmed, alone?"

"I didn't think about it. I acted," she said, keeping her tone reasonable. "You would have done the same."

He gaped at her. "We're *not* the same! I'm a soldier. And when I go down there, I'm armed. I'm capable of twisting a man's head off his shoulders if I need to. I've been trained to kill. I *have* killed. How could you possibly think we're the same?"

"I told you. I admit I didn't think before I acted," she repeated softly. Reaching up, she touched the hard lines of his jaw and stroked the coarse growth of beard. She'd never studied him this close—when she wasn't kissing him, that is. She looked above the stormy black eyes. He had a scar above his temple that she'd never noticed. She reached up to trace it with her fingers.

He caught her wrist and brought her hand down. "Stop distracting me, Phoebe. I'm angry at you, and for good reason."

She'd done this to him. She'd made him lose his temper. "I know. I can tell. This was why I didn't tell you any of this sooner."

There was another scar on his neck, disappearing into the collar above his cravat. Her fingertips longed to touch it, but she was disappointed when he pushed her hand away again.

"What else have you not told me? Let me guess. You've been smuggling state secrets to Tsar Alexander. No? Then I'm certain you're the one who broke the Prince Regent's carriage window with a rock last year."

He'd pulled her onto his lap to lecture her, but she was starting to notice his temper wasn't the only thing being affected.

"Honestly, Ian. You're being unreasonable. You're giving me far more credit than I deserve."

She rolled off the sofa and climbed onto his lap, straddling him. The robe and nightgown rode up on her legs, displaying bare skin in the light of the fire.

"Phoebe, you're trying to divert this conversation. You're trying to seduce me."

"I'm not doing any such thing. I am all ears." She raised herself on her knees and undid the belt of her robe. Slowly peeling the garment off one shoulder and then the other, she let it drop onto the floor.

She chanced a look at him. Ian's eyes were closed, but his face was almost touching the curve of her breast through the nightgown, as if he were breathing her in.

Excitement rushed through her as wicked thoughts raced through her mind. Their wedding—five months away or next week or tomorrow—was far too long to wait.

No regrets, she told herself as she eased down onto his lap again. His hardening manhood indicated he was definitely open to the possibility of seduction.

He was gripping the cushion of the sofa. "Phoebe, do you have any relevant response to the issues we've been discussing?"

The wanton warmth in her belly was spreading through her. Flushed and determined, she edged closer until their loins were separated only by the fall of his trousers. Her position was completely shameless, and she felt the thick ridge of his sex nestle into the cleft between her thighs.

Even to her own ears, her voice had taken on a husky tone when she replied. "My response is that the woman who acted impulsively and recklessly was the old Phoebe. The new Phoebe would never do such a thing."

She moved her hips slightly and the intimate pressure of him against her caused a silken ripple of heat to run through her. She tried to edge even closer, but he took hold of her waist.

"Tell me what would the new you do in the same situation?" He tried to sound strict and focused, but his voice was strained and tight and belonged to a stranger.

She began untying the strings holding the neckline of her nightgown closed. He watched the progress of her fingers. "In the same situation? I thought you didn't want me to return to the Vaults ever again."

"I don't. Ever." He moved a hand from her waist to her wrists, holding them still. But she knew he'd already lost the battle, for he was staring at the open neckline of her garment. "I need to know you'll think first, before you act."

It occurred to her that his earlobe was perfectly shaped. She leaned forward and nipped at it.

She sat back. He was still staring, his eyes smoky.

"In a similar situation, I would lift that curtain into the opium den—the one I'd never go anywhere near—and I'd cry out 'Help! Bloody murder!' I'd scream so loud they'd hear me all the way to Arthur's Seat."

Anticipation was bubbling up like molten lava inside of her. The question of how far she could push him before he lost control was tantalizing. Phoebe shifted her weight again until he was nestled even tighter against the knot of pleasure in her most sensitive place. She felt him throb against her.

"Is that . . . is that satisfactory to you?" she asked.

His gaze moved languorously up from her breasts. "Is what satisfactory?"

He was losing track of the conversation. A sense of power welled up in her as she freed her hand and continued undoing the ties until the front of her night-shirt gaped open. When she leaned forward, he could see all the way to her navel and beyond. Goose bumps rose on her skin by the way his gaze moved over her slowly, lingering on the shadows of her breasts, making her feel that he appreciated every dip and curve. Phoebe wondered what wicked things he would do to her once he decided there was no stopping.

"My answer. My response. Is it satisfactory?" she asked again.

He struggled but finally managed to raise his eyes to her face.

"Phoebe," he murmured. "I don't want to take advantage of you. We should wait."

She smiled. "There's no waiting, Ian. I have every intention of taking advantage of *you*."

He chuckled out loud, and she realized this was the first time she'd heard him laugh.

"So I'm asking you to be an agreeable soon-to-be husband and allow me to have my way with you."

"And how do I do that?"

"Sit back. Allow me to explore your body. And don't interrupt."

"I don't know if that's possible."

"Try." She untied his cravat, unwinding the starched cloth that still contained the heat of his skin. When his throat was exposed, she touched the long scar that had fascinated her before and traced it with a gentle fingertip.

He could have died from this. And from many of the other wounds he'd suffered in the war. Sarah talked often about her brother's scarred and broken body when he'd come back to them.

"If you're nearly finished . . ."

"Not yet. And I don't wish to be distracted. This is my first time . . . exploring."

She wanted him to know. She was twenty-seven years old, and she'd never allowed any man to make love to her . . . because no other man was Ian Bell.

"If I do something wrong, I don't want to be lectured," she said, trying to make light out of an awkward moment.

She placed her lips against his throat, kissing the scar, tasting the saltiness of his skin with the tip of her tongue.

"You can never do anything wrong."

"Says the man who was taking my head off a few moments ago."

His hands moved along her bare legs beneath the nightgown. He teased and ran a finger along the crack of her bottom to her aching sex, making her rock closer to him with excitement.

"We were on a different subject." He kissed her throat.

Her fingers went to the buttons of his waistcoat and shirt, and she unfastened them in rapid succession. She spread the edges of the garments wide, baring a muscular torso streaked with faint lines of battle.

She stared, saddened but grateful that he'd survived and was here now. Flattening her hands against his chest, she gently felt each line and his skin burned beneath her touch.

He watched her from under heavy lids, and Phoebe's hands moved lower. The texture of his body, rough skin and hard muscle, fascinated her.

"I want to kiss and stroke you everywhere," she said.

She nudged closer to him. The full hard length of his sex fit perfectly between her legs, and she was impatient to feel him, skin against skin.

"Not before I taste you here." He ran a thumb inside the neckline of the nightgown, over her nipple and downward toward her aching center. "And here."

Suddenly breathless, Phoebe grasped the hem of her nightgown, pulled it over her head, and tossed it aside. She sat completely naked on him, the pink tips of her breasts contracting into hard pebbles in the cool air.

He raised his mouth, and she pressed her lips against his, slipping her tongue into his hot mouth. Eagerly, she molded her body against his, wrapped her arms around his neck, and kissed him again and again. And he allowed her to take charge, to do as she wished.

Phoebe wriggled against him again, wanting more, her body feeling more and more an urgent craving she could not seem to satisfy.

He had to sense her frustration, for he levered her higher onto his lap until her nipple brushed his jaw. The texture of coarse beard against her sensitive flesh had her aching. His mouth opened over the tender nipple, and he drew it deep into his mouth. She leaned her head back and sighed. The feel of his tongue, the gentle suckling seemed to send waves of pleasure straight to the junction of her thighs. An exquisite tension was building within her, pulsing like the beat of a heart.

His mouth moved from one breast to the other while his hands caressed her back, the soft curves of her backside, the firm flesh of her legs. His fingers slid gently along her sex. Her body arched against his hand as he softly stoked the raging fire within her. She rocked against his touch, gasping at the growing frenzy taking hold of her body. She was caught in an uncontrollable race where she couldn't see the end, and yet she knew she had to run faster and faster.

"Ian," she called his name, not knowing what to ask and yet aware that only he could give what she sought.

She gasped when he suddenly stood, lifting her with him and wrapping her legs around his waist.

"Where are you taking me?" she asked, knowing full well the answer.

"I've been a good soon-to-be husband. Now it's your turn to be a good soon-to-be wife."

In the next moment, she was flat on her back on his

bed, sinking deep into the mattress. He rolled onto his side.

"I love you," he murmured, one hand trailing downward in a seductive path. When his fingers slipped into the cleft between her thighs, Phoebe raised her hips instinctively, arching her body, giving herself completely to his touch.

As he kissed the hollow of her throat, he teased and played with her slick flesh below, and the pulsing heat in her continued to build and build. Phoebe's body pressed restlessly against him as his mouth latched onto her distended nipple.

She held her breath as his lips moved slowly down along the softness of her belly. He moved to the edge of the bed and parted her legs. Their eyes locked when he reached under her buttocks and lifted her to his mouth.

Blood roared wildly in Phoebe's head. When she thought she couldn't take another moment of this sweet, sensuous torture, he still held her down, tasting, probing, and teasing her until she cried out and clutched at his hair.

Moments later, as she felt him move up next to her on the bed, Phoebe opened her arms to him. "I want all of you."

"Phoebe." He kissed her. "We can wait until—"

"No," she protested. "Your soon-to-be wife demands it."

She'd waited too long for him. Raising herself onto her knees, she tugged his shirt off of him as he kicked off his boots. Pushing him onto his back, she let her hands travel, exploring his shoulders, his arms, his chest, tracing the scars and muscle as he pushed off his trousers.

Ian groaned when she followed her fingers' trail with

her mouth. She took her time, watching him, waiting for his reaction to the effect of her mouth on his skin. He tried to touch her again, but she pushed his hands away. She was in command of her curiosity, his body, his mind. He belonged to her.

Slowly, she lowered herself in front of him, and as her mouth traced a path down his stomach, he took a deep breath and held it for so long that he finally gasped for breath. His cock was large, wondrous in its thickness and length. This too was hers now. Their gazes met.

"What are you doing to me?" he growled.

"Practicing what I just learned," she said, taking him in her hand and rubbing the warm crown against her cheek and her throat.

Ian groaned.

The moment she slid her lips over him, taking him into her mouth, he moved with the speed of a panther.

Pulling her up, he rolled her under him, and she felt him pressing himself against the portal of her sex.

Phoebe gasped as entered her, slowly at first, backing out and sliding in again, taking his time as her body grew accustomed to him. Gently, he slid into her again and again until she'd taken him in fully. Then he stopped, his lips on hers, his weight held above her. As they lay still, his arms tightly wrapped around her, she knew what it felt like to be cherished and loved.

When Ian began to move again, Phoebe went with him. Looking up through the haze that clouded her vision, her hands moved over his chest to his face, and she clung desperately to him as they rose together, two birds in flight.

She embodied love, enticement, beauty, seductiveness.

The gentle summer breeze blew in through the open windows and brushed across their naked forms. Tonight was her first time, and yet they'd made love twice. And if it wasn't because of exhaustion, they'd be at each other again. Ian felt himself stirring again at the thought and imagined a lifetime of nights like this.

But he first had to find a way to tame the haunting guilt that dogged him over Sarah's death. Just because he was getting married, just because he was in love, the blame would not simply go away. And the thought of leaving Phoebe alone at night as he chased after his demons shook him to the core.

It was always at night that the restlessness attacked him. Even tonight, while the household slept, he'd been downstairs, unable to shut off his mind. It was the sound of footsteps and the knock at his door on the floor above that drew him up the stairs.

Phoebe. He never imagined what awaited him. He snuggled closer to the warm back that had fit itself to the contours of his abdomen. Her leg lay between his own. His arms encircled her body, his hand resting on her perfect breast.

"I can hear you thinking," she whispered.

"You can't hear someone think," he reminded her, lifting his head and placing a kiss on her shoulder.

"I can," she challenged him. "And I have been doing some thinking of my own too."

He rolled Phoebe onto her back. Her hair spilled out across his pillow, a tangle of silky black curls. Her lips were swollen from his kisses, her eyes dreamy. His body stirred again.

"You're supposed to ask me, 'What have you been thinking, my loveliness?'"

She did make him laugh. He kissed her lips. "Tell me, what have you been thinking, my loveliness?"

"My article about the Select Committee's visit from London and other things."

He could have teased her that it pained him that his lovemaking would make her think of stuffy old Englishmen strutting through Scottish poorhouses, but he wouldn't do that to her. She was proud of her writing. And he respected what she'd set out to do.

"Tell me."

"This may be my final article for the newspaper," she said, glancing up at him.

She never failed to surprise him.

"I'm more of a storyteller than a journalist. I want to use my talents to the best of my ability. Mrs. Edgeworth has been writing novels about the problems plaguing Ireland for decades. I think it's time someone wrote novels about the struggles of the poor in Scotland. Not broad tales of adventure like Walter Scott, stories with heart about personal struggles to overcome tragedy and injustice."

He was relieved and happy for her. Even though he'd been ready to support her writing for the *Edinburgh Review*, Ian knew each topic she chose would present new challenges, new dangers, and new enemies who'd be going after her.

"I think you'll be brilliant," he said. "But are you still going to write this last column?"

"I am." She turned and faced him, propping herself on one elbow. "But I want to change the focus of it. From the evidence I have, the City Parish directed the poorhouses to do wrong, but why blame the charity institutions when they reject those instructions? Blame must be placed where it belongs."

He waited for her to say more.

"With your help, I'd like to do a commendatory article about the Orphan Hospital and all they're doing for the children of this city. I'll include information about how the other institutions are providing valuable services, as well, but the main thread of the column will be how the work in Bailie Fife's Close continues to go on without interruption, regardless of the pressures of the parish committee. And the message I'll convey is that we Scots need no interference from outsiders in taking care of our own."

"And what if the other institutions in the city did not act as the Orphan Hospital chose to do?"

"If they didn't, a positive representation of Bailie Fife's Close will encourage them, or shame them, to do what they should be doing."

Since they were talking business, Ian decided to tell her what he'd done already. "I've already sent the letters I spoke to you about earlier to the administrators and directors of the other institutions in the city. And when we get to Edinburgh, I'll make sure to follow up with them. Perhaps you'll have a number of places you can reference in your article."

"You did that already?" she asked, wide-eyed. "And will continue to pursue the matter with them?"

"Of course. And I think your new approach is positive and constructive. In fact, it's brilliant."

She smiled, pushed him onto his back, and slid on top of him.

"Excellent," she purred and nuzzled his throat.

⚜ 18 ⚜

M RS. B ELL AGREED to accompany them back to Edinburgh, bringing Mrs. Young with her. The morning of their departure, Dr. Thornton decided to ride in with them as well. It was clear that Alice was the main cause of his enthusiasm about joining the company on their journey to the city.

Nonetheless, the trip went off without her or the doctor verbally or physically assaulting each other, and she and Millie were deposited safely at the Pennington's Heriot Row townhouse.

Upon their arrival, Phoebe was delighted to learn her parents were due in the city in a day or two. Since giving up traveling to London to sit in Parliament, Lord and Lady Aytoun enjoyed coming to Edinburgh for part of every July to attend the annual races at Musselburgh, the theatre, and a few social engagements. With Mrs. Bell in town, Phoebe was relieved Ian could speak with them here rather than go to Baronsford. A consultation had been immediately arranged with the specialist Thornton knew.

Phoebe felt it would be best if their news could be kept private until everyone was together, and she'd sworn Millie to secrecy. She wanted the engagement to come fresh to her parents and not as a foregone decision. She'd also tucked her ring away for now, until the formal announcement could be made.

Once Lord and Lady Ayton arrived, a dinner was arranged that included Ian and his mother and a handful of other guests. If her parents were surprised by having the Bells attend, they said nothing to Phoebe about it.

The evening of the gathering, Millicent Pennington could not have been more genuinely and evidently pleased to visit with Mrs. Bell. The two chatted away amiably in the salon before dinner, and Phoebe kept a polite distance from her intended, who was constantly sending teasing looks at her from across the room.

During the dinner itself, she felt her nerves beginning to fray but managed to carry on a reasonably coherent conversation with a family friend who was seated next to her. After retiring with the other ladies to the drawing room, Phoebe caught her mother giving her worried looks as she realized she was pacing back and forth between the pianoforte and the windows like a caged tiger.

As the men filed in and rejoined the ladies, Phoebe felt the blood drain out of her body entirely. Ian and her father were not with them, and she heard someone tell her mother the two men had disappeared into the library a quarter of an hour earlier.

Minutes ticked away like hours, and Phoebe's agitation grew. Staring at the mantle clock would not make the hands move quicker, no matter how hard she tried.

What was taking so long, she anguished. The request for the earl's permission should have been brief. The answer even briefer.

Her father wouldn't refuse him. He couldn't.

Ian was the perfect matrimonial candidate for any young woman. What he lacked in title, he made up for with his military record, his civic service as Deputy Lieutenant of Fife, his substantial holdings in Fife and in Edinburgh, and the fortune his father had made in America.

Damnation. If there was a more ideal man, she'd never encountered him.

Phoebe stopped pacing, realizing several guests standing nearby were looking at her. She smiled weakly, praying she hadn't said any of that out loud.

Still, the hands of that clock would not move, and Phoebe was beginning to wonder if the blasted thing was broken.

Two of the women approached her and asked Phoebe if she was familiar with the new novel *Persuasion,* and whether she'd known it was the work of a woman. She tried twice but couldn't focus enough to make an intelligible answer. Another lady approached and asked her to play a piece on the pianoforte. Phoebe went immediately to Millie and whispered, "Please. I beg you. Save me from them."

Gracious as always, the younger sister nodded and sat at the instrument. A moment later, the sounds of music filled the room, and Phoebe slipped out the door.

"What's the matter with you?" her mother called out, catching up to her in the hallway outside of the drawing room.

"I need air, Mother." Phoebe looked in the direction of the library, then back to her mother.

"Are you unwell?"

Where they were standing, they were protected from the eyes and ears of their dinner company. Phoebe looked back at the library door again. How long had those two been cloistered away in that room? Her father had a temper, but he had no reason to be critical of Captain Bell. None whatsoever.

"Mother," she said, "I think you should go right in there and tell Father he is being rude, ignoring the guests as he is."

Millicent put a hand on her hip, one eyebrow raised, looking at Phoebe as if she'd grown a second head.

"Tell me, young lady. What is it?"

Phoebe took a deep breath.

"I'm to be married," she whispered, although it sounded more like a squeal. "To Captain Bell. That is, if you and Father agree to it. But I'm worried. I don't under-stand what is taking them so—"

The rest of the words were lost as her mother pulled her into her arms.

"But what if he says no?" Phoebe said in panic, holding tight. "I'm disagreeable, temperamental, independent, impertinent. What if Father tries to talk him out of marrying me?"

"Good gracious! My Phoebe. A married woman."

Millicent was talking as if their marriage were a real possibility. Phoebe wished she could share her mother's enthusiasm. Still, she held on to the thought that the countess had a great deal of influence over her husband.

Before they could exchange another word, the door of the library opened, and Ian emerged. She and her mother were standing with their arms around each other's waists. He gave no sign to her but closed the door behind him. Her father wasn't with him.

"No," she sighed. Leaving her mother, she walked toward Ian, a million arguments coming to mind that she was going to barrage the earl with.

Compromise. The word came to her like a bolt from heaven. Compromise was the order of the day.

She would beg her father, promise to change, to be the daughter he wanted her to be, but in return, he *must* agree to this marriage.

She was too upset to notice the smile on Ian's face until they met in the middle of the hallway.

"Well?" she whispered as he took her hands in his.

"He didn't refuse. But he'd like to speak to you before he says anything more."

Phoebe looked toward the library and braced herself. There was no time like the present. With a glance back at her mother—who nodded to her encouragingly—she walked directly to the library, knocked once, and entered, closing the door behind her.

The Earl of Aytoun was standing in the center of the room, clutching his walking stick with the carved lion's head handle. He frowned fiercely at his daughter.

"Phoebe," he began brusquely, "what are you doing ruining this young man's life?"

"Ruining?" Objections arose in her, but she could not voice them. His words stung her.

Her father didn't waste any time, however, and continued.

"I've been having you followed. I know what you do. Where you go. I know you're writing for the *Edinburgh Review*. I know *what* you write and under what name. I know you employ a former constable as a bodyguard. He's a good man, but that's not enough, apparently. I know you put your life in danger."

His sharp tone made it clear that all his information had come from a paid informant, and not from Grace and Hugh.

"You've had me *followed?*" she asked, fighting through an avalanche of emotions as she tried to fathom his first statement.

"You showed up at your sister's wedding last month, battered and bruised. And you would not say a word about how it came about."

She recalled the argument with her father the day after she arrived back at Baronsford, following the incident in the Vaults. She'd offered no answers to his questions, not even attempting to fabricate a story, as she had with Ian. It was only because of Jo and her wedding that the two of them had put their quarrel aside.

"Of course, I've had you followed. What father wouldn't?"

Phoebe recalled the moments while she was sitting in the carriage in the Grassmarket when she thought she was being watched. There was also the day at Bailie Fife's Close, feeling that someone was following her. And there had to be other times.

He leaned on the walking stick, suddenly looking tired. "I was worried about you. I still am. Not a day goes by that I don't imagine some trouble you might be getting into. And I understand your desire for independence. I respect it. This is the way your mother and I raised you. Raised all of our children. But a line exists between pursuing a life for oneself and risking that life unnecessarily."

For all that he'd learned about what Phoebe was

doing, she realized he wasn't censuring her for her work but for the dangers she was exposing herself to. She looked up at the tall, imposing man that she'd always adored and yet had made miserable for much of her adult years. Her mother always said the two of them were "cut from the same cloth." Headstrong. Proud. Passionate. Looking at her father now, she also saw him aging, tired, but stoic in the face of his advancing years. And still loving her, despite all the trouble she'd given him.

Her heart ached for what she'd done to him and to her mother; she knew no pain was endured by one without the other feeling it as well.

"Father, I've always viewed you as a great man." She took a step toward him. "A man of vision, a romantic, a hero, a voice for justice and good. I can name a hundred qualities that I've always known to exist in you and Mother. And as an adult, I've wished I could emulate a portion of who you are and what you've done."

Phoebe struggled to keep her voice steady as she said words she should have spoken long ago.

"I am sorry," she whispered, meaning it heart and soul. She took another step toward him. "For all the pain. For all the worry. For not thinking through my actions and seeing how they affected those who love me, those whom I love."

He stretched a hand out to her, and she closed the distance, moving into his embrace.

"Captain Bell," he said gruffly, holding her. "The man is still grieving his sister's death. When I said ruin—"

"I know," she interrupted, remembering her own thoughts when she'd been ready to lose hope in the well. How her death would affect him had tormented her. But her love for him had also strengthened her. "I cannot be reckless, not any longer. He means too much to me. Caution, attentiveness, and responsible action. This is your daughter from now on."

"And you're willing to do all of this? For him? For yourself?"

"I'm more than willing. I'm determined," she told him, pressing her face to his heart. "I love him, Father."

He smiled and hugged her fiercely before letting her go.

"Do you know," he told her, holding her hand as he sat back against a writing table, "I tried to warn him about your stubbornness and uncontrollable nature. And he told me there is nothing about you that he doesn't know. Without blush or stammer, he said that in all you are, and all you do, he loves and cherishes you."

"He said that to you?" she asked.

"Phoebe . . ." Her father smiled. "Ian Bell is the perfect man for you."

EVEN WITH THE normal smoky haze that hung over Edinburgh and the gathering mass of clouds, the South Bridge with its fancy shops looked far different from the last time Phoebe had been here. Standing inside the dressmaker's front shop, she scanned the activity on the street. It was no longer a dark, empty avenue, where the fog and mist cloaked every sound but the wheels of Ian's carriage taking her away from the Vaults. Today, the street was filled with color and the busy sounds of pedestrians, carters, and conveyances of every size and description.

As always, she marveled that this bustling and prosperous city thoroughfare and the tall buildings that lined both sides actually sat upon a bridge . . . and that the lowliest of Edinburgh's poor languished in the Vaults beneath its glittering street.

Phoebe reluctantly shook off the thought, however, and turned away from the large glass window of the shop. She didn't want to spoil the excursion for her mother and

Millie. Today, she needed to have a dress made to wear when she married Ian.

The church in Melrose Village was about to host another Pennington wedding. The notice of their engagement was perfectly succinct, as far as Phoebe and Ian were concerned. *Captain Ian Bell of Bellhorne, Fife, is to wed Lady Phoebe Pennington by special license.* They were both relieved the families deferred so amiably to their wishes. Only immediate family and close friends would be attending the ceremony. A much larger celebration was planned for the days preceding the Christmas Assembly at Baronsford.

Phoebe had given a letter containing the news to Wynne, asking him to give it to her sister once they arrived in Jamaica. She'd also sent letters to Gregory and Freya in Torrishbrae in the Highlands. They'd just returned to Sutherland with little Ella after Jo's wedding. Phoebe couldn't even ask them to come back to Baronsford so soon, considering Freya was now six months into her pregnancy.

"A week," Phoebe repeated under her breath as she walked by her mother and Millie, who were busily inspecting bolts of painted satin and cotton and muslin cloth, as well as embroidered silk. She couldn't get excited about new dresses and sashes and shawls and hats and gloves. It didn't matter what she wore. But thinking of marriage to Ian . . . she let out a sigh of pleasure.

Tonight, her family was having dinner with his family at the Bells' Melville Street house. Phoebe imagined a day very soon when she'd be sharing that house with him. They'd go to Fife together. They'd dine together every day. They'd walk in the gardens and ride in the fields together. They'd sleep in the same bed. Her face warmed as she remembered their last night in his rooms in Bellhorne. The passionate and insatiable love they'd shared still heated her blood.

She walked to a counter and let her hand trail absently over rows of ribbons.

"Six days to be exact," she whispered under her breath. Six days to have a husband and friend and lover for eternity. Six days before she could climb into bed with him at any hour of the day or night. In six days, she could call Mrs. Bell 'Mother' too and sit with her and read to her and help her find her way through the grief.

The doctor from the university, a friend of Dr. Thornton, had come to Fiona. Another expert was to see her in two days. But this trip to the city—or perhaps it was the bright activity of nuptial preparations—had already improved her health. Mrs. Bell appeared sturdier in body and far more stable in mind. The confusion was gone.

Unfortunately, she still did not feel strong enough to join them on this outing today.

The tinkling sound of the door opening onto the street drew Phoebe's attention to the young lad who tumbled in. Her heart broke a little at the sight of the filthy face, the tattered clothing, and the large eyes peering from his thin face.

"Out, rascal. Out, this moment. Do ye hear me?" the shop owner called from behind the piles of material.

Dropping a stick at Phoebe's feet, he turned and ran out with the same urgency as he'd come in.

"Just a street urchin, Lady Phoebe. My apologies. The Old Town has gangs of them overrunning entire neighborhoods. There is nothing we can do to stop it. I hope he didn't distress you, m'lady."

Phoebe's attention had already shifted from the

owner's apologetic complaints to the stick that lay at her feet. A cane with an ivory handle, carved with a partially opened rosebud. She picked it up and stared at it. It was Mrs. Bell's walking stick. Or one that looked exactly like it.

She went to the door of the shop, pulled it open, and looked out.

"Where are you going?" her mother called.

"I'll be right back."

The sidewalk was filled with crowds of shoppers, and the lad seemed to have evaporated into thin air.

It was possible, she supposed, that others owned a similarly carved cane. But it seemed so unlikely.

Phoebe continued to scan the throng for some sign of the lad . . . or Mrs. Bell, for that matter. As she stretched up onto her tiptoes, someone bumped her from behind with such violence that she would have fallen if not for a set of strong hands that caught her by the elbow, steadying her.

"Oh, my . . . Lady Phoebe!"

She was astonished to find herself looking into the handsome face of the minister. She hadn't realized his eyes were hazel. He tipped his hat. "Why, Mr. Garioch."

Ian had told her the minister arrived from Bellhorne yesterday and was staying with them. "I heard you'd come to town. What a surprise to run into you here. We'll be dining together tonight, I understand."

"I must apologize, m'lady, for being so abrupt." The man looked past her down the street. "But I cannot tarry. Mrs. Bell and Mrs. Young are looking at hats in a milliner's shop only five doors down, and some street rat absconded with—"

"This?" Phoebe asked, holding the cane up.

"You have it," the man said excitedly. "You appre-hended the thief."

"Not exactly," she explained. "He seemed to take a wrong turn and found me."

"Well, we must return the walking stick to Mrs. Bell immediately. She's quite attached to it, you know." Garioch looked back over his shoulder. "She's just up the street."

"Where?" she asked, looking in the direction the minister was indicating, but the crowds blocked her view.

He took Phoebe by the elbow and started leading her that way. "Mrs. Bell will be so delighted to see you. I actu-ally think the milliner's shop was simply an excuse to join you and your family."

"I know choosing ribbons and lace is not the way you'd prefer to be spending your afternoon," Ian's mother said. "But I'm truly appreciative of you taking me over here."

"Absolutely, Mother. Don't even mention it."

He was quite happy to be accompanying his mother on this little shopping excursion. Initially, when Fiona decided she didn't feel well enough to go out with Phoebe and her family, Ian's cousin Alice had arranged to walk a little in Charlotte Square with Dr. Thornton. But later, feeling more game, his mother changed her mind. Ian didn't need any better reason. He wanted to see Phoebe, regardless of the occasion.

His mother absently patted the seat next to her, feeling for her missing cane.

He took her hand. Her favorite walking stick had been misplaced today, and she was lost without the comfort of it. Before leaving, he'd asked the servants to fetch a different one, but Fiona refused to take it.

"There once was a day when I imagined I'd be taking Sarah shopping for her wedding dress." She looked out the window at the crowds of people. They were passing Tron Church and Hunter Square and were approaching the South Bridge. "But it wasn't meant to be."

The heavy hand of responsibility once again clutched Ian's gut. After three years of searching, he'd never found the answer. The mystery of his sister's death was still unresolved. From this street, from these same shops, she'd disappeared. He wondered if he ever would be able to let go of the guilt.

"But now"—she smiled, brightening as she turned to him—"Phoebe is going to be my daughter."

And his wife. Phoebe was the key to a future that could one day conquer the tragic past. That was his hope.

"And you should know that your cousin is planning to accept Dr. Thornton's offer today," his mother said, tapping Ian on the knee. "That's the reason for their walk this afternoon. With you marrying, and Phoebe in our lives, Alice feels more secure that she won't be leaving me without a companion. I told her, however, that she is always welcome at—"

"What is Mr. Garioch doing on the South Bridge?" he asked as their carriage rolled past. The minister said he was spending the afternoon going through the archives at St. Andrews Church on George Street.

More importantly, why was Phoebe walking alongside him?

The minister nattered on about the crowds and the shops and the beggars on every corner, but Phoebe couldn't comprehend much of what the man was saying. An invisible hand held her stomach in a tight grip, and she couldn't understand why. But with every step she took away from her family at the dressmaker's shop, the tighter that hand squeezed.

The cane. Mrs. Bell's cane had been brought into the shop and dropped at her feet. Why?

Phoebe slowed down. "I think we've gone more than five doors, Mr. Garioch."

"You're correct, m'lady. Running after the wee scoundrel, I lost track and misspoke. But here we are." He motioned to a building ahead. Phoebe could see a display of hats in the window. "Mrs. Bell and Mrs. Young were to wait in that shop."

The minister tried to direct her steps toward an alley that ran along the side of the building.

"I left them right inside the door off this wynd. The side entrance is right down here, m'lady. Quite convenient."

Phoebe stopped. "One moment, Mr. Garioch."

Fear clawed its way into her throat. Sarah left a shop and disappeared near here. She had to know her assailant. Someone she trusted. Phoebe's nightmares came rushing back. Faces changing into other faces. Men becoming monsters.

She glanced into Garioch's eyes, and she knew she was right.

"Give my regrets to Mrs. Bell." Her words were rushed. She needed to get away from him, but he was herding her closer to the alley. "My mother and sister . . . I need to return to them."

Phoebe tried to edge around him, but he cut her off. Light glinted off his knife as he pulled the weapon from his coat. She stared, frozen in time, at the blade.

She saw the attack play out in her mind. Here, in daylight, with throngs of people around them, if anyone paid the least attention to a woman bent over in pain, Garioch would calmly reassure them that they were together, that she would be fine in a moment, and that he needed no help.

Phoebe leaped back, avoiding the point of the knife by a hair, but stumbled into the wynd. As she regained her balance, he kept coming, his blade held low, backing her down the alley. Phoebe tripped over a discarded box and fell backward, rolling over onto her hands and knees. She was quick to jump to her feet, but he continued to move toward her. She glanced behind her into the darkening alley. A few yards more and the wynd turned. In the murky distance, she saw steps descending between crumbling walls.

The Vaults.

"Why? Why are you doing this?" she yelled at him.

His face was impassive. He said nothing but came on unrelentingly.

She recalled her promise to Ian and shouted for help, but no one could hear her. The wynd was too secluded. No one was coming. No one seemed to hear. She couldn't believe she'd fallen prey to his trick so easily.

He was the one. The chill of evil grew more distinct with every step. The way he held the knife. His size, the way he moved purposely, inexorably toward her brought back that horrible night.

"I saw you. I fought with you when you tried to kill the boy. That's why you're doing this, isn't it?"

Still no answer. In the corner of her eye, she spotted a doorway in the wall. Perhaps, she thought desperately, it opened to a shop. People. She threw her shoulder against it, but it didn't budge. Barred from the inside. She saw another and ran toward it. Before she reached it, she heard him behind her.

"Garioch!"

Phoebe turned and threw up her arm in defense as the knife arced toward her.

"Garioch!"

The shouts startled the killer, and Phoebe slipped to the side, fending off the blade's downward stab.

Ian! He was here. He'd found her. He'd save her.

Garioch's head jerked around as Ian raced toward them.

"Stop!"

The minister jumped past her, and before Phoebe could move to Ian, she felt the edge of the blade at her throat.

"No stopping. I've been chosen. *Chosen!*" Garioch shouted. "She meddled with God's work. She needs to die. For I must avenge them."

Blast him, Ian cursed. Blast the devil. The minister. The man who had been welcome in their home. A monster in the house of worship. The invisible evil, trusted by all. No wonder Sarah had walked into his trap. Phoebe had nearly done the same thing.

"The voices come to me," Garioch told him, backing away down the wynd and taking Phoebe with him. "The five martyrs. They died at the hands of the corrupt ones.

They were pure and innocent, but the heretics butchered them and burned them.”

Ian didn't want to hear about heretics or butchers. He wanted the man to let Phoebe go.

The despicable fraud had her in his power. He looked at Phoebe's face, at the knife in Garioch's hand. Blood was dripping from where he held the blade against her throat. He moved closer.

“They command me. I have no choice. I must do their bidding. I'm a soldier of God. Surely you can understand that.”

“I don't understand. You must let Phoebe go. She has nothing to do with this.”

He was backing away, dragging her with him.

“She's the meddler. She's not Sarah. Your sister was never supposed to die. It was an accident. She shouldn't have seen me.”

Ian's fury roared for blood, but he had to control it.

“Stay where you are,” Garioch warned him. “One step closer and I'll take her head off right here.”

They'd almost reached the steps leading down to the Vaults.

Ian gave him a few steps, but he was not about to let him take her down there. Once they passed through the door into the labyrinthine darkness, they'd be gone. He'd never get to her in time.

“I'll go mad if I don't do their bidding,” the monster said, the intensity in his voice rising. “I have no choice.”

“You always have a choice.”

This was insanity. He was the same height, the same weight, and wearing the same clothes. But a different creature lived beneath his skin.

“My hatred of her is my choice,” Garioch roared,

jerking Phoebe's head back. "She is the devil who thinks she has nine lives."

"You pushed me into the well," she spat through gritted teeth.

"You should have died there, but it's not too late. I will teach her how to die."

The man stopped. A dozen paces separated Ian from them. Dread washed through him. He couldn't lose her. Not now. She deserved better. She deserved life.

He wouldn't argue with a madman. But Ian couldn't fail her. For all his life, he was a lost man. Wounded, crushed by war, by grief, and she saved him. He couldn't let her go.

Garioch backed toward the open door. "Men must die. Men must pay for the blood of the martyrs."

As Ian charged, a tall, thin lad came out of nowhere, swinging a cudgel hard, and it sang in the dim light as it glanced off the killer's head. Garioch staggered backward for only a second, but it was enough. Ian was on him, driving the knife still clutched in his murderous hand straight into the monster's heart.

❧ 20 ❧

Two Months Later

PHOEBE STOPPED READING for a moment and inhaled deeply. The September breeze carried in from the hills the sweet, earthy smell of heather. The afternoon sun warmed her face in this protected spot. She loved Bellhorne.

In the garden below the stone terrace where Phoebe sat reading to Mrs. Bell, a solitary figure was toiling away, digging the soil, adding compost, turning it, and preparing the ground for the bush sitting in the grassy lane nearby.

"We have gardeners capable of doing the hard labor," the older woman said, following her gaze.

Phoebe closed the book and patted the slender hand of her mother-in-law. "I believe he needs to do this himself."

Sweat soaked the back of Ian's shirt. His sleeves were rolled up over muscular forearms. He stood, stretched, and ran his dirt-covered fingers through his uncombed hair, completing the roguish, unruly look that she loved. She understood his need to complete this task, to work in these gardens, to explain to Sarah how her killer had finally received the punishment he deserved.

Peter Garioch, a man who led two lives so different that no one during his fourteen-year ministry here ever had the slightest suspicion of the corruption existing in the brain behind his attractive face.

From the day Ian's father brought Garioch to Bell-horne, his wife, his children, and everyone who came in contact with him in the village loved and respected the man. But even as he left his mark preaching the word of God here in Fife, in Edinburgh he was leaving his horrid signature on scores of bodies. Many of them were never identified.

It was several weeks after the minister was killed that Ian and a constable from Edinburgh discovered Garioch's journals hidden under some floorboards in the rectory office. It was a clear, unemotional record of the murders he'd been committing for decades. His madness was chilling.

Phoebe trembled as she recalled how close she'd been to becoming one of his victims.

Ian looked up at her, but even from here, she could read the poignant edge to his smile in the set of his handsome mouth.

Mrs. Bell stood, peering at her son. Her voice quavered as she realized which of the plants he was determined to replace today.

"He's replacing the rose Sarah herself planted on her twentieth birthday." She leaned on her cane. "I think . . . I think this means she will know she's welcome to continue visiting us."

Ian's mother knew the truth, but at the same time, she was committed to believing in Sarah's presence at Bellhorne. No one found that strange, especially not Phoebe.

"A white, double-bloom Scots Rose," she told her mother-in-law as she stood too. She'd been with her husband when he chose the plant to be brought to Bellhorne.

Her husband. She cherished the sound of those two words. They were truly husband and wife, their hearts connected, their souls joined. The invitations would soon go out for the celebration of their nuptials at Christmastime in Baronsford, but that was simply an added nicety for family and friends. To Phoebe and Ian, their union could not be more loving or secure.

With Garioch's violent demise, Ian's restlessness and guilt had subsided. He no longer haunted the Vaults, except to help Duncan gather up the gangs of street urchins so he could speak with them. A new school with dormitories was already in the works, financed by Ian and Phoebe and a few others who had been eager to join the cause. To see to the immediate needs of some of the older boys, a temporary arrangement had already been established and seven students enrolled, the first one being Jock Rokeby, who had helped save Phoebe's life that day on the South Bridge.

Phoebe knew what they were doing was a drop in an ocean of misfortune. The world did not change overnight. Her final published article had received a few nods of approval, but the politicians she was critical of continued to sit comfortably in their positions of power. Still, it was a start.

The voices of Dr. and Mrs. Thornton reached them through the open doors to the house.

"Our dinner guests are here early," Ian's mother said.

The doctor's company was more tolerable now that Alice was in charge of the man's life. There were times when Phoebe actually found him entertaining. The husband and wife lived nearby, and many a day Alice walked over and sat with Mrs. Bell.

"I believe the doctor wishes to examine you first, before we sit down to dine."

Mrs. Bell waved her cane in the air dismissively, as if all this attention was unnecessary. The doctors in Edinburgh could not offer anything more than they already knew. Fiona's heart was weak, and she had to be mindful not to do too much or worry too much.

Phoebe and Ian made sure of that, especially now that they spent more time in Bellhorne.

"You go get that husband of yours and tell him I expect him to be washed and dressed and ready for dinner. I don't want him to be late."

"I'll tell him." She placed a kiss on her new mother's cheek and watched her walk inside with more vigor than they'd seen in days.

Phoebe turned around to Ian as he stamped down the soil around the newly planted rose bush.

There were words Ian wanted to say to his sister. Apologies and clarifications. He also wanted her to know that from the time she'd gone missing until the moment Garioch died, he'd never doubted her.

Working the same bit of earth where Sarah had

planted her favorite rose bush, Ian sensed that she knew all of this. As he knelt and pushed his fingers into the soil, he felt her sitting beside him.

In the breeze, he heard a whisper. In the graceful dance of the falling leaves, he heard laughter. The signs were there, and he understood their meaning. His sister had passed away, but her presence would live forever with him, with them, at Bellhorne.

He pressed down the dirt one last time and looked up to find his wife crouching next to him.

He'd been struggling for a way to say to his sister what was in his heart. Replacing the rose bush had been Phoebe's idea.

"It's done."

She leaned forward and kissed him as she cradled his face. "I'm proud of you, and I love you."

He smiled at the smudge of dirt that had rubbed off his face onto her nose. "Thank you, my love."

He stood and helped Phoebe to her feet. She wrapped her arms around him, paying no regard to the dirt and dust and sweat. "It wasn't only Sarah that you made happy today. You also cheered your mother."

He looked back at the rose bush. "What happens if this one dies like the last one?"

"You'll plant another one in the spring."

"And if that one dies?"

"We keep replacing them." She linked her arm with his as they started for the house. "Hope is the flower on the shrubs we plant. What else can we do but start them and nurture them and pray they will produce . . . for your mother, for our families, for the less fortunate in Scotland . . . only the sweetest of flowers."

As they walked together, Ian watched three leaves fall and rise and tumble and swirl through the air.

"I think Sarah would approve," he said, pressing her hand.

Phoebe listened to the breeze for a moment. "I think she already does."

THANK you for reading *Sleepless in Scotland*. If you enjoyed it, please leave a review online.

And be sure to check out *Dearest Millie*, the next install-ment in the Pennington Family series.

One reader wrote,

"a beautifully written tale... filled with a depth of emotions that run the gambit of poignant, sadness, disbelief, laughter, hope and a forever love. I laughed at Dermot's pranks and cried at Millie's illness. I had hope that they would achieve an HEA, and the author did not disappoint. It is a loving, heartwarming story of two people who fall in love under less than ideal circumstances. Loved the last chapter. I highly recommend this story."

More about *Dearest Millie*...

Lady Millie, youngest of the Pennington family, has always lived in the shadow of her talented and powerful siblings. She's been the rock of stability and order for her sisters and brothers. Her future looks bright until fate deals her a tragic hand.

Dermot McKendry is a former surgeon in the Royal Navy who has returned to his home in the Highlands to open a hospital. As disorganized as he is passionate, he is

a man with wounds and a secret past he has worked a lifetime to hide.

Providence brings them together, but their future may
lie beyond redemption. *Dearest Millie* is a poignant tale of
two lovers, life's calamities, and the healing power of the
human heart.

We hope you enjoyed reading about Phoebe Pennington and Ian Bell in *Sleepless in Scotland*.

Edinburgh in 1818 was a vibrant and dynamic place. In the years since the fall of Napoleon, this medieval town had rapidly grown to be one of the most important cities in Britain. Known as the "Athens of the North," the city was home to Henry Dundas, Lord Melville (who ruled Scotland for the English crown), and Walter Scott, friend to the Prince Regent and a rising literary light. Its university had made it a leading force in medicine, science, and law. And with its growing wealth and influence, it had also become a tumultuous, overpopulated city where underworld kings, Jacobites and violent reformers, journalists, police, and self-serving politicians clashed in an ongoing struggle for survival and dominance.

As novelists and historians, we couldn't help but try to capture a piece of this amazing city.

We've borrowed the ghost and the gardens and some

of the history of Kellie Castle in Fife for our creation of Bellhorne Castle, which we situated near Kinghorn.

For his friendly assistance with questions we had about the Firth of Forth and the crossing at Queensferry, we'd like to thank Richard Hopper. If we erred in any way, don't blame Richard.

For readers who are new to the Pennington Series, *Sleepless in Scotland* is one of ten novels and novellas that comprise the multi-generational Pennington Family series.

If you're interested, here is the complete list:

— The Promise (*USA Today* Bestseller) - Running for her life on a desperate journey to America, Rebecca Neville promises the dying wife of the Earl of Stanmore to raise and care for her newborn son, James. Ten years later, the Earl of Stanmore learns of the boy. He sends to the colonies for his young heir so he can raise him as a peer of the realm. With no intention of forsaking her vow, Rebecca returns to England with James to face a future without her beloved charge, but she must also face her tumultuous past.

— The Rebel - Jane Purefoy, daughter of an English magistrate, takes on the guise of the notorious Irish rebel, Egan, and leads a secret band of revolutionaries against the brutality of the colonial troops. Sir Nicholas Spencer is on his way to Ireland to court Jane's younger sister. When he runs afoul of Egan, Sir Nicholas unmasks the legendary rebel, only to uncover Jane. Bewitched by her, he decides to keep her secret and embarks on a risky plan of seduction that will throw her family into chaos, a country into rebellion, and his heart into the throes of a love that can never be.

— Borrowed Dreams *(RT Award for Best British-Set Historical)* - Driven to undo the evil wrought by her dead husband and facing financial ruin, Millicent Wentworth must enter into a marriage of convenience with the notorious 'Lord of Scandal' Lyon Pennington, the Earl of Aytoun. Lyon is a man devastated by a tragic accident that killed his first wife and left him gravely wounded. Filled with despair, he reluctantly allows himself to be lured into the unwanted marriage. A fresh twist on Beauty and the Beast.

— Captured Dreams - Portia Edwards will go to any length to find the family she's never known. And when she meets merchant Pierce Pennington —the estranged younger brother of Lyon Pennington—Portia has the perfect chance to ask for his help. But her stubborn pride keeps her silent. That is, until she recognizes her strong attraction to the brave man who, by night, is known as the infamous Captain MacHeath, smuggling arms by sea under the pall of darkness, all in the name of liberty...

— Dreams of Destiny - Wounded by scandal and the unsolved murder of his sister-in-law, David Pennington is outwardly insolent and arrogant. But nothing will stop him from escorting his childhood friend, Gwyneth Douglas, to Scotland to save the Scottish heiress from fortune hunters. But with their arrival in Scotland comes terrible danger. Now, if they ever hope to satisfy long-hidden desires, they will need to thwart the evil that threatens to destroy both their lives...

— Romancing the Scot - Hugh Pennington, a hero of the Napoleonic wars, is now a grieving widower with a death wish. When he receives an expected crate from the continent, he is shocked to find a nearly dead woman inside. Her identity is unknown, and the handful of American coins and the precious diamond sewn into her dress only deepen the mystery. Grace Ware is an enemy of the English Crown. Trying to escape from her father's murderers, she never anticipated bad luck depositing her at the home of an aristocrat in the Scottish Borders. As she strives to keep her identity a secret, a duel of wits quickly turns to passion and romance...until danger comes to the very doors of Baronsford, threatening to tear the two lovers apart or destroy them both.

— Sweet Home Highland Christmas (*RITA© Award Finalist*) - Freya Sutherland is a desperate aunt trying to keep custody of her precocious young niece, Ella, even if it means marrying for security instead of love. Recently retired Captain Gregory Pennington wants nothing more than to make it home in time for Christmas, but he's asked to escort some travelers from the Highlands to the Borders. His plans do not include a wife and child, and Freya has responsibilities as Ella's guardian. With Ella conspiring to get them together, Penn and Freya might just experience a little Christmas magic.

— It Happened in the Highlands - Lady Josephine Pennington's life was nearly destroyed when rumors spread about her questionable parentage. Years later, when she receives a package from the Highlands containing sketches of a woman who looks eerily similar to herself, Jo believes she might have found a clue to the identity of her birth mother. When Captain Wynne Melfort was forced to end his engagement to Jo Pennington sixteen years ago, he never imagined he would see her again. More than that, he never expected feelings long thought dead to resurface. As they strive to unravel the mystery of her birth, Jo must learn how to trust Wynne. And as secrets of the past begin to surface, evil forces will stop at nothing to keep Jo from uncovering the truth and reclaiming her legacy.

— Sleepless in Scotland - Lady Phoebe Pennington risks her life to expose Edinburgh's corrupt political leaders, even descending into the city's seething netherworld. Then one night, she narrowly escapes death and lands in the arms of the brother of her murdered best friend. Captain Ian Bell is a tortured man fighting through grief and guilt over the loss of his sister, and he still hunts for her murderer. Fate has thrown them together, but trust is elusive and danger lurks in the dark alleys of the city. For Phoebe is the only one who has seen the face of her friend's killer, and the sinister shadows of evil are closer than she and Ian imagine.

— Dearest Millie - Lady Millie Pennington's future looks bright until fate deals her a tragic hand in the form of cancer. Dermot McKendry is a former surgeon in the Royal Navy who has returned to open a hospital in the Highlands. Providence brings them together, but life's calamities will sorely test the healing power of the human heart.

— How to Ditch a Duke - Lady Taylor Fleming is an heiress with a suitor on her tail. Her step-by-step plan to ditch him is simple. But there is nothing simple about the Duke of Bamberg. Taylor tries to escape to the sanctuary of the Highlands, but her plans become complicated when the duke arrives at her door and her loyal allies desert her. And even with the best-laid plans, things can go awry...

Finally, if second-chance romance with a twist interests you, be sure to check out *Jane Austen CANNOT Marry!*

As authors, we love feedback. We write our stories for our readers, and we'd love to hear from you. We are constantly learning, so please help us write stories that you will cherish and recommend to your friends. Please sign up for news and updates and follow us on BookBub.

As always, if you liked *Sleepless in Scotland,* please leave a review online, and don't miss Millie Pennington's story in *Dearest Millie.*

ABOUT THE AUTHOR

USA Today Bestselling Authors Nikoo and Jim McGoldrick have crafted over fifty fast-paced, conflict-filled novels, along with two works of nonfiction, under the pseudonyms May McGoldrick, Jan Coffey, and Nik James.

These popular and prolific authors write historical romance, suspense, mystery, historical Westerns, and young adult novels. They are four-time Rita Award Finalists and the winners of numerous awards for their writing, including the Daphne DeMaurier Award for Excellence, the *Romantic Times Magazine* Reviewers' Choice Award, three NJRW Golden Leaf Awards, two Holt Medallions, and the Connecticut Press Club Award for Best Fiction. Their work is included in the Popular Culture Library collection of the National Museum of Scotland.

facebook.com/MayMcGoldrick

twitter.com/MayMcGoldrick

instagram.com/maymcgoldrick

bookbub.com/authors/may-mcgoldrick

* 9 7 8 1 9 6 0 3 3 0 1 2 3 *